DEATH ON THE SMALL SCREEN

JO ALLEN

Author Copyright Jennifer Young 2025
Cover Art: Mary Jane Baker

All rights reserved.
No part of this book may be reproduced in any form or by any electronic or mechanical means, including information storage and retrieval systems, without written permission from the author, except for the use of brief quotations in a book review.

This book is licensed for your personal enjoyment and may not be resold or given away.

This story is a work of fiction. The characters are figments of my imagination and any resemblance to anyone living or dead is entirely coincidental.
Some of the locations used are real. Some are invented.

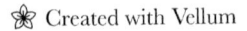

❦ Created with Vellum

AUTHOR'S NOTE

While the characters in this book are entirely figments of my imagination, the same can't be said for the locations. Beautiful and varied though Cumbria is, its geography doesn't always fit my plots. For this reason, along with my superstitious dread of setting a murder in a building where someone actually lives and because I didn't want to accidentally refer to a real character in a real place or property, I've taken several liberties with the map. Jude's home village of Wasby, for example, is entirely fictitious, and while you might take a reasonable guess at where Gerry Cole's cottage *might* be, you won't be able to place it exactly.

Despite playing fast and loose with distances, views and buildings, I've tried at all time to remain true to the overwhelming and inspiring beauty of the Cumbrian landscape. I hope the many fans of the Lake District will understand, and can find it in their hearts to forgive me for these deliberate mistakes.

ONE

Autumn scented the air on this, the first day of the rest of Lexie Romachenka's life. Opening the car door she got out, stretching arms and legs after the long journey, and paused to take in the smoky breath of burning wood and a whiff of freshly-spread muck that rode the September breeze like a pair of gunslingers on the Oregon Trail. She had been on a long journey and at times a damaging one, but it had ended and here she was, free at last, unencumbered by any baggage save for the couple of cases she'd brought with her to see her through her month in the country.

She left the bags in the boot of the car for now, ensuring that she was in the right place (Wasby End Cottage, rather than Wasby Cottage which was to the left and Town End Cottage on the other side of the road) and then checking the instructions for access. That done, she freed the keys from the small metal box on the wall and wrestled her way past the stiff front door (*you will need to push!* the instructions had warned her) and into the cool interior.

On the threshold she paused to take stock. First impressions mattered and, thank God, her response was overwhelmingly positive. The curtains had been drawn but not quite closed, so that a shaft of light speared like a spotlight across a hallway with a mix of stained wood and grey stone that spoke of age, and of a builder who'd wrought this building from the land with the sweat of his brow. Her creative appetite satisfied, Lexie smiled. There had been many places that were both cheaper and more convenient, but who wouldn't want to pay the premium for the character and the promise that came with this cosy cottage for two?

For the length of her tenure, however, it would be a cottage for one. Her sense of well-being was momentarily overshadowed at the brief thought of Nico entering this paradise and making it his own. He would have loved it and yet he would have overwhelmed its nuanced charm. His personality was too big for somewhere so thrifty with space. His voice would have boomed off the low rafters and rung from the polished horse brasses over the fireplace, and his long-armed, expansive gestures would have spelled disaster for the primary-coloured prints of the fells that hung on the walls, for the old-fashioned lamps and the artily-placed slate ornaments on fireplace and windowsills. It was just as well he wasn't here and she'd never make that fatal mistake of falling for his charm again. For the next few weeks, longer if she liked the place, Wasby End Cottage would be her sanctuary, definitely not the country love nest the brochure had tried so hard to sell. It was her opening scene, her new chapter. When all was done, she would have her happy ending.

The room had a dual aspect. She threw open the curtains and looked out. The garden, narrow, long and not too large, had a patio with a table and two chairs. At one side was a large apple tree bowing under the weight of red fruit, with bird and squirrel feeders hanging from it. The grass sloped away towards a wire fence reinforcing a scrawny hedge, on the far side of which was a field with Belted Galloway cows bunched furtively in one corner, and then up to the open ground of Loadpot Hill and Bampton Common, behind which a spectacular sunset was beginning to form. At the edge of her vision two women, one about her own age and the other rather older, stood in deep conversation by the wall that separated the cottage from that next door. No doubt she'd soon be their topic of conversation, if she wasn't already, Lexie was depressingly accustomed to being the subject of speculative, and often vicious, gossip. Everybody in the industry was, and many saw it as a necessary evil in their upward climb. Wasn't that what people meant when they said the only thing worse than being talked about was not being talked about?

She stepped back from the window and took a brisk turn around the cottage. The kitchen was small but well-equipped. A quick glance into the cupboards showed that she was well-provided with teabags, sugar, and coffee (real coffee, and a cafetière to put it in). There was a cardboard hamper on the counter with bread, biscuits, apples and a jar of home-made bramble jam, and there was milk and a bottle of (cheap) Chardonnay in the fridge door. The thoughtfulness of it touched her, although not without a trace of irritation when she realised it removed her reason for approaching one of her neighbours to find out a little about the village and tell them a lot about herself, but when had she ever needed a reason? As her mother said, she'd never been backward at coming forward and in her line of work you had to talk about yourself or the rising tide rolled over you and someone else rode the wave of popularity.

Upstairs the bedroom was cosy and romantic, with flounced white bed covers on a brass bedstead and far more pillows than was practical, a scattering of rugs on a polished floor, and walls hung with glass ornaments in the shapes of fairies, birds and flowers. In the window a particularly egregious glass heart dangled in the light and cast pink shadows onto the white rug. Turning up her nose, Lexie tweaked it down and laid it to one side. She would remove the rest of them later. In the street below her, the two women were still chatting, snatching quick glances at Wasby End Cottage with the air of those who think themselves unseen.

It was good to be curious. Lexie took the briefest of glances in the mirror, happy that for once it didn't matter what she looked like, decided she was respectable enough not even to need to brush her hair, and ran lightly down the stars and out into the front garden.

The older woman was retreating up the path of the cottage opposite. The younger, in the act of removing her bag from the boot of her Fiat 500, had stopped to place her hands on her hips and seemed to be administering a telling-off to a haughty-looking grey cat that sat on the adjacent wall staring at her in the manner of a being who owed no-one anything. Lexie liked cats and was always keen to make their acquaintance so it seemed as good a time as any other to introduce herself to her neighbour, especially when the cat, if it proved attentive, would give her something to fuss over during the conversation.

I'm such a fidget, she chided herself. It was a habit Nico had once found charming but which had latterly come to irritate him. He had suppressed it, to a degree, but she'd increasingly spotted him opening his mouth to speak whenever she was playing with a cork from a bottle, or a pen, or her cuffs, and when she'd picked up the cue and stopped he had closed it abruptly. That was only one of many signs, some of them seemingly trivial, others more significant, that had prompted her to end their relationship. If she hadn't he would have done, and she knew how brutal that would have been. Nico was a man who loved well, but he left ruthlessly and without regrets and this way at least the scorched-earth policy of his loving left her self-respect intact.

'Good evening,' she said to the woman, with her best film-star smile. 'What a lovely evening. And what a beautiful cat!'

The woman, as she expected, responded immediately to this overture with a genuine smile of her own. At close quarters Lexie could see a lanyard around her neck but it was turned inwards and she couldn't read the name.

'It really is a beautiful evening.' Her new neighbour pointed a forefinger down at the cat. 'But please don't say things like that to Holmes. He's big-headed enough as it is.' She beamed indulgently down on the animal.

'I'm Lexie Romachenka.' Lexie bent down to fuss the cat, which rubbed its chin against her hand in ecstasy.

'Becca Reid.' The woman closed the boot of the car and her lanyard twisted around. *Becca Reid. District Nurse.* 'Are you renting End Cottage, then? For a holiday?'

'Yes to renting, no to the holiday. I'm here for a few weeks, maybe longer.' Lexie straightened up but left her hand down for the cat, who nudged it with its head. 'I've just come out of a relationship and I needed to get away from town so as not to keep bumping into him, which would be embarrassing for both of us.'

'Oh dear.' Becca cast a strange look, not towards Wasby End Cottage but across the road to where the other woman had disappeared. 'Yes, getting away is a good thing to do, if you can. Though in the country you bump into them all the time.' As if she had a lot of exes. She wasn't, Lexie noticed, wearing any rings, but maybe that was because she'd just come from work.

'Yes. Nico — that's his name — was so lovely, very special, but you know how it is. That kind charms everybody and it goes to their heads because everybody loves them. They start taking you for granted and mess you around, thinking you'll always forgive them.' Thinking they could get away with anything. Nico always had, until he'd crossed Lexie Romachenka. She smiled.

'Hm.' Becca hovered on the path. 'Oh dear. Though having said that I'm sure Wasby is the very best place to go if you want to escape someone who's in town. You mean London?'

'Yes. I live in Clapham.' Naturally Nico had a crash pad in Battersea, though Lexie had never been sure quite how he'd managed to afford it. Not that she thought he couldn't; it was just that his sources of income had always been somewhat obscure, and when it came to money his public lavishness was over-compensated for by a mean streak as hard as a vein of quartz in Lakeland slate.

'What a contrast,' said Becca and laughed. It wasn't brittle or sarcastic, just a normal laugh as if something had amused her and not at anyone's expense, and Lexie's response was instant and warm. She and Becca would get on. 'You'll love it here. But why Wasby? Do you know this area well?'

'Not this bit in particular, but I do know parts of Cumbria very well.' Lexie leaned on the wall, not caring if the damp moss that crept between the cracks left a mark on her jeans. Her sense of freedom was absolute. For all his professed love for her, Nico had never cared enough about anyone to follow them out of London to somewhere where the pubs closed at eleven (or maybe earlier, she wasn't sure) and you had to drive halfway across the county if you wanted something Michelin-starred to eat, with the added irritant of either not drinking or paying a fortune for a taxi. She felt safe, so much so that she had to suppress the urge to twirl around as if in *West Side Story*. *I feel pretty*, her heart sang to her. 'I'm a location scout and I was up here for several weeks a while back. I stayed in Windermere and I was up over towards Langdale, mainly, but I did come to the Eden Valley, too.'

'Goodness me,' said Becca, in what seemed like genuine admiration. 'That's very glamorous.'

It wasn't, really. The job involved long, dull meetings in which everyone talked over everyone else, hours watching videos badly-made by others, and endless treks to potential locations only to discover at the next endless meeting that most were entirely unsuitable for the purpose. 'Only sometimes.'

She waited for Becca to ask her more, which anybody at the endless parties and drinks receptions she attended in London would surely have done without hesitation (*Tell me about the film. Who was in it? Who did you meet? Oh my God, what was he like?*) but Becca merely nodded. Perhaps in the country people weren't so brazen, or just not interested in the ways of strangers, only themselves and the intricacies of their own tedious lives.

'And so,' went on Lexie, 'when I decided it was time to end it with Nico and have a break, naturally I thought of here.'

'Why Wasby?' Becca flicked a look at the village, barely more than a single street without a shop or a church or a school, just a handful of cottages, a farm at either end and a dilapidated-looking village hall sitting in isolation like a leper on the road to Askham. 'I mean, I wouldn't live anywhere else, but I was born here and I'm used to it. It's hardly a metropolis, is it?'

'That's the attraction.'

'I suppose. Especially if you're off men.' Becca looked at the other cottage again with a scowl.

Lexie wasn't off men — the opposite, in fact — though it was easy to see how Becca had come to that assumption. Without a man she felt isolated and alone. Her mother scolded her for this weakness, for being too much of a people-pleaser, for needing the attention, but it was what it was. She was always careful never to lose her heart, which had been another reason for leaving Nico, whose dangerous attraction and extreme good looks were only enhanced by his mysterious wealth, but she loved the admiration and security that came from a beau on her arm. 'I wouldn't say that. I'm thirty now, and ready to settle down and he wasn't the type. Sometimes you have to look out for yourself, you know?'

Becca's responding laugh was hollow. 'Yes. I do.'

'Why don't you come round for a drink?' asked Lexie, on impulse. 'The people who own the cottage left me a bottle of wine and it would be a shame to drink it on my own.'

Becca's face, as free of make up as Lexie's own and all the clearer for it, flared into pleasure and then disappointment. 'I'd love to, but I've a village hall committee meeting tonight.'

Wasby was that sort of place, then. Everybody would be public-spirited and involved, consumed by a desire to help the community rather than improve their own careers, trampling on other people on the way up. 'Tomorrow? We could invite your neighbour, perhaps.'

'Linda? Oh yes, that's a good idea. She's lovely. Or you could come round to me and I could make a cake.'

Of course she would. Lexie hadn't expected anything else. Her heart warmed. 'Tomorrow evening?'

'Come at seven,' said Becca, picking up her bag and turning to the door. 'So nice to meet you, Lexie. But now I'd better go and feed my lord and master.'

The cat had become more vocal during the conversation. Lexie watched as Becca followed the animal up to the door then headed back into her own kitchen, got out her laptop and did her online grocery order. Then, remembering a promise she too often failed to fulfil, she texted her mother. *made it 2 Wasby found a friend already*

Nico's number was still in her phone, taunting her, but finally she found the courage to delete it. She would never need to use it again.

TWO

'Am I through to a detective?'

'Yes, you are. Detective Sergeant O'Halloran speaking.' Ashleigh O'Halloran sighed. Sometimes it took just a few words to know you'd struck unlucky and she was already wishing she'd left the phone for someone else to answer. On the other side of the open-plan office half a dozen detectives were engaged in small-talk after a routine briefing meeting, and if she hadn't strayed away from the chat those few seconds too early any one of them would have been closer to the phone than she would. *C'est la vie*, she said to herself with the smallest shrug. 'How can I help you?'

'My name is Annabel Faulkner,' said the voice at the other end, clear and assertive, 'and I wish to report a missing person.'

'Okay.' Ashleigh sat down and pulled a pen and a sheet of paper towards her. 'Let's get some details, then, Ms Faulkner. Who is missing and under what circumstances?'

'My husband,' said Annabel Faulkner and there was contempt in her tone. 'His name is Simon Morea — that's

DEATH ON THE SMALL SCREEN

pronounced *Moray*, emphasis on the second syllable, spelt M-O-R-E-A.'

'Okay.' An unusual name. Had she ever heard it before? 'And may I ask, how old is your husband, and how long has he been missing?'

'Simon is fifty. I last saw him a week ago, last Monday. Since then he has been absent.'

'I see. And he's missing from…where?' Even as she noted down the details Ashleigh knew how this matter would be dealt with, and she also had the sense that Annabel Faulkner wasn't going to take kindly to it. The word *absent* was the giveaway. It didn't mean he'd disappeared, just that his wife couldn't find him. She'd seen that film before, too many times.

'We live in London but we have a house at Troutbeck, outside Windermere. He came up here to stay last Friday, I believe for the weekend, and he hasn't been in touch since.'

'You didn't travel up with him?'

There was a snort from the other end of the line. 'Simon and I spend as little time together as possible. When I hadn't heard from him and he wasn't even interested enough to argue with me, I drove up from London to see what he was up to. I arrived this morning and he isn't at the house.'

'Okay.' It was best to proceed cautiously with this one. 'And does Mr Morea have any vulnerabilities?'

That snort again. 'Women. Drink. Living the high life. Probably the odd illegal substance, though I couldn't possibly comment on that to a police officer. You might call those vulnerabilities. He sees them as strengths.'

'I was thinking more of any mental or physical health issues,' said Ashleigh, as pleasantly as she could. Already the picture was forming in her mind, a man with a roving eye or in the throes of a mid-life crisis who, for whatever reason, no longer wished to be with his wife and wasn't prepared to do her the courtesy of telling her to her face that he was leaving her. Annabel's suppressed fierceness suggested he might be wise.

'Simon was at the very peak of his fitness, a man in his prime,' said his not-very-happy wife, 'at least in his own opinion.'

'I see. And when you arrived at the property, Ms Faulkner, was there anything that caused you to think your husband's disappearance was in any way suspicious? Had he left his phone, perhaps, or his jacket?' It was September and even in good weather anyone who knew the Lakes would be mad to go out without some kind of outer wear. 'Or were there any signs that he'd left in a hurry?'

'No.' Perhaps because she was being taken more seriously than she might have expected, Annabel Faulkner had calmed down a little. 'His car was parked at the house, but his coat and boots were missing. There's no sign of his wallet though his phone was there. There was food in the fridge but most of it was out of date.'

'If he took his wallet and coat it sounds as if he left the house for a normal reason, then. Was he a hillwalker?' The most likely reason for the man's absence was that he'd gone for a walk, forgetting his phone, and had an accident. After a week, that wasn't good news but without knowing where he'd gone there wasn't much they could do about it.

'Simon didn't walk,' she said, dismissively, 'or not anywhere that required any exertion. The boots were for purely for show. He came to the country to get away from town and so that he could preach to gullible young women about nature and try and persuade them he had a beautiful soul. In reality all he did when he was here was sit in the house and drink.'

You wouldn't want to get on the wrong side of Annabel

Faulkner, but Ashleigh had a suspicion that was exactly what she was about to do. 'Is it normal for him not to respond to your messages?'

'For a day or so, maybe. Not for a week.'

'And is there any sign that he might have left the area and gone somewhere else? Has he perhaps taken any money from joint accounts, or are there any bank transactions for train or flight tickets, for example?'

'No. But we have separate accounts as well as our joint one.'

It was a pretty straightforward missing person enquiry, then. They could alert the Mountain Rescue to keep an eye out, and ask around to see if anyone had seen Annabel's errant husband, but Ashleigh reckoned not. If he'd chosen to disappear he'd have made sure no-one saw him go. 'Okay, Ms Faulkner, could you give me some details about your husband? A description, perhaps, and what he might have been wearing.'

'I'm surprised you haven't heard of him. He's a well-known producer and director of art house films.'

Who had time to read the credits at the end of a film? Come to think of it, when did Ashleigh last have the time to go to the pictures? 'I'm afraid not.' Even as she said it she thought Annabel might be quietly gratified to hear her errant husband so belittled.

'Google will give you a better description of him than I can, and much more quickly. As for what he was wearing, I've no idea, apart from a green Barbour jacket. Whatever it was will have been expensive, flashy and painfully trendy, which doesn't necessarily mean it will have suited him, or been particularly practical. The opposite, in fact.'

'Exactly when did you last see him?'

'At our house in Fulham, a week ago yesterday, Thursday. We ate dinner together. He was still in bed when I went to the office the next morning.' Annabel reeled off the details of her address and workplace. If nothing else, she was admirable in her supply of detail. 'That's all I can tell you. I trust you'll treat this matter as a high priority, given his position.'

His position. Who did these people think they were, and why should the problems of the privileged take precedence over those of the vulnerable? 'Obviously, Ms Faulkner, I appreciate your concerns. But as Mr Morea is an adult without any vulnerabilities, and as there are no indications of foul play or accident, I'm afraid there's very little we can do other than keep an eye out for him.' The Lake District was a huge place and Morea had been gone for a week.

'That isn't the answer I was expecting to hear from you, Sergeant,' said Annabel Faulkner, an edge of steel in her voice.

Ten years in the police had more than equipped Ashleigh to deal with the entitlement of a certain segment of the public. 'I understand that. But I'm afraid that's how it is. It's by no means unusual for adults to…take some time out…and it's not illegal. From what you say, and particularly given that Mr Morea is extremely unlikely to have gone up onto the fells, it sounds as though he may have gone off somewhere of his own volition, for reasons of his own.'

'Yes, and I know exactly what reasons those would be.'

'I understand. But if I'm honest with you, Ms Faulkner,' said Ashleigh, incautiously, because she guessed she was dealing with a woman who might not respect honesty from others as much as she claimed to value it in herself, 'I expect you'll hear from him, once he—'

'Once he runs out of money. Yes. But that could be a while. So let me be absolutely straight with you, Sergeant O'Halloran. Nothing untoward has happened to Simon.

No-one's killed him. He hasn't killed himself. He hasn't got lost on the fells. He's disappeared because he knows I'm hell-bent on divorcing him and he wants to seize the initiative. I'm the one who brought the assets to our marriage and I've no doubt he's taking the chance to salt away as many of our joint assets as he can. I imagine there's a burglary due to happen in our London home very soon, if it isn't happening already, and that my jewellery and many other things will fall victim to it.'

'I'm afraid that isn't a police matter, Ms Faulkner.' From across the room Jude Satterthwaite, Ashleigh's boss and (these days occasional) lover threw her a questioning glance, to which she replied with an extravagant shrug.

'A burglary isn't a police matter?'

'If I understand you correctly, no burglary has occurred, and as your property you refer to is in London any issue would be dealt with by the Metropolitan Police. I'm afraid that as your husband is an adult and there's no evidence of anything suspicious, there's nothing we can do.'

'Fraud is a criminal offence,' said Annabel, in a steely tone.

'Are you saying fraud has been committed? Do you have any evidence for that?'

In the ensuing pause, Ashleigh watched the knot of her colleagues on the other side of the room begin to break up, amid laughter, and get back to whatever routine task they had been engaged in.

'I do not,' said Annabel, eventually.

'Then, as I say, I'm afraid it's not a police matter. We'll take a note and keep a look out for him.'

'May I ask what exactly we pay you for?'

That old chestnut. At least she hadn't said *I pay your wages*. 'I'm sorry I can't help you any further.'

'My next step will be a private investigator,' said Annabel, as if Ashleigh cared, 'and if it turns out that Simon's absence has cost me anything, or if a robbery occurs and he's responsible, then I will be considering my legal options with regard to your highly unsatisfactory response.'

Good luck with that. It wasn't hard to imagine what the Professional Services Department would make of Annabel and any putative complaint. 'I'm so sorry I can't help you, Ms Faulkner,' said Ashleigh again, and waited for the inevitable click as Annabel cut her off. When it came she dropped the receiver back in its cradle, tossed the pen down, pushed the notepad away and sighed.

'Is everything okay, Ash?' Jude, hands in his pockets, came strolling over. Annabel had been scathing of her husband's dress sense; it was difficult to imagine what she might make of Jude, who always opted for the formal but understated look and never failed to carry it off. 'I wouldn't say I'm a body language expert, but judging by the way you looked when you were on the phone I'd say someone just wasted ten minutes of public resources on a triviality.'

'You guessed right.' Ashleigh pulled back the pad, tore off the sheet of paper on which she'd written the details, and handed it to him. 'Angry wife, errant husband. He's missing, but she's not remotely concerned about his personal welfare. She wants us to chase him down so she can serve him with divorce papers.'

'Missing?' he inquired, interested.

'There are no suspicious circumstances. It's technically possible he might have got lost on the fells because he was last seen at their house in Troutbeck, but she's adamant he never goes walking for pleasure. He's done a runner, by the sound of it, and I have to say I don't blame him.' She'd come across this type of caller before. The difference was that none of those she had met previously had had the determination and entitlement of Annabel Faulkner.

Jude scanned the sheet of paper. 'Simon Morea. Do I know that name?'

'You might do. He's in films, apparently.' No doubt if Annabel was the one with the money a good chunk of her wealth might have found itself invested in his various projects. That was what people did when they were young and in love; they invested in one another. As they grew older and squabbles led to infidelities and breakdown the investments became restraints or, worse, weapons for them to use against one another. Annabel's call represented just one side of what sounded like a doomed marriage hurtling to its bitter end. You didn't have to be rich to endure that.

'I'm not that into film,' admitted Jude, 'but I imagine Doddsy will know.' He turned and flourished the sheet of paper at DI Chris Dodd, known to all as Doddsy, who was on his way out of the room. 'Have you got a minute? We need to pick your brain about the arts and culture sector.'

Ashleigh grinned. That was one of the attractive things about Jude. Annabel's call indicated an open-and-shut case, one in which they could reasonably take no action, but if his interest was triggered he always found a minute to follow up. 'It's not important.'

'No, but it's interesting. Maybe more interesting for the newspapers than for us, but a missing celebrity, even a minor celebrity, is always worth keeping an eye open for. You can bet your life if it does get into the papers they'll be on the phone to us before you can say BAFTA, demanding to know what we're doing about it, so it's best to be prepared.'

'What's the crisis, then?' asked Doddsy, as casual as Jude. It seemed to be one of those rare moments when the place was quiet. Policing in Cumbria was never as high-stress as it was in major cities but even with a relatively low crime rate they were never short of work — and in particular, as Jude was wont to complain about, paperwork. 'Nothing serious, I hope.'

In a few words, Ashleigh recapped her phone conversation. 'Jude reckons he's heard of Simon Morea, but I confess I never have.'

Doddsy nodded, sagely. 'I can't tell you a lot, but he does films. Low-budget art house stuff, mainly. Lots of soft-focus landscape shots and weird goings on. Think *Wicker Man*, but less popular and with plenty of overt left-wing social commentary. And the plots are a bit more convoluted. There's always a twist. I think he's more than a producer, though. A producer-director, if there's such a thing. I'm not sure I know the difference but he's pretty hands-on, and he invests.'

'I'm impressed.' Ashleigh took the piece of paper and frowned at it. In truth, if the man was that well known, and if he had disappeared, it would be difficult to justify doing nothing if popular pressure demanded that something should be done. How long might it be before someone other than Annabel realised he was missing and came to the police for comment? 'I didn't have you down as a film buff.'

'I'm not, but Tyrone is. You have to try new things, don't you?' Doddsy looked a bit pink. His much-younger partner was rather more on trend than he was himself. Ashleigh suspected he worried about it more than Tyrone did, but that was natural enough when one of the pair had almost twenty-five years in the police and the other was only in his mid-twenties. There must be relationships on the planet that were uncomplicated, or she supposed there must, but she'd never come across one. 'We go to the Alhambra occasionally if there's something like that on, but I can't say I pay a lot of attention. It's more of an opportunity for a snooze when you get to my age.' He laughed.

'You haven't heard of the wife? Annabel Faulkner?'

'No, that level of detail is beyond me. I can't tell you much more about him than the name and the films. Difficult, was she?'

'Difficult, vengeful and hard as nails,' said Ashleigh, wondering what Annabel Faulkner was like and how far she might go to punish the man she thought had wronged her. 'I tell you one thing. I wouldn't want to be Mr Morea when he finally pops up again.'

THREE

'Mum tells me you've got a new neighbour.' Jude Satterthwaite loitered on the grass verge that passed for a pavement in Wasby and cursed his timing.

'Oh,' said Becca, looking as irritated about it as he was, as if she was frustrated at his attempt to breach the awkward silence that too often descended between them these days. 'Yes. I certainly have.'

There was a pause — yet another one — in which Jude looked towards Linda Satterthwaite's cottage, saw his mother wave in his direction, waved back and decided not to head up to the front door straight away. 'From down south,' he said, helpfully.

'You are so nosy,' said Becca, in a sudden burst of familiarity that reminded him of when they'd been lovers rather than the tentative friends they now were.

He smiled at that. She'd almost sounded affectionate. 'I can't help myself. It's my inquisitive nature.'

'Is that what it is?' said Becca, and shook her head. He thought she was trying not to smile but these days he could never be sure. 'You get more like Holmes every day. Or is it that he gets more like you?'

He still loved her, that was the problem. They'd been together for a long time. The break-up had been at her instigation and he was sure she now regretted it, but too much water had gone under the bridge in the intervening few years for them to go back to the way they'd been. He'd tried, and had been brutally rebuffed, so now if there was to be any movement it could only come from Becca. So far there had been no positive sign, and yet these difficult encounters persisted. Every time he came to Wasby to visit his mother, which he did more often than was strictly necessary and on the slenderest of excuses, he'd find Becca in her garden or fetching something from the car, or on the front step calling in Holmes from whatever hunting expedition he was on underneath the shrubs that formed a tangled thicket beside the wall. Throughout it all, he continued to dally in that on-off relationship with Ashleigh, who herself was still in love with her ex-husband, while Becca watched from the sidelines as the dance went on, endless and graceful as a Celtic knot.

'Okay?' he asked, to prolong the contact.

'You mean Holmes? Or the neighbour?'

'I already know Holmes is okay.' He laughed.

'My neighbour seems pleasant enough, I have to say.' Becca flipped an irritated finger at Holmes, who ignored her. 'But somehow the set-up seems a bit odd to me.'

Nothing intrigued him more than an odd set-up, the more so when it meant he could string out the few minutes in her company. He shuffled a little on the spot. 'Tell all.'

Becca glanced at Wasby End Cottage and lowered her voice, even though there was no car outside and the cottage, like the rest of the village, had a forlorn, autumnal look about it. It was a grey September day with a bank of cloud in the west and a rising breeze. A spit of rain completed the threat. In the Satterthwaite household, Linda flipped a lamp on, though it was barely six o'clock. 'I hope it doesn't rain. I've got my washing out.'

'I'll help you get it in, if you like.'

She looked up at the sky, where a helpful break in the clouds exposed blue sky only to snatch it away again. 'It'll be fine. And I expect you'll be in a rush. You always are.'

He didn't think that was intended to be as bitter as it had sounded, but Becca had always been resentful of the amount of time he spent at work and he thought that had been one of the things that both counted towards the end of their relationship and prevented her taking any steps to rekindle it. If he had his time over again, would he do things differently? Who knew? 'It's quiet at work at the moment. I haven't been down to see Mum and Mikey for a while, so I thought I'd come along this evening. But apparently the little blighter's off to some book launch or other in Grasmere, so I'll hardly see him.' Mikey's car was still there so he hadn't yet left, but if Jude wanted a chat with his younger brother he should probably go and do it straight away.

'He does get around.'

Still Jude lingered. Mikey would be there another day. 'You were saying,' he reminded her. 'About your neighbour.'

'There's not really that much to tell. Lexie — that's her name, Lexie Romachenka — moved in at the beginning of last week. She came round a couple of days ago and we had a glass of wine and a chat.'

'That's an unusual name.'

'She's Russian by descent, or Belarussian or something. Her grandfather or great-grandfather or whatever came over during the war. The Russians had an air base in Shetland, did you know that?'

Jude wrinkled his brow. 'History's not my strong point.'

'It was something to do with the Atlantic convoys. He was a prince or something, but his family lost all their money after the Revolution except for whatever they managed to smuggle abroad, jewels sewn into their clothes and so on, and now it's all locked up in a trust somewhere that she's waiting to inherit. He was posted to Shetland, but his family all died in the siege of Leningrad so he had nothing to go back for.'

'He was definitely better staying where he was.'

'Well, quite. Anyway, he met this land girl and married her and stayed.'

'A prince!' said Jude, and looked again at Wasby End Cottage.

'I know, I know.' She flapped a hand, amused. 'I don't imagine it counts for anything much, or ever did. There were thousands of Russian aristocrats.'

'I imagine they cling to their titles in exile. They'd have not much else.'

'And I imagine family stories get embroidered. Anyway, that's her background. She works as a location scout for films and TV. She scouts for everything — property programmes and feature films, TV ads, corporate videos, everything. And she knows so many people!'

Jude never trusted a name-dropper. In his experience anyone who had to borrow someone else's reputation was either hiding something or else was usually deeply dissatisfied with their own life. 'What's she doing out in the sticks? Working?'

'She says she's had enough of the hurly-burly of London life and it isn't good for her so she's taken the cottage for a few weeks to get away from it all. She does look a bit peaky, I have to say, and so unnaturally thin. I'd worry about her if I was her mother.'

'The fresh country air will do her a lot of good.' Jude sniffed the air and appreciated it. He'd lived in Cumbria all his life and couldn't imagine living somewhere where there was never a chance of a moment's silence.

'She's planning to take lots of long walks and eat healthy home cooking and plenty of cake. Yes. But the real reason she's here is that she's dumped her boyfriend and, as she says, this is the last place he'd come to find her even if he wanted her back. I get the impression he doesn't know what the countryside is.'

He looked at her, trying to pretend it was Lexie Romachenka he was interested in. It was true, up to a point. He was interested in everything and everybody, because it was part of his job and you never knew whether some nugget of information might come in handy at a later date. People saw things, and knew things, and talked about them. 'She doesn't seem to have held back with her conversation.'

'I think,' said Becca, considering, 'that she likes to talk about herself. Some people do. Your trouble is that you spend too much time talking to people who have things to hide so you assume it's true of everyone, but she wasn't like that. She reminded me a little of some of my patients, the ones who live alone. When I call on them all they want to do is talk about the utter trivia of their lives, because they're lonely. Lexie struck me as being a little bit like that. It's not that that she's selfish or self-absorbed, or I don't think so. It's just that she doesn't really know how to have a proper conversation and she doesn't know how to talk about anything other than herself.'

He nodded. His chats with Becca were always mundane, lingering on into inconsequence when with anyone else he would have cut the conversation short and moved on. Mikey, who was a good fifteen years younger than him and a whole generation more gregarious, worked in marketing and was as nosy as Jude himself though a much more natural networker, but even he occasionally complained about the vacuous conversations he so often ended up having as part of his job. 'I've never been to a showbiz party but I imagine they're all like that.'

'I'm sure you're right. No-one's going to ask about you so you have to tell them regardless. I imagine you soon learn not to be self-effacing. Your mum and I were listening open-mouthed at some of the tales she had to tell. Parties on yachts in Monte Carlo, publishing soirées at the Groucho Club, film premières at Leicester Square, the lot.'

'A few pints at the Queen's Head will come as a bit of a shock to her.' He grinned. He fancied a pint himself, but as Mikey wasn't around he'd have to do without, or wait until he got home.

'I got the impression she was looking forward to it. I think she's rather hoping to get to know some the local menfolk, as well.'

'She's not nursing a broken heart, then.'

'Definitely not.' Becca shook herself slightly, as if she was judgemental and annoyed with herself about it. 'And hats off to her. Who wouldn't want to find a better alternative to the man they just dumped?'

There was a pregnant pause while Jude thought about how Becca had dated his former best friend to spite him and she, judging by the deepening pink of her face and the increasing irritation in her expression, thought the same and was chiding herself for her clumsiness.

'You should introduce her to Adam,' he said, risking a joke about the man in question.

'Don't laugh, but I already have done. He came along

while we were chatting in the street so I could hardly not. And of course when she was here your mother had to go and mention you and sing your praises to the heavens, so now Lexie must think the whole of Wasby is paved with the broken hearts of my former admirers. Which, of course, is anything but the truth.'

'Is she good looking?' he asked, to tease her.

'She is, very much so, and she'll be even better looking when she's had a few decent meals. Though it shouldn't matter to you because you're spoken for, as I made an effort to point out to her. But yes, she'll be quite the shot in the arm for any eligible males.' She shook her head. 'She made me feel quite dowdy by comparison.'

He looked at her and she looked away. Becca was no classic beauty, for sure, and lacked the overt attraction of Ashleigh O'Halloran, but there was something about the curve of her figure and the tilt of her head that had always attracted him and her smile (rarely bestowed on him these days) lit up her face so that even now he couldn't look at her without a tug of regret. Love wasn't about looks but about personality; it defied quantification and evidence. He and Becca had been compatible and in love and yet somehow they were apart. Somewhere in his head there was a string of words that were the answer to this, an answer he thought she was waiting for, but what could he say that wasn't too clumsy, that didn't breach the stricture she'd set him the last time he'd made a move: *don't ever ask me about that again?*

The front door of the Satterthwaites' cottage burst open and Mikey bounded down the path.

'Hello lovebirds!' he yelled joyfully. 'Chatting about sweet nothings again?'

'Seriously, Mikey?' Normally Becca took Mikey's teasing calmly, but today something — Jude himself, possibly, or the arrival of a beautiful stranger giving her a sigh of regret that she was single and homely — had set her onto an unusually sensitive path. 'Don't be such an idiot. Imagine if someone heard you and told Ashleigh? That would put Jude in a really awkward position.'

Mikey, who had known Becca all his life and treated her with exactly the same lack of reverence he displayed to Jude, made a face. 'It was a joke. Anyway, who's going to tell her?'

Jude would, later. He and Ashleigh were lovers but not in love and so he tended to tell her everything, because there was neither risk nor reward in keeping secrets. Besides, Ashleigh was so intuitive she'd guess even if he stayed silent. She always did. It was better to be honest. 'Have a good evening, Mikey.'

'See you.' Mikey got into the car, slammed the door and shot off down the road like a boy racer, leaving Jude and Becca staring at each other.

'I'd better get that washing in, then,' said Becca, eventually, and they turned their separate ways without another word.

FOUR

In the Queen's Head in Askham, a couple of miles up the road from Wasby, Lexie was making the acquaintance of the locals. Her self-imposed exile from London had in no way diminished her gregariousness; strangers never intimidated her and it was an added bonus to discover that in this place, where the same people might have been coming to the same pub, sitting in the same seats and drinking the same drinks since before the dawn of time, she was fresh and different and, therefore, the centre of attention. It was a welcome change from her usual routine of hanging round on the fringes of film parties, trying to catch the attention of this actor, that producer or the other journalist, attracting only the extras and the hangers-on. Crossing her legs demurely at the ankles she settled in the comfortable banquette in corner with her negroni (the barman had found that more of a challenge than he ought to have done, but he'd made a decent job of it in the end) conscious that the eyes of the place were on her.

And that was exactly as she liked it. Without being too obvious, she looked around and immediately spotted exactly what she was looking for — a handsome man of around her own age, elegant in smart jeans and jacket and a crisp white shirt, heading in her direction. Even better — it was Adam Fleetwood, to whom she had briefly been introduced by Becca Reid, and he was heading across the room towards her with a drink in his hand.

'So, the new girl on the block has come along to join us,' he said smiling at her. 'It's good to see you again, Lexie.'

'I'm just visiting for a few weeks,' said Lexie, more for the benefit of any listeners than for Adam, who appeared already to regard himself as suitable company for her in the way that country people seemed so easily to do. When she thought about it she was confident that the bush telegraph would already have transmitted everything she'd told them about herself; if it hadn't, the two women to whom she'd revealed her life story weren't doing the village grapevine the justice it deserved.

She and Adam gave each other a quick once-over and she concluded from the way he was looking at her that he'd be interesting company but not a nuisance. 'Do sit down.' Graciously, she indicated the empty seat next to her. 'Unless you're with someone. Though of course they'd be welcome to join us, too.'

'Nope,' he said with a grin that didn't reach his eyes, and sat down. 'I'm Billy No-Mates tonight, so I'm glad I bumped into you.' He took a packet of cigarettes out of his pocket, looked at them hungrily and put them back again. It was a trick Lexie recognised, one she'd used herself in the past, the cigarettes offering a way to excuse herself from an unwelcome situation should the need arise, but she didn't usually telegraph it quite so clearly. Adam was interested in gossip and being seen with a glamorous and mysterious young woman (Lexie knew her exact value and never did herself down) and no more. The cigarettes were his escape route. Which was fine. The way he looked around the pub and smiled and nodded as if he were the King indicated he had plenty of contacts and that was what she was after.

She cast a quick look around again under the pretence of picking at the garnish on her negroni, which looked suspiciously like the last shout of mint from the pub's garden. There had been a ripple of attention among the onlookers when Adam had approached her and she'd greeted him, as if she'd dropped a stone in a deep, deep pond and disturbed something long left sleeping. It almost felt as if they were more interested in him than in her. Becca had been disappointingly short on the details about who Adam was and where he came from after he'd strolled along the street to introduce himself, but Lexie was never afraid to ask an interesting man a question.

'Tell me about yourself,' she said, straight up front so that he laughed after a moment of alarm. 'I know everyone's talked all about me but I have a lot to learn about everyone else. You're a good place to start.'

He shook his head. 'I'm surprised you haven't heard my entire life story, seeing you hang out with Becca Reid and Linda Satterthwaite and neither of them lets anything past them.'

This was undoubtedly true, but Lexie thought both women also seemed able to resist the temptation to tell all of it. In Adam's voice it sounded harsh, as though he disliked both Becca and Linda at some base level, for reasons of his own. *Text and subtext*, Nico used to say with a sneer when people said something and so often meant something less pleasant. He himself never bothered pretending to be polite.

'It's okay,' she said, fluttering her eyelashes at him and sipping at her negroni. 'I'm not looking to cause any trouble. Just to make some friends.'

'Friends is all,' he said, and tapped the pocket with the cigarettes in it. Lexie knew the type. She came across it often — in her job you came across every sort and most of them were drunk and didn't show themselves off to the best advantage. Adam Fleetwood wasn't interested in a relationship with her (though as a man he might not be averse to a little casual sex) but he was crucified by curiosity and he needed to know everything and be seen to be at the centre of things.

'You're spoken for?' she asked, sweetly. It was a strangely old-fashioned phrase but Nico had used it on her when they first met a few years before, and so she found it comfortingly seductive and always effective. And it had always worked for him.

'In a manner of speaking.' He sat back, drank deeply and, when he was done, put his glass down and smiled. 'I'm the local villain and yes, I'm spoken for.'

She met his eye. Did he look like a villain? 'Villains are far more interesting than the good guys. Don't you know that?'

He laughed. 'It certainly seems that way around here.'

'So what did the local villain do?' she dared him. The cocktail had gone straight to her head and, as it always did, drove her to speak frankly. It was so refreshing to be able to speak without worrying about whether someone present might know her boss or Nico or, in the worst-case scenario, Nico's wife. Here in Wasby she was her own woman and not responsible for anyone's business or unjustly held to account for a man's tomcat morals.

He laughed again. Either he was amused by her or else it hid his true feelings. 'I'm astonished Becca didn't tell you. But maybe her own part in it is something she doesn't want to think too much about.'

'Oh?'

'The local villain did time for dealing drugs,' said Adam, with the clipped disinterest of a bank manager reading out a list of figures to a customer. 'Unjustly, of course.'

'Unjustly?' she asked, feigning breathless interest.

'It was possession for personal use.' He shrugged. 'Everyone does that.'

'Surely the police don't come down on hard on you for that?' In London, in the circles in which she moved, drugs were as much a fact of life as alcohol. Arresting and charging users would be an overwhelming task and she never gave the legality of the matter a second thought.

'It depends on the police.' His lip curled and his handsome face darkened, so that for a moment an ugliness appeared where before he had been craggily good-looking. 'I'd been sharing some weed with a few mates and one of them was a copper's brother. You know what the pigs are like. This one in particular. They bear grudges and they have power.'

'*Bozhe moy!*' said Lexie, and threw up her hands as she imagined her great-grandfather might have done. 'I mean, goodness me! And did you really end up in prison because of a bit of weed?'

'I did. And naturally Becca didn't tell you about it because although she's an old friend of mine she was the cop's partner at the time. Though to be fair she didn't take his side. She broke up with him over it.'

It was no wonder Becca had remained tight-lipped on the subject. 'That's terrible!'

'You think so?' Adam gave her a searching look, and not altogether a friendly one. 'I thought you'd have been all over it, it being such a good story and you being in films.' He cocked his head to one side, inquiringly.

'Injustice so often is the core theme of a good story,' she said, putting down her empty glass and warming to her theme. 'The tensions, the jeopardy, the decisions. All of that.' Adam's choices, Becca's, the policeman's. 'And then at the end the redemption of the hero—'

'I'm not pretending I didn't do it.' He, too, put his glass down and looked at it. 'But that man never forgives and he never forgets.'

Lexie looked across to the bar to the barman. 'Excuse me!'

'Same again?' he shouted and raised a thumb as she nodded.

She turned her attention back to Adam. 'It would make a wonderful movie. A mini-series, even. I can see it being filmed here. The hero, moody against the darkening sky.' Not unlike Heathcliff in *Wuthering Heights* which, though a well-worn trope, was nevertheless an enduringly popular one. 'The villain, plotting in some tiny office — dark, of course — determined to make his enemy pay—'

'He did make his enemy pay,' said Adam, bleakly, 'though not in the way he maybe thought. I fell in love with a wonderful girl and now she's locked up, too.'

'For trying to defend you?' asked Lexie, breathless at this possible twist.

'No, though I'm sure she would have done if she'd had to. She tried to kill someone, and that bastard Jude Satterthwaite could have stopped it if he'd been a bit better at his job.' Adam scowled.

'Satterthwaite? You mean——?'

'Linda's son. Aye. And Becca's ex.'

'Wow! I mean, that's a real twist isn't it?' In Lexie's head the credits whirred. She would play the part of the heroine, naturally, though on the basis of what he'd said she wasn't quite sure whether the heroine might turn out to be Becca or Adam's unfortunate girlfriend, but whoever it was, there wouldn't be a dry eye in the house. She was a sucker for a good story, and there was nothing more wholesome than dreaming of stardom. Who didn't see themselves at the Oscars, stepping up to collect that golden statuette? 'I know exactly where I'd film it.' There was that walk she'd done with Nico when she'd been up the previous year and he'd found an excuse to slip away from his wife for a couple of days. She might be over him but the memories weren't all bad and Lexie was hard-headed about it. Nico was gone and would never trouble her again but she wouldn't spite herself by ignoring what she'd learned from him.

Adam's grin suggested he was indulging in fantasies of his own, no doubt imagining what his enemy's response would be if such a film ever made it to the screen. Lexie was too wise to be completely taken in by a one-sided version of what was no doubt a complicated and highly nuanced tale, but he'd clearly enjoyed telling it and she was entertained by it, so where was the harm? 'Then I won't ask you to introduce me to him,' she joked.

'He wouldn't be interested in you. Don't take it personally but he was too high-minded for that kind of thing. And anyways he's already *spoken for*, as you would say. With a buxom blonde detective who's as depressingly civic-minded as he is. So you'd better not have brought any of your cocaine-fuelled London habits with you, especially given I now work for a drug rehabilitation charity and would feel obliged to offer you advice and support, for your own good.'

Better and better. What a perfect redemption. 'Your detective sounds a bit too goody-goody,' she said as the barman delivered their drinks. We'd better give him a nasty streak in the film. We wouldn't want the public being too sympathetic.'

He laughed, uproariously. 'Don't worry about him. He isn't worth your time. I'll find you some friends. I know just about everybody and everybody knows me. And in the meantime, why don't you tell me a little more about yourself?'

Later, when she'd gone back to Wasby End Cottage and fixed herself the tiniest chicken salad and a negroni that was both larger and stronger than those served in the pub, Lexie sat in the living room with the telly on, watching a French art house film and critiquing its peculiar camera angles and the gauche plainness of its leading actress. In the street outside, in the gathering dusk, Becca Reid walked briskly past on her way somewhere doubtless wholesome and community-minded and in the cottage over the road Linda Satterthwaite was in deep conversation with a man who must be her son, but was too young to be the one who'd aroused Adam's deep enmity. Lexie sighed, contentedly. It was wise to steer clear of a detective with too much of a nose for things she might not want him to know but perhaps one day she'd conjure something out of this story and pitch it, and in the end she might become credited as its director rather than its star. They'd all be in awe of her then, all the people who'd been too busy hanging onto every word spoken by people more important than she was.

It was a dream of course, and she knew the odds against success and the need for a slice of good luck along with everything else, but what was wrong with dreaming?

The film bored her. Linda Satterthwaite drew the curtains against the autumn dusk. Other people's lives were so much more interesting than her own; the silence and the stillness she'd previously welcomed momentarily oppressed her. In London she was never more than a call or a text away from a party and a wild night and here she was in her pyjamas at nine in the evening where the only person expecting to hear from her (apart from Adam, who had already texted to invite her along to a shoot — a shoot!) was her mother.

She reached for her phone. Her mother was horribly, sometimes embarrassingly, over-protective and Lexie spent a large part of her time deflecting interest in a city life that her dour parent would have considered scandalous. Inevitably her mother would worm the truth out of her too late to make a difference and her interventions, though well-meaning, were rarely helpful in the longer term. In fairness, Lexie had been glad enough to have someone to turn to in the aftermath of her chaotic break-up with Nico but her mother, having thought the affair with Nico had been a terrible mistake, now seemed to think that running away to Cumbria was an even worse one. It wouldn't be a bad time to call home with some reassurance.

'*Dorogaya Mama,*' she said as the call connected, and patted her hair. *Dearest Mother*. 'I thought you'd like to know how I'm settling in. I've met the neighbours and they're all lovely, and tonight I went to the pub and met a most intriguing man who's going to introduce me to lots of interesting people, and later this week he's going to take me grouse shooting. Imagine that! And do you know what else? I have the most wonderful idea for a film script…'

She prattled on across her mother's many questions, not really caring what she was saying but certain of only one thing. Nico wouldn't be anywhere near this rather remarkable cinematic tale of injustice and revenge.

FIVE

'I'll get it,' said Jude, with more than a degree of relief, and dived for the phone. Normally it wasn't something he'd do when there were plenty of other officers closer to it, but on this particular occasion he was seeking a rapid exit. Dropping into the open plan office where Ashleigh and a number of the other detectives were based, he'd got more than the quick catch-up he'd bargained for and had run into Faye Scanlon while he was there. Faye, who was his boss, was thin-skinned at the best of times and today she'd proved particularly irritable and in the mood to pick a fight. After fifteen minutes spent standing in a corner defending himself over the trivialities of staffing and budgets — something in his opinion better done in private if it had to be done at all — the opportunity to interrupt the conversation was too good to pass up.

'Jude Satterthwaite speaking,' he said, and almost sighed with relief.

'I have a visitor in Reception,' said a female voice sounding both strained and resigned, at the other end of the telephone, 'and she is insisting on speaking to a detective.'

The reception staff were skilled at triaging the serious and the vexatious, presenting an all-but-impenetrable barrier between busy officers and an aggrieved public. If they called through to a detective it was important, but today Jude's experienced ear picked up an underlying resentment. That indicated a difficult member of the public, one who wouldn't be put off. He imagined the sigh the receptionist didn't dare breathe out loud and his relief at escaping from Faye was somewhat tempered. 'Okay. I'll get someone to come down and speak to her. Do you know what it's about?'

'No,' said the receptionist (warily, he thought, as though this member of the public was standing over her tapping her fingers and trying to listen in), 'but she says she spoke to one of your detectives on Friday and hasn't yet a had a response.'

It was Monday morning. Whoever was making their presence felt in reception had no idea of how much work they had to do and probably expected them all to work seven days a week. 'What's the name?'

'A Ms Annabel Faulkner.'

He should have guessed. 'Okay. Thank you. I'll get someone onto it straight away.' He replaced the phone and turned away.

'Annabel Faulkner?' said Faye, who had followed him to the phone and had been listening in. 'Isn't she the missing film director's wife?'

Jude had a lot of issues with Faye, whose personality and working style were in direct contrast with his own, but he could only admire the grasp of detail with which she kept so tight a control on everything that went on on her watch. 'Yes, that's right. She called in a few days ago and spoke to Ashleigh.'

'And has Ashleigh done anything about finding this missing person?' Faye shot a look across the room to where Ashleigh was sitting typing frantically away at her laptop.

'She explained to Ms Faulkner that there's very little she could do, other than put out a call for people to keep a look out for him. There's no evidence of foul play and Ms Faulkner herself said she didn't think her husband had come to any harm. I believe he has form in terms of running off with other women and he always comes back.'

'Then why is she demanding to speak to a detective?'

He shrugged. From what he'd heard it was a fair bet that Annabel Faulkner was the type of woman who expected everybody to jump when she shouted and regarded the police as her own personal security service. 'I expect she's wondering why we haven't wasted police resources looking for a grown adult with no vulnerabilities and a history of going walkabout.'

His choice of words had hit all Faye's buttons, as he'd known it would. 'I see.' She nodded. 'That's a level of entitlement off the scale, by the sound of it. You'd better go down and speak to her.'

'I was going to ask Ashleigh to deal with it. For continuity.' Usually Faye, who was a stickler for protocol and obsessed with giving the taxpayer value for money, got antsy if he took on jobs that were below his rank. Talking to random members of the public about non-crimes fitted into exactly the category, and he was wary of it.

Today, he was wrong. Another of Faye's insecurities had come into play. 'Not on this occasion. We need to be seen to be taking this seriously.'

Ashleigh was more than competent when it came to dealing with a missing person inquiry, and could handle bolshie members of the public with ease. For a moment Jude toyed with pointing that out, but thought better of it. 'Do we? I don't see what more we can do.'

'Yes. Because while I completely understand what you're saying and Ashleigh was correct and under the circumstances there's very little we can do if we think the man has gone off of his own accord, this case needs to be handled with care. The man in question is well-known in certain circles — very well known, in fact, in the film industry — and you know what that means.' She paused, waited for a response, but she got nothing more from him than a raised eyebrow. He knew what was coming next.

'Press interest,' she said, when she finally realised she wouldn't get a reply.

Faye hated and distrusted the press. It was her fatal weakness and led her down too many paths that were better left untrodden. That was what came of indulging in an affair with a junior officer followed by a departure from a previous post under a blanket of disgrace. Because that affair had been with Ashleigh O'Halloran and coincidence had subsequently brought the two women to the same workplace, Jude had become a party to Faye's guilty secret and an unwilling accomplice in her desire to stifle press interest in anything untoward, at any cost.

'Yes. I see that.' When it came to her own personal life he thought she over-rated media and public interest, but this case wouldn't attract the normal level of press interest, instead catching the attention of the celebrity-seekers and scandal-mongers, the red-tops rather than the broadsheets. Faye's concerns, unspoken in this room where others might overhear, were suddenly relevant because a journalist chasing a non-story might have to resort to different material for the internet clicks and likes. 'I'm going to guess Ms Faulkner doesn't want the press involved, though. If she did, I think they'd know all about it by now, and so would we.'

Faye's eyes narrowed. He could imagine what was going on her head: worst-case scenarios, not involving the missing man but the tabloid headlines that might run if they didn't get a grip on them. *Scandal of Top Cop in Missing Film Producer Drama…Morea Case Boss Left Husband For A Woman…*

'Nevertheless,' she said, after a moment, 'she could make our lives very difficult. I want you to go and speak to her. You can reassure her we're doing everything we can, and when you've done that you can make damned sure we are doing something.'

Our lives. Jude almost laughed. She meant her own life. He didn't care what the papers printed about her. 'I'm not sure there's much—'

'We have to be seen to act. Get Ashleigh to check car hire places and see if he's hired a vehicle and make sure you tell the wife we're doing that. Tell Ms Faulkner we're looking at CCTV but it'll take a while because we don't know which route he might have taken. She must be expecting him to turn up. The woman's play-acting. We'll do the same.'

But she might not be. Jude, who was incurably inquisitive, had made a point of taking a quick trawl through some of the more lurid gossip sites on the internet in an idle moment and it was clear that Simon Morea was a man who cared a lot for women and nothing at all for fidelity. He'd earned that reputation early in his career and his marriage to Annabel post-dated it. If, in this case, rather than any previous one, she was so keen for him to be found, perhaps this time was different. 'Okay. I'll go down and have a word with her.'

'Don't commit us to anything we can't afford to do.'

Even in moments of apparent crisis, Faye never forgot her budgets. 'But tell her we're doing our best. Tell her we'll be checking with his workmates. Tell her anything, as long as it doesn't cost too much.'

After leaving a note on Ashleigh's desk he left the room, hiding a smile at this instruction, and headed down to the reception area. Annabel Faulkner, dressed in a blue suit that screamed designer and a scarf of pale silk so fine that it shimmered, was sitting with her handbag (he was no expert but even he could see that it was at the top end of expensive) on her lap. As he came in, and as the receptionist turned towards him as if to introduce him, she got up and faced him, holding a paper cup of coffee in her left hand as if it were a grenade.

'Ms Faulkner?' He shook her hand. Annabel Faulkner was tall, blonde, attractive, and unquestionably assertive. She looked at him with no shadow of the awe with which so many people treated the police, or the contempt that others did, but as if he were a junior bank clerk about to arrange for a transaction involving an absurdly large sum of money. 'I'm DCI Satterthwaite. I understand you wanted to speak to a detective. Is it about your husband?'

'It is.' She looked him up and down and nodded, as if he'd passed a test. He sensed she'd noted his rank and approved of it, that she felt she was being treated seriously, as if the bank clerk had called for the manager.

'Room 4 is free,' said the receptionist, helpfully, effectively destroying his plan of offering Annabel a few platitudes and then seeing her off the premises. Instead he led her to the meeting room and waved her to a chair.

'It's good of you to call in, Ms Faulkner.' He pulled out a chair and looked at her. 'How can I help? Do you have any more information on your husband's whereabouts?'

Annabel set the paper cup on the table and stared right

back at him. 'I was expecting some information from *you*, Chief Inspector. I'd assumed that, despite what your sergeant told me, you'd be making every effort to trace him.'

'We're following the usual sources in this case,' he reassured her, 'but unfortunately we have a very heavy workload and these things take time.'

'My husband's disappearance is of the most immediate importance to me.' She sipped at the coffee, fingers curled elegantly around the cup. Her nails were neat and perfectly polished and a diamond and emerald eternity ring and a huge solitaire diamond formed a guard on either side of the wedding ring on her fourth finger.

'I understand you're upset, Ms Faulkner—'

'I'm not upset. I'm angry. I don't want him back because I care two hoots about his welfare but because I'm concerned he's going to try to defraud me of my investments.'

'With respect, I think that's something you're best taking up with your financial advisors,' he said, shaking his head in apparent regret. 'And if it's a matter of your personal finances—'

'I don't think you understand. I'm exceptionally wealthy. Yes, my lawyer and business advisors insisted that Simon signed a very restrictive prenuptial agreement, but of course when you're young and in love you're foolish. I invested heavily in his film career in the early days of our marriage and although his work was critically acclaimed his creativity always ran away with his budgets and his films made a loss. Simon will never make money without a wealthy backer and I've told him, in no uncertain terms, that this particular tap is turned off. He knows our marriage is over and he knows the prenup is watertight. That means that the only way he can continue to finance his films, and the only way he can continue living the life he lives and doing the job he does, is by taking me for every penny he can before he goes. That's why he's disappeared. I want him found before he can do me any financial damage.'

'As I say, that's not a matter for us. We can't act unless a crime has been committed.' A stubborn streak hardened within him. Despite Faye's strictures he had no desire to give this woman any preferential treatment purely to assist her in her power struggle with her husband. Ashleigh's tactic of repeating the same thing over and over again in response to each of her demands had been the correct one and so he persisted with it.

'I see.' She folded her lips into a thin line, closed those perfect fingers on the empty paper cup. 'So all this talk about crime prevention is hot air, then, if you don't respond to warnings of potential crime.'

'It depends entirely on the nature of the crime.' And the credibility of the person reporting it, but he was too diplomatic to say that.

'I see,' she said again. The paper cup crumpled between her fingers. 'Oh, there is one other thing.'

There always was. He inclined his head, questioningly.

'Simon was never violent,' said Annabel, avoiding Jude's eye. 'I can't in all conscience say that. But he has a terrible temper and when he's angry he can be very threatening. He's used to having his own way. Directors always are. Everybody fawns over him and as far as I know I'm the only person who's ever stood up to him.' She fluttered her hand in front of her breast. 'He's dead set against the idea of a divorce. Not because he loves me, but because he's become very used to our lifestyle and he'd be unable to sustain it for himself. Money, as I'm sure you know, is a powerful driver and makes men do things they wouldn't otherwise do. When I first raised the subject of a separation, he threatened me with violence.'

In the ensuing silence, she folded her hands demurely on that expensive handbag and looked down. Of course she did. If she'd looked Jude in the eye he'd have seen confirmation of what he already suspected — that she was lying.

'I don't believe you mentioned that to Sergeant O'Halloran,' he said, dryly.

'I was ashamed. I'm not used to admitting I'm afraid,' she said, fiddling with her rings. 'I have my pride and people see me as a resilient woman, which I am. But at the end of the day I'm a woman and he's a man and if he does turn violent, what chance would I have?'

It was Jude's turn to look away. If he waved aside the threat of violence and violence did, by some terrible chance, occur, he'd never forgive himself, and he'd be out of a job into the bargain. For a moment he gave in to a moment of irrational speculation of which Faye would have been proud, imagining the headlines. *Cops ignored murdered woman's plea for help*.

Annabel Faulkner had him checkmated. She'd spotted the chance to force his hand and there was nothing he could do about it.

'She was lying,' he said to Faye when he'd tracked her down in her office half an hour later, 'but I could hardly challenge her on it.'

'No, you're right. Oh God. I can't abide these people who think they own us. But there are way too many cases like this and too many forces that don't take violence against women seriously enough.' She scowled. 'I should have gone down to speak to her myself.'

'Would you have dealt with it differently?' Sparks would have flown between Faye and Annabel, two women used to having their own way and neither with any patience for those who did things differently.

'No, but I'd like to have had a look at her. She sounds like a piece of work, as my mother would say. Not that I should say that of members of the public, but there you have it. Did she give you any examples of these so-called threats?'

'Once she'd shed a few crocodile tears of relief at my sudden conversion to her way of thinking, yes.' He'd spotted the motivation behind that, too — Annabel giving herself time to think up something to back up her moment of inspiration. 'There was never anything specific, and he never did anything in public.'

'Surprise, surprise,' said Faye, sourly.

'Indeed. He drinks heavily and is aggressive, though has never before been violent when drunk. When she raised the matter of the divorce he told her she'd never get away from him. He said she'd live to regret it. He said she wouldn't get away with treating him like this.' None of which he had believed and none of which, even if true, meant that Simon Morea had either the intention or the capability to kill his wife. 'I took her statement and offered her advice about security, told her to call us immediately if she felt threatened, and that we'll do our best to trace him in the meantime. And that was all I could do.'

SIX

Rather to her surprise, up in the high hills of the Pennines Lexie was having the time of her life. Adam's invitation to come along to a shoot and meet some interesting people had come at exactly the right moment and she'd snatched at it. It had required immediate action (a quick trip into Penrith first thing the next day to kit herself out with a Barbour jacket and some sensible tweeds from the local outdoor shop) but she loved the unexpected. It wasn't that she particularly approved of shooting — the opposite, in fact, and she'd struggled to suppress her generalised disapproval when Adam mentioned it — but it wasn't that hard to be noncommittal on the subject while playing the enthusiastic novice, making sure that the only chance of her injuring some poor innocent creature was entirely accidental. That way she could fit in with those among whom she found herself without compromising her vague, urban principles, with the added benefit of some observation of a sector of society to which she was a complete stranger.

The shoot would give her plenty of social contacts locally and it meant she wouldn't be sitting staring out into the garden, getting bored and regretting what she'd done. She thrived off human company; that was one thing she hadn't factored in when she'd made her grand gesture and run away, but having made the error she didn't hesitate to address it. The day had been a huge success; she'd been surrounded by admiring men, several of whom seemed to be on the market, and it was easy to overlook the scowling stares of the other two women in the party, both of whom were sturdy country types, dull brown birds clearly unprepared for the exotic bird of paradise who had landed in their midst.

'Well done, Lexie. You're not bad for a beginner.' One of the group, a stocky, bearded man with a twinkle in his eye and a wife who was already fretting impatiently with her car key, thrust a hip flask towards her. 'Have a dram to warm you up.'

'Thank you.' She offered him the demure little smile she kept for men's wives to keep them from being consumed with jealousy, and took a larger-than decorous swig.

The wife (Sonia? fretted Lexie, who was normally good with names but hadn't paid her enough attention) smiled at her. 'I'd offer you a lift home, but my taxi's full. It always is on these occasions.'

Damn. The scotch, too large a mouthful of it for peace of mind, was still burning in Lexie's throat when she remembered. She lived in the country, now, in a village where the only bus ran once a week, on a Thursday, and was only any use if you could get whatever business you had in the town done and dusted within two hours, barely enough time for a bite to eat and a run round the M&S

Food Hall. In London she never had to think twice about taking a drink. 'Oh God. Of course. I have to drive.'

'I'll run you home.' Another of the shooters stepped forward from the back of the group. He was blushing slightly, she saw with amusement, like an embarrassed teenager not a man whose slightly greying hair suggested he was approaching his fifties if he wasn't already there.

'Oh, but I couldn't ask you to do that.' She remembered his name. He was Hugh Cameron, not as Scottish as he sounded but rather your archetypal posh English countryman and he'd devoted a few moments to showing her how to shoot, though she'd spent enough time in films to have picked up the basics of at least looking competent, even without having ever touched a gun in anger. He had been shy and self-effacing, failing to ask her about herself or talk about his own life, and after that brief interaction this was the only moment he seemed able to summon enough courage to speak to her directly.

'It would be a pleasure. I'm not so far from you if you're going back to Wasby. I'm only just the far side of Bampton.'

One of Lexie's skills was a firm grasp of geography and the logistics of getting anywhere by road. She had passed through Bampton on her previous trip and in practical terms it was a long way from anywhere. 'But Wasby's so far out of your way.'

'It wouldn't be a…' He stumbled to a halt. 'I'm sorry. I shouldn't have offered. I don't want to make you uncomfortable. You don't know me.'

'I'd offer,' said Adam, intervening, 'but I'm heading off elsewhere.'

Lexie looked at her car. She had no idea how much of that stuff she'd thoughtlessly swallowed, or how strong it was. Better not to risk it. She turned back to Hugh.

'I didn't mean to sound rude,' she said, surprised by how genuine her embarrassment was at the thought of hurting his feelings. 'Thank you. That would be wonderful.'

'We're all very lovely people,' said Adam, who had no hesitation in taking a sip from his own hip flask, 'but of course, you don't know that. I can vouch for Hugh, though. I've known him for years. And besides, we all know exactly where you are so we can point the finger at him if you disappear.'

That wouldn't do you much good if he's a wrong 'un, said Lexie's mother in her head, even as everyone around laughed and Hugh's blush deepened. In London she wouldn't have dreamed of taking a lift from a stranger but here, where everyone had been so kind, it seemed insulting not to. Hugh didn't seem like a wrong 'un. Then again, Nico hadn't seemed like a wrong 'un to begin with, only misunderstood.

'But my car,' she said, apologetically. 'That's the problem. It'll still be here and I won't be able to come up and get it.' She'd just have to sit by the side of the moorland track for an hour until she was sure she was safe to drive.

'I can run you up to pick the car up tomorrow,' offered Adam.

'No,' said Hugh, 'I'll do it. My time's pretty much my own tomorrow.'

'Thank you. That's kind.' Adam, standing behind Hugh, directly in her eye-line, winked and held out the flask. She smiled again, committed, took and savoured a decent but not desperate slug. It was buttery smooth in her mouth but passed down her throat with the fire of a Roman candle. 'That's good!'

'It's local,' said Adam, and took the flask back, screwed the lid on and pocketed it. 'Right. I'm off.'

The other shooters clustered round, shaking her hand; the women kissed her on each cheek, far too obviously glad to see the back of her, and she followed Hugh down to the mud-spattered Land Rover Discovery parked next to her hire car in a lay-by.

'Lovely to see you, Lexie. You're a breath of fresh air.'

'We'll see you again? Next shoot's in a month.'

'We must have lunch,' said the second woman (Marge, her name was, though Lexie thought that had to be a nickname) and seemed to mean it.

Londoners intimidate country bumpkins, Nico had said once, with a sneer. That had been the point at which Lexie had actively begun to dislike him. He was a Cumbrian himself and yet he pretended to be so modern and cosmopolitan.

Yes, that had been when she realised quite how ruthless he was, how he adopted a chameleon's garb, how he appeared to everyone as whatever he thought they wanted him to be. Lexie wanted a man who was decent, kind, uncomplicated, someone who adored her for herself. She'd fallen for a false version of him and now she regretted it. These strangers who had welcomed her, who couldn't do enough for her, were all just the type of person her heart yearned to spend time with. Even Sonia and Marge had got over their obvious jealousy and accepted her after a fashion, and that was something she hadn't expected. No wonder Nico had gone on all the time about northerners being the salt of the earth, much more honest than soft, superficial southerners. He hadn't been right about much, but maybe he was right about that — though, being Nico, his comments had been entirely at odds with his behaviour and she thought he only praised them when there were soft southerners around to take offence.

Hugh opened the door of the Land Rover for her, then went down to the driver's side and started the engine. With a degree of trepidation, Lexie saw her hired car disappearing in the wing mirror. It was too late, now, to worry about whether she should have trusted her judgement.

'Tell me about yourself,' she said to him, because when she'd been telling them all her life story he'd hung around the fringes of the conversation, saying little when the others had tripped over their tongues, so keen to tell her about their work in the countryside, or in high-end property, or on sports and leisure development. Hugh seemed not to like to talk about himself, and she didn't know many men like that.

'Oh, I'm not very interesting!' he assured her, bumping the car down the track. 'You see it all, as my dad would say.'

She rather liked what she saw: a face that wore the pink glow of the fresh air rather than the sallow look of a man who spent too long under studio lights; long limbs, not the slightly hunched posture that came with film editing on a computer; a lean, muscular body that suggested he worked out in the real sense, under the sun and in the wind, not on the soulless treadmill that was too symbolic of her life. 'What do you do?'

'I'm a farmer,' he said, 'over by Bampton as I said, so I'm not too far away from you if you're in Wasby. I'll happily pick you up tomorrow and take you up to pick up your car.'

'I'd really appreciate that.' Everything worked differently here: time, distance, people. She was still recalibrating. The distance might be significant but it could take less time than a rush hour taxi between her flat and Nico's in London.

'It's no trouble. I'd just be doing stuff around the farm and you're much more interesting to talk to than cows.'

She burst out laughing. 'I don't think anyone's ever said

that to me before. I'll take it as a compliment.' And, now that she thought about it, working with cows was something they had in common.

'Cows are fine. Friendly little things, mostly, though they can turn on you. But they're a little short on conversation. Even Buttercup. She's my favourite.'

'You have a favourite cow?'

'Any farmer who tells you he doesn't is lying,' he said, a twinkle in his eye. At the wheel he seemed more comfortable, less abashed. Lexie studied his profile, furtively, and liked what she saw. There was a permanent shadow of a smile on his face.

'Do you have a family?' she asked, because why not? If he had a wife she wanted to know and she'd run a mile. Once bitten, forever shy.

'No. I never married. There was someone, once, but she said she didn't want to be shackled to the land. I don't see farming like that. It's a fairly fundamental disagreement, under the circumstances.'

Lexie digested this. 'Have you always lived up here?'

'Unless you count boarding school. I said I lived beyond Bampton and that's right, but the farm's a hell of a way even from there. The local school was good but there were too many times when I couldn't get there and it was difficult for me to make friends, so my mother thought I might be happier at boarding school. I wasn't, but I did make some lifelong friends.'

Lexie's butterfly mind swung through a collage of Harry Potter and Malory Towers, of innocent adventure and austere and brutal repression. Everyone had a story. 'I don't think I know anyone who went to boarding school.' Except Nico, and she was reluctant to think about him.

'It didn't change me,' he said, and laughed. 'I'm what I

always was, a simple farmer. Tell me about London. What do you like so much about it?'

Safely back on her own territory, Lexie filled him in with tales of parties and premières and the doings of people she suspected he might never have heard of. If he wasn't interested he pretended to be, convincingly, and by the time they got back to Wasby they were both laughing.

'It would be nice to see you again,' he said, as he stopped the car outside Wasby End Cottage. 'Apart from tomorrow, I mean. I thought we could go somewhere for lunch at the weekend. Or dinner, perhaps.'

She hesitated for a moment, but only a moment. He was so unlike Nico, such a breath of fresh air. 'That would be lovely.'

'Shall we say dinner? I'll pick you up. We can agree a time and a place tomorrow.'

'Perfect.' She got out of the car and watched as he drove away. A warm glow that wasn't just the sun and the whisky washed over her. What a genuinely nice man. He was older than her, of course, probably by the better part of twenty years, but what did that matter these days? There had been a similar gap between her and Nico, and it hadn't been the cause of the problems between them. Besides, men her age were always in such a hurry. It was exhausting trying to keep up with their ambitions.

She looked around. A navy blue Mercedes drew up outside Linda's cottage, and Becca's inquisitive cat streaked across the road and jumped onto its bonnet almost before the engine had stopped. A man got out and made a fuss of the cat. This must be Adam's nemesis. She'd ask Hugh if he'd heard the story and see if there was some alternative angle on it that Adam hadn't revealed, a product of the local gossip. Though putting the idea to Nico was now impossible, there were plenty of other people in the industry who might take it up if she could make it good enough and commercial enough, and some of them would be all the more enthusiastic if they thought her success meant they could pay Nico back for other misdemeanours and perceived slights. He always left a lot of collateral damage in his wake.

With a last sly look at the detective, who had strayed across the road like a man drawn by an invisible thread to where Becca was dead-heading her roses, she opened the door to End Cottage. (The locals, she had noticed, never bothered to call it by its full name.) The corner of an envelope poked out from the letterbox. Odd; she hadn't given her address to anyone, even her mother, who was never one for letter-writing at the best of times and who, in any case, was never off the phone to her long enough to write a letter. She tweaked it out of the jaws of the letterbox and opened it.

GOLD DIGGER, it said in red ink, bold and a huge font size, probably 100pt or more. She walked through to the kitchen and thrust it into the recycling. That hadn't taken long. It must be someone local, too, because there was no address on it so it had been hand-delivered. Maybe Wasby wasn't such a pretty little village after all; or could Marge or Sonia conceivably have got here before her? Hugh had been pleasingly slow in his driving, as if to spin the journey out, but surely not so slow that they would have time to execute this kind of trick on someone they'd only just met.

She stepped back out. Becca and the man were still talking, though both of them stood well back from the wall that divided them, out of touching distance. 'Sorry to interrupt,' she called, before she reached them.

'I'll need to go,' the man said to Becca. 'I only came down here to help Mum move some furniture. The decorator's coming tomorrow and Mikey's doing something else.'

He nodded towards Lexie and smiled, a clipped smile that suggested he was both delighted and disappointed at the interruption. 'Evening.'

'I'm sorry,' said Lexie, approaching the front gate. 'I hope I didn't scare him off.'

'No.' Becca looked after him with a half scowl. 'He was just looking for an excuse to get away. Is everything okay?'

'Someone left me a lovely *welcome to the village card*, but they forgot to sign it. I don't want to seem rude and not acknowledge it. I just wondered if you'd seen anyone at the door.'

'I'm sorry, no.' Becca tore her gaze away from the Satterthwaites' cottage. 'I've only been home a few minutes. I just wanted to get the roses done before it rains.'

'Do you think it will?' Lexie looked up at the clear sky.

'Probably not, now that I've done it.' Becca sighed. 'Sorry I can't help.'

'No problem. I'm sure whoever it is will make themselves known soon enough.' Lexie stepped away, just as the man had done, but Becca was still looking across the street with a frustrated expression.

Back in the cottage she retrieved the note from the recycling and examined it carefully, but there were no clues so she put it back again. Realistically it wouldn't be anyone from the shoot, unless Adam had told them about her beforehand, and even then they were hardly likely to come after her this hard before they'd met her and made their minds up. So that meant it might, after all, be someone from the village. She was still too much in love with the idea of the place to want to think ill of it, but the alternatives were far more sinister than mere hostility from a jealous neighbour. It couldn't be Nico, but it could be his wife. How had she found out about the affair? How had she tracked Lexie down?

She sighed as her phone pinged with the usual evening message, her mother wondering how her day had gone. There was plenty to tell her, for sure, but this last bit of it was something she would definitely keep to herself. She'd come a long way to get away from all that nonsense of jealousy, duplicity and revenge, but it seemed she hadn't come far enough.

SEVEN

'Go through and take a seat,' said Ashleigh, waving Jude in the direction of the living room. 'I'm all but done. I'll just set the dishwasher going and then we can chat.'

There was a reassuring feel about the evening. These days it was rare that Jude came round to the house Ashleigh shared with an old school friend. Until relatively recently it had been commonplace, a coming-together of the personal and the professional that she'd found easy and reassuring, but in recent months those comfortable moments had fallen foul of the creeping dissatisfaction that came with a fading relationship. They were, she knew, coming to understand that the flame that had burned so promisingly between them was fading and had never been strong enough to banish the failed love affairs both had in their past.

These days if they were discussing work in a way that took them beyond their contracted hours they tended to stay late at the office and do so in a neutral environment but today, when Ashleigh had approached Jude at the end of the day for a quick catch-up on Annabel Faulkner and her missing husband, he'd been in a hurry to leave. She was under no illusions about the big attraction of Wasby and it certainly wasn't doing some minor chore for his mother, but it turned out that neither was he able to leave as fascinating a topic as Annabel undiscussed. He'd suggested a drink and she'd offered to cook. The meal had been accompanied by a glass of wine and there was every chance it would end, satisfactorily, in bed. It was almost like old times, except that it was impossible to be unaware of the elephant in the room. Jude wasn't Scott, Ashleigh's ex-husband, and Ashleigh wasn't Becca.

It was an impossible conundrum, and one that required one of them to have the strength to act on that shared and inconvenient knowledge and put their faltering relationship out of its misery, but to do so would be to acknowledge failure and, worse, would leave her free and single. If that happened, the irresistible Scott would be circling within hours of hearing of it and she, as she always did, would weaken and go back to a man she loved but who barely even pretended he'd be faithful. It felt mean-spirited to use Jude as a shield against her past but he'd know exactly what she was doing and wouldn't mind. And besides, Ashleigh was protecting him from the same folly.

It was a deadlock that suited them both. She slammed the dishwasher closed and listened to it whirring into action, wiped her hands on a tea towel and tossed it into the washing machine, then picked up the wine bottle from the table and went through to the living room, where Jude had made himself comfortable on the saggy old sofa.

'That was one of your better efforts,' he teased her. 'You do turn out a passable lasagne, I'll say that for you.'

'Think yourself lucky it wasn't bought pizza.' She poured them both a second glass of red wine from the bottle he had brought, and stood for a moment, deliberating on whether to sit next to him.

'You again!' said Lisa, Ashleigh's housemate, poking her head around the door and directing her comment to Jude. 'Though having said that, I haven't seen you around for a while and it's always nice to see your cheery face. It's okay, Ash, I'm not stopping. I have an urgent appointment with a pint of Timothy Taylor's and it just wouldn't do to be late.' She ducked out again with a wicked smile.

Jude was swirling the wine round in his glass, the tiniest frown on his face. Ashleigh recognised and interpreted the look. He would have seen Becca when he was down in Wasby, as he always did, with such an inevitability that she suspected it was deliberate though Becca seemed neither to want to reciprocate nor to send Jude on his way. At least, she consoled herself, Becca wasn't toxic in the way Scott was — just too proud or too angry to have him back and so spiting both of them in the process. One day one of the four of them, locked in this uncomfortable but perfectly balanced set of circumstances, would make a move to upset everything, but she didn't think it would be that night.

'Okay,' said Jude when the front door had clicked shut and Lisa had gone. 'Let's get to business. What do we make of Annabel Faulkner and what do we know about her wayward husband?'

The September night was closing in. Ashleigh placed the bottle on the table and drew the curtains shut, then took her seat in the armchair by the window. 'Shall we start with Annabel? I formed a pretty clear opinion from speaking to her on the phone, but you're the one who's looked her in the eye. What did you make of her?'

'For a significant portion of the time I wasn't looking her in the eye. She wouldn't let me.'

'Right?' said Ashleigh, interested. Annabel hadn't struck her as the furtive type.

'Yes. That was at the point in the interview when she was telling me what a brute her husband is to her and how he'd threatened her and how she's terrified of him. I didn't believe a word of it. If there's something in the world scary enough to frighten that woman, I don't want to meet it.'

Such fierceness might be telling in itself. 'What about the rest of the story? Was it much the same as she told me?'

'Even more blunt, if anything.' He drummed his fingers on the arm of the sofa for a moment. 'I don't know quite what I was expecting from her but I don't think I was surprised at what I got. She's very much a stereotype of a successful businesswoman and I think it might be deliberate. She's good looking — handsome, I think you'd call it, rather than beautiful. She claims to be very wealthy and shows all the trappings of it. I'm going to guess she has no time for humility. She probably thinks it's a sign of weakness. She's extremely well-dressed, and must spend a lot of time as well as money on her appearance. The hair was immaculate, the manicure was perfect. And she didn't allow the crocodile tears to damage the make up.'

'You don't think she was lying about him going missing, though?' Ashleigh had a sixth sense for a liar and Annabel's fury had struck her as raw and genuine.

'No, I don't think so. She said he'd left his phone, which is the only thing that you might think unusual, but she also said that didn't surprise her. Nor did she seem particularly perturbed by the fact that he'd left the car. That makes me think he's the kind of man who has more than one phone and probably more than one persona too, even if not more than one legal identity.'

Ashleigh had come across plenty of people like that in

her time. Usually but by no means always men, they thought they could have their cake and eat it, put off the difficult choices between different lives and different lovers by pretending to be different people. In the end some of them might even have come to believe in the illusions they created for others. 'Do we reckon Mr Morea is nesting with some other bird, then?'

'I'm not sure. If he was a nobody I'd certainly think so. It's easier for people to slip away for a while if no-one's going to notice that they're missing, but Morea is anything but anonymous within his own world.'

'Lisa knew who he was,' noted Ashleigh, 'though I grant you that's not an extensive sample.'

'Yes. I asked my mother and Mikey, and they'd both heard of him, though neither could say anything more than the name and a vague connection with the film industry and I'm pretty sure neither of them could have told me what he looked like.'

'If he isn't off with another woman then Annabel might be right about the divorce and him salting away money as quickly as he can.' Ashleigh reached onto the table and nudged the pile of magazines that had been sitting there, so that they spilled into an untidy fan of glossy images and screaming headlines. *Soap Star Ivy's Baby Heartbreak. Amy's Double Life. My Vicar Husband Was A White-Collar Criminal.* 'Lisa was at the hairdresser's today and she picked up a few of these for me. They've all got a snippet or two about our Mr Morea. He seems to have been quite the Svengali. And, oh dear me, you don't have to go too far down a few internet rabbit holes before you get the scandals.'

He wrinkled his nose in distaste. 'This isn't really my kind of policing.'

'No, it's frothy and mostly untrue, but I did spend a bit

of time looking our friend Simon up earlier, while you were at your mum's.' She couldn't hide the hesitation in her voice, the meaningful pause that meant *while you were with Becca.*

'What did you find?'

'I don't like policing via celebrity magazine any more than you do, but I have to admit there's something strangely compulsive about it.' She reached for the topmost magazine, opening it to the page where she'd folded down the corner. 'He isn't an A-lister in the broader sense of the phrase, although he does seem to be highly regarded in his own circle. But it does seem to me that wherever the A-listers hang out, he's there too.' She passed the magazine over. 'Here he is at last year's Oscars, for example.'

Even after Faye had pushed the probably-not-very-mysterious case of Simon Morea up Jude's to-do list, he hadn't made it his priority. There had been so many more immediate things to do; he had confined himself to asking Ashleigh and their colleague Chris Marshall to try and discreetly identify the film director's whereabouts. 'Right. This is the first time I've had a proper look at him. Interesting.'

'He's not what you expect, is he?' The photograph of Morea posing on the red carpet with Annabel on his arm had taken Ashleigh by surprise. 'The less sympathetic commentators call the pair of them Beauty and the Beast.'

He squinted at the picture with a characteristic slight frown of concentration. Annabel Faulkner was dressed to kill in a midnight blue gown that flattered her rather straight figure, and a river of diamonds around her neck that drew attention from her broad, bare shoulders. Her blonde hair was swept up into a towering mass in which diamond pins, almost certainly real, sparkled like the gems on her finger as she laid a hand proprietorially on her husband's arm. She was the one who drew the eye. By contrast, he was squat, square and graceless. His hair was smoothed down; his eyes were hard as obsidian behind huge, black-framed glasses; his suit was ill-cut and badly fitted and his body language as he turned to the camera was charmless and grudging.

'Is he like this in all of the pictures?' he asked.

'He certainly is. Even in their wedding photo. He makes no effort at all. It seems to be a trait of his.' She reached for her iPad and begin flicking through the links she'd bookmarked, celebrity websites and showbiz blogs. 'My ad feed is going to be hell after this. What a bore. I don't care who's sleeping with who unless they've committed a crime on my patch, and even then I only care if it's relevant. But it seems to be what sells.'

Jude was still looking at the picture. 'And we're supposed to think this man's a babe magnet for gorgeous, talented young women who could do much better? Being an alleged philanderer is bad enough—'

'There's no *alleged* about it. He's definitely a philanderer. But in the circles he moves in there are a lot of people with good looks and talent, way too many for them all to succeed. You need more than that. You need contacts, which he has in spades. You need influence, which oozes from him in every article I've read. And you need money, which by all accounts he isn't short of even if most of it is his wife's. Power is an aphrodisiac, as they say. And do you know something else?'

'Go on,' he said, interested.

'I think he's rather deliberately ugly,'

Jude looked at the picture again. 'I'm not sure what you mean.'

'If you can see beyond the hair and the clothes and those spectacularly hideous glasses, it wouldn't take a lot for him to brush up quite nicely, as my mother would say.'

'I'm no judge of a man's looks,' said Jude, looking again at the picture, 'but it just seems to me—'

'Look again. Look at that slouch. I thinks it's deliberate because it's not quite the same in all the pictures. Without it he'd be much taller and much more imposing. If he stood up straight, got himself contact lenses and smiled he might even be quite good looking. But then he'd be just like all the rest of them. He needs to stand out.'

Jude tossed the magazine down. 'Ah. Beauty and the Beast is a bit of a selling point for him, then.'

'Maybe. Look, here are the wedding photos. A whole magazine feature on his wedding to a gorgeous woman and he can't even muster a smile.'

Jude took the iPad and looked at it. 'No, that's odd. Most people smile on their wedding days, don't they?'

He didn't say *did you*? It was a reminder, if she'd ever needed it, that a wedding photo — any photo — told a truth that lasted no longer than the split second in which it was taken, and sometimes even then it was fake. 'Annabel looks like the cat that's got the cream, doesn't she? I wonder what they saw in each other.'

'There's no accounting for attraction,' he said. 'What do we know about her? I asked Chris to do a quick check, but I haven't had time to look at what he sent me.'

'She's not the arty type at all. She runs a PR agency which she set up and made a success of, but most of her money comes from inherited wealth. Her father made a fortune buying up uninhabitable property in the cheaper parts of London and doing it up.' One of the articles about the wedding had described him, rather picturesquely, as *riding the crest of a gentrification wave*. 'There are a couple of articles in the business magazines about her and it does seem like she plays hardball a lot, both in her public life and her private one. There was a first husband and he tried to take her for a lot of money when he left her. He didn't get much.'

'Hence the vicious prenuptial agreement with Simon that she seemed so proud of. Okay.' Jude put the iPad down. 'It's a great tale, isn't it? Full of drama and lies and sex and money and all the rest of it. But that's all it is.' He indicated the pile of magazines. 'It feels performative. People who love attention and drama and spend their lives being pandered to, living out their own film scripts. If you're right about Morea's appearance, that's another example. But while I can't deny it's fascinating in a psychological sense, I honestly can't see anything that suggests that a crime has actually been committed, or is likely to be.'

'I know.' Ashleigh shook her head. 'It's almost like we've been dragged into it as part of their power play. He disappears with another woman or for other reasons, she gets the police involved just to show him how influential she is.'

'Yes. It's so much more ballsy than calling in a private investigator, which is what he's probably expecting. What a coup for Annabel to show him she's got us at her beck and call.'

And she had. It wasn't just that hint at a threat, vexatious though it had been. It was that Faye's paranoia had meant they had no alternative but to buy into it. 'I feel a little better now we've done this. At least if we're asked we can say we've done an investigation of the background and found nothing.'

'I'm sure that won't be enough for Annabel,' said Jude

with a laugh, 'but with a bit of luck her man will turn up in the next couple of days and we can leave them to fight it out between themselves.'

EIGHT

Hugh was forty-nine years old, just a few months shy of what would be, he had always thought, a half-century in which being single would be a mark of failure, and he had just realised that he'd never fallen in love until he'd set eyes on Lexie Romachenka. It hadn't, in the strictest terms, been love at first sight. He'd seen her get out of the car and look around her and his first thought had been that she didn't fit in. She was too blonde and too smart, and her outfit was too new, her wax jacket glossy and without tears or patches. In the first few moments as he'd watched her look around and size everybody up he'd thought she was trying too hard but when, after five minutes, Adam Fleetwood had waved him over and suggested he might like to show Lexie the ropes, he'd been overtaken by a wave of emotion that had progressed from interest to fascination to affection so fast that by the end of the day, when he had headed back to the farm to do his night rounds, he was well and truly lost.

Maybe it was love at first sight after all, he'd said to Buttercup, leaning on the gate of the field as the dusk fell, and she had turned her liquid brown eyes on his almost as if she understood, *but she's far too good for the likes of me*. He thought of telling Lexie that as she slid into the passenger seat of his car and clicked the seatbelt, and the smile that rose to his lips was partly self-ridicule and partly a complete failure to control his pleasure at seeing her again.

'I take it you suffered no ill-effects after the shoot?' he inquired as he pulled away from her cottage and moved smoothly out of Wasby towards the blue Pennines. It had been a long day up there and the terrain was pretty rough, probably more than she was used to.

'Goodness, no,' she said, turning her wide blue eyes on him. 'I go to the gym and so on in London and run a little, so I did think I might have tested some muscles I'd forgotten I had. But I came out of it surprisingly unscathed.'

Hugh kept his eyes on the road, resisting the temptation to look at her. He didn't know how to play this. It was barely twenty-four hours since he'd set eyes on her and he had no idea what she thought of him. He was bad at reading people anyway, or so his mother had told him. He was too innocent, too trusting. Other people, she'd always assured him, were more complicated than he was, much more than he could possibly imagine. Maybe that was why he was still single. In a moment of clarity, he saw that as a blessing. It would have been intolerable if Lexie Romachenka had walked onto the shoot the day before and he was shackled to a wife he'd met and married when he hadn't understood what love was.

'I don't know if you have any plans for the morning,' he said, braver than he'd thought possible, 'but I have an hour or so in hand. Perhaps we could go and get a cup of coffee and a bacon roll somewhere? Though of course, if you're in a hurry…'

'My time's my own. That would be lovely. I'll buy, of course. It's the least I can do.'

His smile was more one of self-satisfaction. The first step was accomplished. She hadn't turned him down. He knew for a fact that she didn't have a partner because he'd heard her telling Marge and Sonia that she'd come to Cumbria to get away from a man she didn't love any more and Marge, rolling her eyes, had said she was thinking of going to London for exactly the same reason. At which point, all three women had laughed and shaken their heads at each other.

He shook his own head, feeling like a different person. Normally he wasn't that decisive; in his line of work it was rare that difficult decisions had to be made on the spur of the moment. You didn't buy land or stock, or decide to go away for a few days, or employ part-time help, without thoroughly weighing up all the pros and cons before you did so. There was always a decent interval in which he could think things through before asking around for temporary labour or making that appointment with his bank manager. Knowing that Lexie might at any time decide to head back to London, or that their paths might not cross again, was a mighty impetus. All he'd had was the few hours on the moor to decide he needed to see her again, that second to snatch at the opportunity to offer her a lift, and a five-minute conversation with a bored Frisian cow.

'Tell me more about yourself,' he said, as he turned up towards Askham — an uninspired opening if ever there was one, but he'd already taken more emotional risks than usual and this line, at least, was safe. And it would mean he had the chance of listening to her voice and learning about her.

'I think I talked way too much about myself yesterday,'

she said, and out of the corner of his eye he saw her turn towards him and smile. At that he took his eyes off the road for a moment to smile back. 'Why don't you tell me more about you?'

'There's nothing much to tell.'

'Do we just sit and trade this sort of comment until we've had coffee?' she asked, in a way that would have sounded petulant from anyone else but somehow sounded enticing from her. 'I know the bare facts of your life. You told me that yesterday. But what about you? Deep down Hugh?'

Deep down Hugh. He thought about that. If he was honest there probably wasn't much, deep down. He lived a lonely life and he was suddenly tired of it. 'I've always been a solitary type. Farmers have to be.'

'Surely not necessarily? I've met plenty of chatty farmers in my time.'

'I think boarding school knocked the socialising out of me.' His mother had shaken her head over him one day in the holidays. *We thought you'd make friends,* she'd said. *Can't you try harder?*

'You didn't enjoy it?'

He regretted mentioning it, now. Just that morning he'd thought there was nothing he wouldn't want to talk to her about if it meant he could hear her voice, but it hadn't taken long before she'd picked up on the one thing that he didn't want to think about. *Boarding school was hell* would have been easy to say but he was wise enough to know that she'd only go on and ask him why. Then he'd have to tell her the truth (because he was fundamentally an honest and open man, though not one who didn't have his secrets) and that meant admitting to her what kind of a person he really was. Then his budding romance would surely be over and she would be out of his life with a flick of that blonde hair. One day he might be able to tell her, and if she knew him better she might judge him for his qualities rather than his faults, but it was far too early to show this beautiful woman the side of his character that an unfashionable, spartan boarding school in a Dickensian cleft in the Pennines had wrought.

'I've always been solitary,' he said again.

'I've always thought boarding school might have been…'

'What?'

'Exciting,' she said after a moment.

'The opposite. It was dull. You'll have had much more fun at whatever school you went to.'

'A comprehensive school in Huddersfield. But yes, I always felt I was meant for something more, you know? My dad died before I was born so I never met him and my mum brought me up by herself. I always used to say I'd like to go away to school, but of course she could never have afforded it. My great-grandfather's family on my mum's side had a lot of money, but it's tied up in a long-term family trust and so Mum could never get at it. I used to ask her to try and get it so I could go away to school.' She laughed. 'I see now it must have hurt her feelings, but she never said. She's always been very good to me.'

Would Lexie's mother be as exotic as Lexie herself? 'Is she Russian?'

'She's part Russian. My great-grandmother was from Yorkshire so that's where we ended up. But of course I yearned for excitement and adventure. Who wouldn't?'

She had, he noticed, laid her hands on her lap, fingers spread out. 'And so you went to London.'

'Yes. I've always been very attracted to the city, and to film. I suppose I'm a bit of a romantic.'

'And you'll go back?'

'I expect so. But not for a while.' She twined her hands together. 'Where was your boarding school?'

He internalised his sigh. Why was it that the thing she seemed most interested in was the one thing he'd rather forget? He'd much rather talk about her. 'Up over towards County Durham.'

'Like Dotheboys Hall, in Dickens?'

'Yes.' It was a long time since he'd read any Dickens (under duress, at school) and so he wasn't entirely sure of the reference. While he didn't think there was any way he could impress this sparkling woman with his intellect, he didn't want her to think he was stupid.

'I expect you made a lot of friends,' she said, probing, probing.

'Oh, yes,' he lied, as he had done the day before. 'But we lost touch.'

'I expect a lot of them went off to London and so on.'

Plenty of his former schoolfellows had. Most of them, he thought, were as keen to get away from the place as he'd been, but his escape had been to bury himself in a part of the country he knew and loved and understood and they, like Lexie herself, all seemed to have a taste for the new and the different. They'd wanted to make a mark on the world and he had only wanted to hide. 'Yes.'

'And got lots of exciting jobs.'

'Look,' he said, with a degree of relief. 'There's a café. Shall we stop and get some breakfast?' And while she was having her coffee he would tell her all about the farm and ask her all about herself, and keep the conversation away from his education before she could discover that he knew someone who worked in film in London and, if she was interested enough, get hold of that one person and ask about him. And then she would discover what kind of person he, Hugh Cameron, really was.

NINE

With more than a little regret, Lexie turned to watch Hugh's Land Rover bumping its way down the track where she'd left the hired car overnight. What a nice man he was. How kind. How interested. And how reluctant to talk about himself.

That last one was a bit of a bugger, as her mother would say, in her broad Yorkshire tones, whenever something went wrong. The last time she'd said it had been when Lexie had come home — or rather, after her mother had gone down to London and brought her home — and she knew perfectly well that her mum would use exactly the same phrase if she knew Lexie was seeing another man so soon after the previous relationship had gone nuclear. She would say it with even more emphasis if she thought, as Lexie did, that there was the remotest chance that Hugh might know Nico. There couldn't be that many small boarding schools in that part of the world and Hugh and Nico were of an age.

It was an uncomfortable thought but it had to be a possibility. She frowned. She liked Hugh. She thought she might more than like him, and it was obvious he was much taken with her. This time it didn't feel like any of the casual liaisons she'd fallen into early in her time in London, amplified and manipulated by the need to be seen to be with someone for the sake of contacts and career and being talked about, and it was even less like her complicated, secret and ultimately doomed affair with Nico. In London Lexie had been actively seeking someone who would be able to bring her an advantage but she hadn't arrived in Cumbria on the lookout for a man, or at least, not a man like this. This was different. It was sweet and fresh and unexpected, wholesome and maybe even healing.

She opened the car door and got in but, rather than drive off, she sat for a while and looked at the moors. At this time of year they were purple with heather and dappled with shadow as the wind chased the clouds across the sky above them, but she barely paid then any attention. Her mind was focussed on the time she'd spent with Hugh, on his reluctance to open up about school.

Perhaps he didn't know Nico, or hadn't made the connection. It would be too bad to have something that might be happening fall apart because of a mutual friend who might find out and, if he was still in touch with Nico, might say something about the kind of girl she'd been just a short time before. The anxiety nagged at her, disproportionately. She'd dreamed about Hugh the previous night, woken with a flutter of excitement at the prospect of seeing him, but the nagging worry had been there from the minute he'd mentioned a small boarding school in Cumbria.

They'd talked about all sorts as they lingered over their coffee, but the one subject she hadn't been able to open him up about had been school. Cows, yes (his fondness for Buttercup was already a running joke between them); his family, even the previous relationship that had failed, had been freely spoken of, but at the mention of boarding school he'd closed down, switched the subject, or just shrugged and not answered.

She should have left it. She should have picked up on that chill when it had come up in conversation the previous afternoon. Even then she'd recognised that it made him uncomfortable, but she couldn't stop herself picking away at it. The worst case scenario was Nico's wife finding out about a new relationship; the woman was bitter and vindictive and, no matter how much Nico had protested to his mistress that he'd never loved his wife, Lexie had always had a nagging fear that he'd go back to her. She hadn't been sure whether the wife's triumph or her revenge would be worse. Now neither of those mattered to her, but it did matter if Hugh were to believe that Lexie herself was no better than a common gold-digger. When she looked back she saw herself as being under some kind of spell and wasn't sure quite why she'd wanted Nico, but it certainly hadn't been for his money. It was important that Hugh never thought she was that kind of woman.

For God's sake, she chided herself, *you barely know him. You've been a fool before*. But how did you know it was the real thing? When it was different and unexpected? What if these feelings she was so instantly experiencing for Hugh were love? What if Nico, or his wife, were to ruin it?

Life was so full of uncertainties. She'd solved the problem of Nico but in doing so she'd caused another. There were so many connections that needed to be made for this doomsday scenario to become her truth that it was near-impossible, but that tiny chance, the sequence of coincidence on which many a movie plot hinged, remained. What a twist that would make in a film — but, unlike the idea that Adam had given her, this one filled her with a discomfort so great it amounted to dread.

Perhaps, after all, she wouldn't go straight back to Wasby. It was a beautiful morning and the early fog had lifted from the tops leaving eggshell-blue sky behind it, a day far too promising to waste. Despite her concerns the journey had put a song in her heart, one that hadn't been there for a long time. She'd run away from Nico because she hated the power he exerted over her, the way he treated her like a queen but only on his terms, claimed she was his everything yet refused ever to be seen with her in public. It was over and she would never see him again.

I'm a country girl at heart, she told herself, *and maybe Mama was right. Maybe I was looking in the wrong place all along. Maybe London wasn't what I needed. Maybe what I needed was soft rain and moody fog. Maybe early nights and clean living aren't so bad.*

And maybe what she needed was a country man, of simple tastes and conversation, of decent behaviour, with his muddy wellington boots very firmly fixed to the Cumbrian earth.

She shook her head as she drove through the line of villages strung out like pearls on a necklace along the western foot of the Pennines. She'd been up here the previous year, up back lanes and through tiny clusters of homes, rambling farm buildings clinging to the slopes, white against its green backdrop. Hilton, Murton, Dufton, Knock. Milburn, Blencarn, Skirwith. Just outside the last of them, Ousby, she pulled up in a gravelled lay-by that served as a car park for the church and sat there for a moment wondering if Hugh had got home yet and if he'd mind if she called him, about what excuse she might make for calling rather than have to admit she only wanted to hear his voice.

She wouldn't ask him about boarding school again, for

sure. At least, not yet. She examined herself in the distorting, fly-splattered wing mirror, trying to see if she'd changed, if the real Lexie Romachenka was visible, and thought about what she would do with her life. London was such a world of artifice. When she was there it seemed the centre of everything but now she was here, where the loudest noise was the grumbling of a distant tractor and the most piercing the cry of a bird whose name she didn't even know, she began to doubt herself. The countryside exerted a different influence upon her, brimming with creativity and inspiration. The story Adam Fleetwood had spun her would be a winner, she was sure, if she could find the right person to take it on, but did she have to be in London to pitch it? Couldn't she make her fortune from the north? Couldn't she give herself a fair shot at a different life?

'When I am rich,' she said aloud, getting out of the car and going around to the back to retrieve her walking boots, 'I'll still do this bit for myself.' Scouting for locations was her passion, and she knew just the place where she might stage her final scene, the meeting between good and evil, her Holmes and Moriarty but with the roles of hero and villain reversed. It was the place she had looked at the previous year which hadn't been quite right for what Nico had wanted but which had featured in a few shots in the middle of the film. A path cut down into a sodden dale, past long-abandoned lime kilns and a sinister and twisted line of rusty rail tracks. Here, the path forked, one branch forging left to scale the side of the Pennines and the other meandering into nothingness among unforgiving, featureless bog. It was a perfect place for redemption, where Adam would rescue his enemy from the sodden jaws of the bog and be revealed for the hero he really was, and all would be forgotten and forgiven.

If only life was as simple as that.

When she'd laced her boots she straightened up and looked around. In the field opposite, a curious sheep lifted its head to stare at her, and a smile jumped to her lips. Hugh would tease her if she called him to ask him about breeds of sheep and, thinking about it, she laughed out loud. In the churchyard a ride-on mower came to a halt by the gate and stopped.

'Morning,' said the man who had been driving it. He took off his ear defenders and looked at her, expectantly. 'Going up to Cross Fell?'

In the countryside even other people's nosiness seemed wholesome and sharing one's business seemed natural and polite. 'Not today. I'm just going for a quick walk up to the old lime kiln at Ardale.' Knowing the name made her feel like a local.

'It's right boggy up there at the moment,' said the man, after a while.

'It's been such a wet summer,' she agreed, feeling the keenness of the wind and wondering whether, after all, she had misjudged the weather and should just head back. 'But it's all right. I know the area.'

'Are you from round here?' He frowned at her, as though he'd seen her before.

'No, but I was up here for work last year.'

His brow cleared. 'Work? They were filming up here for some arty-farty thing, weren't they?'

Arty-farty. She could imagine Nico's outrage. 'Yes, that's right.'

'I remember the filming. Did I see you then?' He took off his gloves and laid them on his lap. 'With a man. Your husband, was it?'

Lexie felt herself going pink. Thank God he didn't know who she was. She'd brought Nico up here, keeping her company as she looked for locations, and they'd held hands and laughed as they walked up the path, stopping at every kissing gate for the requisite toll, helping each other over stiles where no help was needed. Finally free of the need to pretend, they had been so free with their affection that they must have seemed newly-married. 'It looks like the weather might turn. I'd better hurry if I'm going to be back before it rains.'

She turned away, sensing the man's unwavering stare on her back. Everywhere you went, someone saw you. Now when she thought of Nico and good times they'd shared here, the idea that she'd actually thought he loved her was as embarrassing as a schoolgirl crush.

She checked her watch as she strode along beside the beck, high from recent rain and lapping at the side of the road. Away to the left the road dipped downwards and the waters swirled over it, a ford that must be a foot or more deep in its centre. As she left the beck behind her, the sun and the cloud continued their running battle and wrestled over a brief rainbow until the sun emerged victorious. Nico was dead to her and Hugh was very much alive, in her present and, perhaps, her future. To her astonishment, Lexie realised that she was happy.

The next gate was chained but the path was a right of way so she had no qualms about climbing over it and tramping up the path beside the old stone wall. Beyond the farm, where there was still signal, she called Hugh. 'I just wanted to say thank you again for this morning. It was such fun.' Like being a teenager again, like being innocent.

'No, it was fun for me,' he insisted.

He's nearly fifty said her mother in her head. *For God's sake, Lexie*. But it wasn't that much older than her, not in the great scheme of things, and young men were so fickle, so naive, so immature. 'I can't believe we've barely known each other for twenty-four hours.'

'It's odd, isn't it? And yet I want to get to know you so much better. I meant to tell you how much everyone loved you. They all said you're a breath of fresh air. Even Marge.'

They'd been talking about her. What else had she expected? *GOLD DIGGER*. The note preyed on her mind, all in capitals, that red ink. They might simper and pretend to Hugh, who was so obviously trusting and would believe them, but she knew how shallow people were and how easily they lied. She did it herself. Once again she revisited the improbable idea that one of them hated her, that that was the reason and that it was too unfair to be borne. 'Look Hugh, there's something I need to tell you.'

In the pause that followed, maybe caused by the failure of the signal, maybe by Hugh himself, she strode along. Thick red mud clotted under her boots and splashed up to the knees of her jeans. 'Hugh?'

'Sorry, I don't know what happened there. Yes, I'm still here. What do you want to say?'

'It's about money. I bet people think that's what I'm after. They think I'm a gold digger.' Take them on. Name the name. Confront the challenge. Even over a broken telephone link there could be moments of drama. 'But actually that's not true. I have plenty of money. I earn a really good wage and I have family money of my own. I mentioned a family trust. That matures next year and I'm the beneficiary of it. It's probably about half a million, maybe more. So you don't need to worry about that, okay?'

'Well, I…' It was hard to tell how he felt, with the wind whistling in her ears and the signal flicking in and out.

Anxiety surged within her. 'I told you I don't have much money,' he said, eventually.

'The money doesn't matter, but you have the farm and people might think I think you have tons of money and that's what's so attractive about you.' Money was relative, and what he had might seem a lot less to some people than it did to the others. Many of the other shooters had oozed the shabbiness of vast unearned wealth. 'I just wanted you to know. That's not what it's about.'

'Then what is it about? What's attractive about me?'

The line shivered again, dangerously so. She'd reached the brow of the hill now, and the ground sloped down to the crouching shape of the lime kiln, crushed into the hillside as if it belonged there. 'You're so nice. Just so nice.' A ridiculous tear appeared in her eye. Maybe it was the wind. 'I just like you.' Such a simple thing. So precious. So rare. For all the compliments she'd exchanged with Nico, all the extravagant praise and all the beautiful lies, neither of them had ever been able to say this of the other. 'That's all.'

'Well...I...' She thought she heard a gusty sigh, or maybe that was the wind, too.

'I hope you don't mind.'

'No! Not at all! It's just that—'

'What?' She'd got it wrong. She'd broken something before it could become beautiful. She was too gauche and clumsy to be allowed to handle love.

'No-one's ever said something as nice as that to me before.'

Relief filled her heart. 'I thought I'd upset you.'

'No! Of course not!'

'Can we see each other again?' she asked, emboldened.

'I'd like that. Shall we meet for dinner tonight?'

'Why don't you come to the cottage? I'll cook.' She wasn't normally so quick off the mark.

'Deal,' he said, and she imagined the smile as he hung up.

Take that, Nico. She thrust the phone back in her pocket and strode down the hill, smiling. In her film (working title: *Adam's Redemption*, though she would change that) this would be where the two protagonists met for their final scene, brought together by the actions of the villain. There would be a pursuit. Adam would be crouched in the back of the kiln in the man-sized niche in which he would have hidden as the day darkened to dusk, and as night fell he would emerge to face his deadly foe and prove his innocence.

The ground dropped away at the bottom of the hill and she skipped across the narrow footbridge over the beck and up the bank towards the kiln. There was a thin whiff of decay on the wind — a dead sheep, perhaps — growing stronger as she approached the entrance to the lime kiln. Her stomach turned, but she ignored it and pressed on, because if anything was to happen between herself and Hugh she would have to get used to the sour smells of the countryside. Standing in front of the building she surveyed it, critically. Yes, it would work. Adam, knowing the land, would take the dangerous route from here into the treacherous bog and his enemy, ignorant of the traps, would follow him.

She stepped into the left-hand kiln. A crow hurled itself at her from the back of it, black wings beating close to her head, and she screamed, hands flung over her head to protect herself, and dived outside. A sick feeling grew in her stomach but she couldn't just walk by. The smell was even stronger inside. She advanced a few steps further.

A boot. A long, tweed-clad leg. What was left of a hand, black with flies.

Screaming, Lexie turned and ran.

TEN

Faye, who was as obsessed by rank as she was by secrecy, generally preferred her senior officers to remain in the office where she could reach them and leave the legwork to the underlings. Regardless of that, Jude headed out from Penrith to Ousby as soon as the report of the discovery of a body filtered through to him. Doddsy would realistically have been expected to go up there but was otherwise engaged, and Ashleigh had been set to the largely cosmetic task of collating all available information on Simon Morea in order to keep Annabel Faulkner at bay.

Jude always relished the unique challenge of a remote rural crime scene and knew the area well, so the opportunity was too good to miss. Sometimes, missing the more interesting quirks of the job outside the office, he wished he hadn't fallen foul of the young man's thrust for promotion. Desk work was too often dull and he was interested in people, listening to them as they talked, watching them make mistakes or fall into confusion, putting the pieces together to see whether they were lying or whether they were genuinely mistaken about what they'd seen.

If he'd been a bit less ambitious, he mused as he drove through Ousby, the personal cost might have been less. Becca's disagreements with him hadn't just been about Adam Fleetwood. There had been an underlying theme of how much time he'd sacrificed to his job when they should have spent it together.

Sometimes, no matter how much you wanted to — and he did — you couldn't go back. He got out of his car where the end of the track up from Ousby petered out in a field. A cluster of police vehicles stood in the churned-up mud of the farmyard, a chaotic scene that meant someone — probably him — would need to calm an irate farmer over the mess they'd inevitably leave behind. He flashed his warrant card at the officer on duty and picked his way through what was now steady drizzle, across a previously-damp surface that had become treacherously slippy. Down in the cleft that the beck had carved there was a flurry of activity: a couple of officers sealed off the lime kiln with blue and white tape while another stood, arms folded, to direct walkers along a different, depressingly longer route back to Ousby. Behind the tape forensics officers in white suits were beginning the painstaking job of assessing the situation before the body could be removed.

He stopped at the outer line of tape, scanning the scene for anything unusual, though there was unlikely to be anything there for him to see. The stench of death was obvious even from where he stood, a good distance away, and he could just make out a thick black blossoming of flies at the mouth of the kiln which told a tale of its own. If the body had been there for a few days it would have deteriorated rapidly in the mild, wet autumn. Even without the recent rain, a few days in this remote spot meant that many clues to what had happened would have disappeared, smoothed away by wind and weather.

After a moment one of the forensics officers spotted him and made her way over to the tape, pulling her mask down so that he could see her face. It was Tammy Garner, one of the senior CSIs. Her mouth was set to professional immobility and her glasses smeared with rain so that he couldn't tell for certain what she thought, but it wouldn't be pleasant. A body left for days in the open never was.

'It's you, Chief,' she greeted him. 'Thanks for sending us out on this one. It's not one of the nicer ones.'

'You'll get your reward in heaven, as my mum would say,' he said cheerfully, but he took her point. Crows, flies, foxes, badgers, rats. There was always something interested in benefiting from carrion. 'You think it's been there a while, then.'

'I'd say a few days at least, but you'd need the pathologist to tell you that.'

Matt Cork, the pathologist on duty that day, was a friend of Jude's and was notoriously cagey about committing himself. *Time of death between when last seen alive and when the body was found* was one of his favourite maxims, but it was a fair bet even Matt would have to be more specific on this one. 'What can you tell me about him?'

'Not much. It's an adult male,' Tammy said, 'height a shade under six foot, in walking gear, but don't ask for details about hair colour or eye colour or anything. You can't see it at first glance, and I didn't want to look more closely at him than I had to. I'll leave that for the medical professionals. I take it you don't want to see the photos.'

He shook his head. If it was an accident, which was the most likely explanation under the circumstances, he wouldn't need to see them. If the autopsy suggested something sinister he'd see them soon enough. 'There's nothing to suggest a cause of death, then?'

'Nothing obvious. There are no wounds that I can see, no signs of broken bones or anything external.'

He took a look around him. The area was popular with walkers who trekked up to Cross Fell, but this particular point lay a little off the main route and even in the best of weather it never attracted the throngs who flocked to the more popular Lake District peaks and dales further west. Those who came might or might not be tempted off the path to explore the lime kilns and any who had done might have been put off by the smell of decay without realising its significance. 'Do an old man a good turn, Tammy. Tell me something that'll help me.' And justify this visit to Faye, if necessary. 'Haven't you got even a crumb of information for me?'

'I've bagged up his belongings, if that's any use to you.' Tammy plodded back to the lime kilns and lifted a bundle of clear plastic bags, sealed and signed, which she handed to him. 'See what you can make of them. I'll leave you at that, if you don't mind. The sooner I get out of this place and get the smell of it out of my nostrils, the happier I'll be.'

Jude watched her go and, after countersigning the bags, turned to check in with the constable on duty, gaining a quick briefing about the circumstance of the discovery of the body and the news that no-one at the farm through which the path passed had seen anything out of the ordinary or, indeed, seemed to have seen anything at all, not even the woman who'd discovered the body heading up the hill. He'd had a wasted journey then, or so it seemed.

Or maybe not. With the evidence bags in his hand, he walked back to the car and got in, sitting there for a moment. An unpleasant thought had occurred to him. He spread the bags out on the driver's seat and reviewed the contents. A black leather wallet, unfolded and bulging with banknotes and cards; a few loose coins; a brand-new iPhone; a set of house keys; a key fob for a Renault. He focussed his attention on the wallet, picking it up and shaking the bag until the contents shifted and a bank card became dislodged. It was a company credit card, for SNM Enterprises Ltd and the name of the card's owner didn't surprise him.

Simon N Morea.

He let out a long, long sigh. It needn't be a crime. Indeed, there was no suggestion of one, unless you counted that spurious one from Annabel, that threat she seemed to have invented on the spur of the moment to force the police to find her husband. And now, it seemed, they'd done so.

He stared at the card for a moment longer. Ashleigh's research had so far uncovered a few innocuous facts that now made perfect sense. Morea was a Cumbrian and despite his love of the city and his fondness for its bright lights, in direct contrast with Annabel's observation, had professed himself in interviews to be a keen walker and nature lover. The existence of the phone, in addition to that he had left at the cottage in Troutbeck, supported the theory that the man was accustomed to switching between one life and another, or at the very least was well-practised in subterfuge. Again, that didn't necessarily imply foul play; it might mean only that Morea liked to switch off from his London life from time to time, yet kept the comfort of a means to contact others without allowing them to contact him.

If he was a betting man, if he hadn't been trained never to make an unwarranted assumption or jump to a clumsy conclusion, Jude would have speculated that this was an accident, a man taken ill in the middle of nowhere, alone and with no phone signal, no-one around, unable to reach help in time, but something seemed odd. His sense of foreboding grew. Surely in that situation a walker wouldn't have crawled into a place where they couldn't be seen, but rather would have done their best to get somewhere where they might find help?

He stared at the bank card for a few moments longer. If it turned out that, in whatever circumstances Simon Morea, if it was him, had died after Annabel had reported him missing and the police had deemed it not sufficiently important for them to take the matter on, the force — specifically himself and Faye —had a huge problem.

There was no help for it. He got out his phone and dialled.

'Okay, Faye,' he said. 'Brace yourself. I've got some really, really bad news.'

ELEVEN

Lexie Romachenka, still quivering with shock, had been driven home by a policewoman and it fell to Jude to follow on and speak to her about what she'd found. *This is your mess*, Faye had said to him as if it was Annabel who'd been found dead rather than the husband she claimed to have been so afraid of. *You can sort it out. At least that way when that woman comes after us we can tell her we've escalated it to a senior level.*

He supposed this was intended as punishment. Interviewing witnesses wasn't his job and he had a million other things to do. At first sight it was straightforward, though time-consuming. Simon Morea had, he suspected, fallen foul of the weather or his ill-health (Ashleigh had uncovered a report of him missing a film première due to a longstanding heart condition) and it would be unfortunate, though not disastrous, if it turned out to have happened after Annabel had demanded they search for him. He still stood by Ashleigh's original decision, as Faye would also have done if she hadn't been so scared of scrutiny, and he still maintained that there had been, and currently were, better uses of his time and public money. But there they were; there was no point in arguing with Faye or nursing a grudge about what some might see as an attempt to humiliate or undermine him. On the plus side he was already out of the office so dealing with Lexie was a reasonable price to pay for that, and at least he'd be able to drop in on his mother for a cup of tea and a sandwich on his way back to the office.

There was another reason he was happy to be sent on this particular errand, one he'd decided not to mention to Faye. He'd raised an eyebrow when he saw Lexie Romachenka's name. That Wasby's newest resident had found the body was intriguing enough, not just because Becca had told him she worked in film. Lexie was a location scout — not an actress or a technician or in production, but nevertheless there was every possibility she'd know something of Simon Morea and their paths might have crossed. He took a moment to think about it as he sat in the car, watching Holmes sitting on the inside of Becca's living room window and stretching up against the glass in what looked like frustration. Was such a connection even a coincidence, or was it just within the bounds of normality? He couldn't be sure.

He got out of the car and headed up the path. The police constable who had brought Lexie home opened the door to him and behind him a liveried police car nosed its way down the street to pick her up and take her back up to Ousby or wherever she might be needed. The constable had been watching out for it and headed down the path.

'Everything okay?' Jude asked her, looking towards the cottage.

'Yes. The poor woman was in a hell of a state and couldn't talk to start with, but I got her home and calmed her down. I was about to take her statement when I saw you coming along. Do you want to do the statement, or should I stay?'

'No, you get on. I'll see what she has to say for herself.'

'I asked if she had someone who could come and sit with her but she said she didn't want anyone,' said the constable, almost apologetically. 'I think she's feeling better now. I gave her a cup of tea and let her cry for a bit.'

'All you can do under the circumstances,' said Jude, and waved her off before he turned and headed into Wasby End Cottage. Lexie Romachenka was in the living room, sitting in an armchair by the window and occupying the only spot of sunlight in the room. The light drew his eyes to her, as perhaps it was meant to do; she was sitting slightly forward, very still, stockinged feet crossed at the ankles, hands folded earnestly around a mug with a cartoon picture of a cow on it. He walked into the room with an acute sense that this scene was staged and this was his big entrance.

'Ms Romachenka,' he said, not liking the idea that someone else had control of the situation when he was used to being in charge. He sensed she was a woman who saw everything in terms of film and that this was a scene she was enjoying, in a strange kind of way, knowing how it would play out with herself as the focus of it. 'DCI Jude Satterthwaite. I've come to have a quick chat with you about what happened this morning, if that's okay.' Though there would be nothing the constable couldn't have got from her about the order of events and it was only the identity of the dead man, if that identity was correct, that he could add. It would be interesting to see her reaction.

'Thank you.' She made to stand up and he motioned her to remain seated, then sat down himself on a hard-backed and uncomfortable chair that was the only one available given that the sofa was occupied by magazines and an open laptop. 'Did you say your name is Satterthwaite? I think I know your mother.' The look she gave him was curious, much more so than an anonymous copper would warrant. God knew what she'd heard about him. He suppressed a grin. His mother could be relied on to sing his praises but Becca, while always impeccably polite, could be waspish when his name came up.

'Everyone around here knows my mum,' he said, and laughed. 'I hope you're okay, Ms Romachenka. That must have been a horrible experience for you.'

'Yes, and I'm afraid I reacted very badly. But I feel much calmer now.'

'I'm glad to hear it. I'd like to ask you, if I may, what happened? And, with your permission, record it.'

He placed his phone on the small coffee table between them and, at his nod, Lexie cleared her throat and began speaking. Her account was admirably succinct. She had left her car up on the hills the previous afternoon so that she could have a drink, and had accepted a lift from a friend to collect it. Once there, she had decided to make the most of what had looked at the time like a promising day and go for a walk; she had driven down to Ousby and walked up to Ardale Beck because it was a walk she knew, having scouted it for a film the previous year. At the lime kilns she'd noticed a smell; the crow had startled her, then the apocalyptic cloud of flies had risen and revealed the body. It had all been very Hitchcockian. She had panicked and had been halfway back to Ousby before she thought of calling the police and when she did so the signal had been too weak. She had eventually called them from her car. She had met no-one on her walk other than the man who cut the grass in the churchyard, who would be able to verify both the time she had left the car and the time she had returned. She'd spoken to him on both occasions.

The tale told, she sat back and gave him the benefit of her full, open stare. 'What happened to the poor man?'

'We don't know yet. So, while there's every chance it was an accident we have to keep an open mind on the matter until we know for sure.'

'I understand.' She set the mug down on the side table and looked beyond him, out into the garden where the fells beyond the village melted into an endless grey mist. 'It was strange, though. So strange. Because when I went there before I was scouting for a murder scene there. It was a Cold War spy thriller and there was to be a chase, like in *The Thirty-Nine Steps*. But it wasn't quite right, and though we did use the place in the end it was only for a few shots and we used the Via Ferrata at Honister for most of the rest of it. So in my mind…well, I went there with a very dramatic mindset and in a funny way I was almost looking for something unusual. I think that was why I went into the lime kilns.'

'It's a very interesting connection,' said Jude, carefully, 'because although the body looks as if's been there some days and isn't in great condition, we do think we know who the person was.'

'Oh?'

'Yes. This is in confidence, and we have yet to verify his identity and inform his family.' Faye, at least, had agreed to tell Annabel Faulkner. 'He had bank cards with him and they suggest that his name was Simon Morea.'

'What?' For the first time he thought she was surprised. The scene wasn't going as she'd expected it to and she'd lost control, but her response was immediate and dramatic. In the time it had taken to say the name, Lexie Romachenka collapsed from confident to helpless. 'No! Oh my God! The film director?'

'Yes. Mr Morea's wife had reported him missing. They

have a property in Cumbria, which is where he was last seen.'

'My God? Simon?' She put her hands up to her mouth. 'I can't believe it! This has to be a mistake.'

'As I say, it is yet to be confirmed. You seem very distressed. Did you know him?'

'Of course.' With care, Lexie reached for the mug again. 'Everyone in the film industry knows everyone else. I wouldn't claim to know him well, unless I was trying to impress someone, of course.' She managed a weak smile. 'In reality I only met him a couple of times.'

She was speaking rapidly now. Watching her, Jude thought the news had genuinely shocked her, but she was fighting whatever feelings lurked beneath that. 'Are you sure you're all right, Ms Romachenka?'

'Yes, perfectly all right. Just taken aback. But actually, if it is him, I think I might know why he was there.'

'Oh?'

'Yes. I know he'd been here before. It was his film that I worked on. That's when we met. After my visit I sent clips and photos to the location manager and she told me that he was struck by the dramatic possibilities of the place, though as I've said it turned out not to be suitable as the main location for that particular project. I imagine he went back up there to see if it was suitable for something else.' She sipped at her tea. 'That's why I went up there.'

'You were working on a second project with Simon Morea?' he asked, watching her closely.

She stared back at him with her chin lifted in defiance and he was surprised to see her flush a deep pink. 'No. It was a project of my own.'

'I didn't know you were—'

'I'm not a director,' she said, cutting him off, 'but I love film. I've always thought I'd like to try my hand at making something, even just at an amateur level. You have to start somewhere, don't you? I have a very strong sense of place and for me the setting is as much a character in the film as…as you might be. Or anyone else. So that was why I was there. To see if it was a good fit.'

He took a moment to think of Ardale Beck, that soggy, remote, undistinguished dale in the foothills of a landscape so much larger and more spectacular and couldn't for the life of him see what made it so much more special than any of a hundred other similar places. 'Did you go up there when the filming took place?'

She shook her head.

'But you worked with Mr Morea on the project?'

'No, not directly. I worked with his location team and they reported directly to him, though we met very briefly.' As if she had boasted about a connection and now, realising she might incriminate herself, was hastening to play it down. 'And I came across him at parties a couple of times. He never really paid me any attention, not more than was polite — well, any more than was unavoidable, because he was never polite. It was a relief, if I'm honest, because he could be a bit of a creep, you know? Older men and young women.'

'That happens a lot in the industry?'

'Yes. There's always gossip about him,' she said, with a degree of disdain. 'There's gossip about everything, but with Simon you always assumed that anything negative you heard was true.'

'Did you like Mr Morea?'

She heaved a deep sigh. 'My mother always says you should never speak ill of the dead, but I suppose this is important. No, I didn't like him at all. The opposite, in fact. He was remarkably talented and probably criminally underrated, but he was arrogant and egocentric. He never saw people as individuals but only as things he could use — as theatrical props, if you like. They were contacts, or beautiful people to be seen with, or women who would fall into bed with him because he was famous. Not without charm when he wanted. But no, I didn't like him. I saw through him.'

Jude thought of the pictures in celebrity magazines, of that carefully-positioned cult of Beauty and the Beast. 'Did you know he was in the area?'

'I had no idea. I hadn't heard anything of him since the film wrapped, except for the usual gossip in the magazines.' The doorbell jangled, sharp and intrusive, and she jumped. 'I'd better get that. Do you mind?'

'No, go ahead. I'm finished now. As I said, I'd rather you kept what I said to you to yourself just now, until the identity is confirmed one way or the other.'

'Of course, yes. I know how to be discreet. I know we film people gossip a lot but we can be close as the grave. We all have secrets we need to keep. Commercial ones, of course.' She got up and went to the front door as Jude ended the recording, stood up and pocketed his phone before following her to the hallway where a tall man, older than Lexie, dressed in a shabby and stained Barbour jacket, was on the doorstep.

'Hugh!' cried Lexie, with what seemed like genuine warmth. 'Surely it can't be—'

'—suppertime already?' He finished for her. 'No, it isn't, but I heard on the grapevine that something had happened up at Ardale and obviously I knew you were there so I went to check you were all right, and some man in the churchyard told me you'd found a body and were in an awful state so I thought I'd come and make sure you were okay.'

'That's so sweet of you. Yes, he was horrid to me. He

said he'd seen me walking up there with a man and kind of sneered at me in an unpleasant way, and it was really awful. I told him he'd mistaken me for someone else and he said I could come and wait for the police at his house, but of course I didn't. As if I'd go off with some creepy stranger! I was so upset and he just laughed at me. So grim.'

'I'm not laughing at you,' said the newcomer, with spirit. 'I've come to make sure you're all right and to remind you you promised me dinner. You don't have to cook. I'll take you out.' At last he took his eyes off her and looked beyond at Jude, who had been politely waiting for the two of them to remember he was there and step away from the door so he could leave. 'Oh, sorry. I didn't...' He looked back at Lexie, questioningly.

'It's the police,' she said, and shuffled a step closer to him.

'I'm Hugh Cameron,' said the man to Jude, placing an arm around her shoulders. 'I'm a friend of Lexie's. Is there something wrong?'

'It's routine. I was just checking with Ms Romachenka what happened this morning.'

'I think you're quite senior. Is that right?'

Hugh Cameron must be local enough to know who Jude was and distant enough not to be known in return. 'Yes, but I came along because I was in the area anyway. What happened up in Ardale looks like a tragic accident, but we have to treat these things as serious.'

'Of course.'

Jude stepped outside, Hugh Cameron stepped in and he and Lexie disappeared into the house leaving him to close the door behind him, trying to remember what his mother and Becca had told him about Lexie Romachenka. She'd left London after an affair, he recalled, though if

Becca knew more she hadn't said. He checked his watch. His mother's car wasn't outside the house, so he wouldn't get that cup of tea after all, and he'd have to go back to the office and face Faye on an empty stomach.

Just before the turning onto the main road he met Becca coming the other way, as if sent by Providence. He squeezed his Mercedes in to the hedge to allow her space to pull up alongside and wound the window down. She, in her Fiat 500, did the same.

'What's brought you down here today,' she asked, resting her elbow on the open window.

'Business. I'm just heading back to the office.'

'And there was me thinking you'd sneaked a cheeky half day,' she teased him. 'Seriously, though. Business? Is everything all right?'

'Yes. At least, it is here. Your new neighbour found a body when she was out walking and I was in the area so I got sent down to check up on things.'

'Foul play?' asked Becca, with an anxious frown.

'It doesn't look like it.' But nevertheless that niggle at the back of his mind made him keep the conversation live. 'But she's very shaken.'

'Oh dear. Do you think I should pop in and see her?'

That was Becca all over. He knew she'd have things to do that evening, because she always did — Brownies or the village hall committee or the Women's Institute, always something that needed to be done and she the one everyone left to do it — but she couldn't resist the thought that someone might need help. 'I'd say yes, but someone arrived just as I was leaving and he seemed to have it in hand.'

'He?' said Becca, with a degree of concern. 'Oh dear. I do hope it's not the ex she ran away from. He sounded toxic and she seemed to think he might come after her and try and get her to give him another chance, which is pretty much code for coercion in my book.'

That was all he needed — another woman scared of a man. If anything happened to Lexie, Faye would be on his back about that, too. 'She seemed pleased to see him.' But, he recalled, Ashleigh couldn't help but be pleased when she saw Scott.

'Good. It's unlikely to be him, then.'

'What was his name, do you know?'

'Oh yes. She's not exactly backward in coming forward, is Lexie. His name's Nico, but I don't know the surname.'

'It's not him, then,' said Jude, grateful for anything that made his life easier. 'This guy is Hugh Cameron.'

'Oh, right. That sounds familiar. Tall? Quite a bit older than her?'

'Yes. You know him?'

Becca sighed, as if she was remembering a time of her life when she wasn't really happy with herself. 'I think he might be a friend of Adam's. Lexie and Adam were chatting the other day and I think he'd offered to take her out with his shooting friends. Hugh's one of them. I met them once, when Adam and I were going out, and I'm sure they're all very nice, but they really weren't my type. I felt like a fish out of water.'

If Hugh Cameron was a friend of Adam's he'd have a very poor impression of Jude, but that would explain how he'd known who he was. 'I can't see you fitting in with the shooting crowd.'

'Well, quite. I don't have time for all that nonsense.' A car, turning off the main road, distracted her. 'I'll get on,' she said, and pulled the Fiat out of the lay-by and onwards into the village while Jude, after a moment's thought, headed towards the office to check in with Faye.

TWELVE

Hugh didn't stay, not (Lexie thought) because he didn't want to and certainly not because she didn't want him to, but because the day's events had been so confusing that neither of them was brave enough to take that first step from the security of their singlehood into the uncertainty of a relationship. She'd hoped he would, because his presence was so comforting and she herself still shocked by what the detective had told her, and he had hinted that he might if she needed help, but she'd resisted the temptation. Not that long before she'd have snatched at this offer but now she was wise enough to see that real love would wait and brave enough to believe it. Hugh was of a different generation and didn't seem the kind of man to grab a bit of skirt whenever the opportunity arose, quite the opposite of Nico. She would have to play this dating game by his rules.

'It was so nice of you,' she said to him as she opened the door for him to leave and let in the breath of fresh air from what had turned out to be a quixotically pleasant night, 'and please don't think I don't want you to stay. It would be very kind of you to look after me. But I think I need to be on my own just now.'

'I understand.' He hovered anxiously on the doorstep, wreathed in the autumn darkness and the thick fragrance of roses and night-scented stocks. 'But if you need me, you know you can call me any time.'

'Thank you.' She went up on tiptoe to kiss him, full on the lips, and allowed the kiss to linger for a moment before she ended it. How ridiculous even to think that way of a man she'd only met the previous day. It was far too soon. Sex would wait. 'Shall we meet again? For a proper date, I mean?'

'Yes. Just let me know when suits you. I'm at the cattle sale in Carlisle tomorrow, but after that I'm flexible.'

'I hope you aren't selling Buttercup,' she said, in mock seriousness.

'Never in a million years.' He grinned. 'Who would I talk to about you?'

She giggled. 'Oh Hugh.' It was a joy just saying his name. Her hand lingered on his sleeve, reluctant to let him go. 'I know you're so busy.'

'There's always a lot to do, but I don't have to do it all at once and plenty of it will wait.'

'Even Buttercup?'

'Even Buttercup, though I don't like to neglect her for too long.'

'Then I'll call you.' She let go of his sleeve. 'Good night, Hugh.'

'Good night, Lexie.'

She watched him get in the car, waved as he drove off, peered along the village street until the tail lights of the Discovery were out of sight. What a strange day. For most of it she'd been flung along on a tide of other people's making, turmoil in her head over what had happened in the morning and in her heart as a result of that evening. Now she was alone after all the time in his company, she didn't know which of these emotions would triumph in the silence after his departure.

The curtains in the living room were open and she left them that way so she could see the moon hanging low in the sky, fat and gold as a baked Camembert. Her phone was on the table and she picked it up, tossing it from hand to hand. It was after ten o'clock and her mother's regular evening message was still unanswered. Lexie spoke to her mother every day and routinely lied to her about her doings, not because she was naturally devious but because her mother was alone, anxious about her and in need of constant reassurance. Today she would have to think carefully about what she revealed and what she kept to herself, how much ground to concede. Her mother would know immediately that she was upset so Lexie would have to tell her something of what had happened, but after the fiasco with Nico, Mary Ford was fierce in her advice to her daughter to keep away from men.

Fair enough. Though Lexie thought her mother's dislike of half the world's population was irrational and probably based on considerable disappointment somewhere in the past, she had to admit she'd proved herself a bad judge of the male sex. This time it was different but Mary wouldn't see it that way, so she need only know about the morning's dramas. Lexie would keep Hugh to herself.

She poured herself a large glass of wine before she settled back in the armchair for the call, breathing deeply and listening to the sound of herself, her beating heart, the throbbing of her blood. In the city these sounds were overwhelmed by the scream of sirens and the hum of washing machines in the flat above, the rush of a bath draining, the wailing of someone else's children. In the country the silence wasn't absolute as some thought, but gentle and comforting, like a thick blanket, its breaths punctuated by sounds that were organic and comforting: the wind, an owl, a distant engine.

The phone had barely finished trilling its first ring before her mother snatched it up.

'I called!' she said, 'and you didn't answer!'

'I know, Mama.' Another sip of wine slipped down like honey. A cloud drifted across the moon. Hugh, driving south, would see it exactly as she did, in all its ripe golden beauty. 'I've had a busy day.'

'I thought something had happened to you.'

She always worried, far too much and usually without reason, but this time she had cause. 'Oh, Mama,' said Lexie, suddenly feeling the tears rising up inside her in a way that surprised her with its suddenness and its irresistibility. 'I've had such a terrible day.'

'What's happened?'

'It's Nico.'

'Is he back? Tell me you haven't agreed to see him!'

'No. No, it's worse than that. He's dead.' Was that really worse that being tied once more to that toxic pretence at romance?

'What?' said Mary, in a sharp, shocked voice.

'I went for a walk,' said Lexie, rapidly, knowing her best chance of getting through the tale without breaking down was to do it all at once, just as she had explained it to the detective. 'Somewhere I went to with Nico once, though that isn't relevant. I went back up there and I found this body in a lime kiln. It was awful, all covered in flies and rotting, and the smell…and I ran back down to the village because there wasn't any signal and then one of the policewomen took me home and then a detective came to ask me what happened and he told me that they thought they knew the name of who it was and it was Nico. Except obviously they never called him that because they don't know that's what I always called him, but it is him, he's dead. And it looks like he had some kind of an accident and it's awful.'

'Truly awful,' said Mary in her grim mother-in-crisis-mode voice, 'for him and his family. But not for you. It's a blessing for you.'

'I know. But I can't help…I hate myself. Because I hated him and now he's dead and I'm glad, and I feel terrible.'

'Alexandra,' said Mary, firm and sensible. 'I'm going to get in the car right now and come and bring you home. I told you should have stayed here longer and let me look after you.'

Then someone else would have found Nico, which would have been a blessing, but she wouldn't have met Hugh, which would have been a disaster. 'I don't want to come home. I'm fine. I like it here.' It had been one thing when Lexie had decided to break with Nico and her mother had come down to London to pack her stuff and bundle her onto a train before she could change her mind. She'd been glad of the comfort and the protection, knowing she need do nothing but cry and if Nico did turn up Mary would have seen him off. Here there was no threat to her — at least, not that sort. 'But it's awkward because now I wonder if I should have told the detective about Nico and me.'

'Why didn't you?'

'It was just too complicated. It was such a shock. He

asked me if I knew Simon Morea and of course I had to say yes because people know we worked together and if I'd said no he'd soon have found out I was lying, but how could I explain that I'd just found the body of a man I'd been having an affair with?'

And fallen out with, badly. She sipped again. Nico had always been determined to keep their relationship secret. She'd gone along with it because she enjoyed the thrill of an illicit romance and because he was such a compelling man, and in doing so he had made her a liar. She'd always suspected that the reasons behind it were convenient for him rather than for her, and his devotion had come at a price. She wasn't just another in a succession of several girlfriends; she was the one he'd wanted to leave his psycho of a wife for. Thank God the woman hadn't seemed to fix on Lexie as her possible rival; that would have been a terrifying prospect. And thank God Lexie herself had seen the trap of commitment before she had fallen into it.

'I don't know what to do,' she said, though she knew the pause at the end of the line was nothing more alarming than the comforting sound of her mother reviewing the next in her daughter's series of distressing life choices and considering the options. Stay or go? Confess or deny? Act, or pretend it never happened?

'Nico was always discreet, I take it?' said Mary, after a while.

'Oh God, yes.' Lexie had always been extremely glad that her lover and her mother had never met. She'd suggested it, because it would have to happen some time if they were to make a life together, but Nico hadn't wanted to and so it hadn't happened. He had layer upon layer of excuses for that and for everything else, three reasons for being in every place he was at every time, a deliberately chaotic lifestyle which hinged on a completely fake lack of organisation and memory. *I'll tell her I forgot*, he would say to Lexie with that captivating grin as he slipped into her bed when he was supposed to be meeting Annabel for lunch, *and she'll believe me. I told her I was working on something and lost track of the time*. Sometimes he'd try that trick on her, too. *Oh God, did we say today? I can't make it.* 'He never wrote anything down. He even had a different phone for me so there was no way his wife would catch him messaging me from the one he used for her. I don't think she'd know me if she saw me.' It had been a measure of the regard in which he held her. He picked up other women and indulged himself, then dropped them and took the flak from his wife with a shrug and a dismissive remark about the latest jilted mistress, but he'd been serious about her. He'd said she was the one his wife would be afraid of, the one he really loved.

On reflection, she wished she'd spent more time thinking about why he behaved like that and why he thought she was different, or wondered why he was prepared to fight his wife over some wannabe actress he'd picked up at an awards ceremony and then blatantly flown to Cairo or wherever before dumping her at the airport, but not prepared to take her on over Lexie, the woman he'd claimed to love. It would have been interesting to know what he'd have said if he was challenged, but she had never dared challenge him. That was why, in the end, her mother had urged her to make the break final and she had succumbed.

'In that case, I'd keep your mouth shut,' said Mary, as if the decision was made. 'If nobody knows, nobody's going to let the cat out of the bag, are they? You never even called him by his name in your messages, so even if they trace them…'

This was the trouble. Lexie had watched endless films in

every genre. She had no favourite. She devoured romance and horror, epic and fantasy, kitchen sink drama and crime. From the latter she'd learned everything there was to know about how to structure a story and how to keep the audience's interest, at precisely what point in the plot a detective should make a crucial discovery, but when it came down to it she had no idea how the police actually worked. They couldn't find out everything, because some crimes remained unsolved. She breathed deeply. She kept forgetting that her over-active imagination often overran the truth. 'The detective said it looked like an accident. So it doesn't matter. It's just private between me and him and it means it isn't relevant to what happened. So maybe I should tell them after all.'

'Best not.' Mary was brisk at the other end of the line. 'You know what some of those characters you work with are like.'

'Yes.' They would delight in her downfall. Worst of all Annabel Faulkner, who had come to hate her husband and yet remained so possessive of him, was notorious for the ruthlessness with which she ruined the chances of success for Nico's other women. Without a doubt Lexie would be forced out of the career she loved. 'You're right. They don't need to know.' But even as she agreed to this elegant solution, something else occurred to her. 'The man in the churchyard might say.'

'What man?'

Lexie explained about the encounter, how he'd claimed to remember seeing her. 'I went up there with Nico, once, so that we could look at the place together. I didn't think anyone who matters had seen us, but he must have done.' Curse the man and his memory. And curse Nico, who wasn't the kind of man you passed over even when he was playing it down. You couldn't hide charisma under a waterproof jacket and a black beanie hat. 'He might tell the police and they'll work out that Nico was Simon and then they'll tell his wife and—'

'They've no reason to tell her, or anyone. You didn't do anything wrong.'

'Just immoral,' said Lexie, miserably.

'They're not there to judge your morality, lass, only whether you've broken the law. Just keep mum, eh?'

Outside the cloud thickened across the pale moon. The breeze had picked up. Somehow that reminded Lexie of the contentment she'd felt that morning, sharing a bacon roll with Hugh in a country cafe, of how comforting it had been to have him with her that evening and how difficult it had been to let him go.

Hugh was a little bit older, perhaps a little old-fashioned. Her behaviour in London might scare him off and she didn't want that. There was all the more reason to keep quiet and let Nico's unfortunate accident blow over. Later, perhaps much later, if the relationship became settled and strong, she might tell him. Her anxiety of the morning had vanished. It didn't matter if Nico had ever known Hugh. A dead man could do nothing to destroy this golden new relationship. 'Yes, you're right.'

'Maybe you want to come back home for a bit, lass. You must be lonely up there by yourself.'

'I'm fine. I love it up here. The cottage is beautiful and the people are so nice. My neighbours keep an eye out for me.'

'Maybe I could come up.'

No, that would definitely not do. The risk of crossing paths with Hugh or hearing about him from one of those oh-so-friendly-but-rather-too-talkative neighbours was much too great. 'I'm actually enjoying being by myself right now. But maybe we could meet up for lunch in Settle or somewhere. I could get the train down.'

'You know I care for you.'

'I know.' Just as Nico had always claimed to care but never really did. But no man could ever care for you as much as your mother.

THIRTEEN

Faye had changed her mind (or, as Jude uncharitably thought of it) chickened out. When he went into work the next morning he found her hovering impatiently at the coffee machine, like a spider ready for a fly.

'Don't take too much time over that,' she said, not quickly enough to stop him dropping coins into the slot and hitting the button with a satisfying click. 'I have a job for you that you're not going to like, but you've brought it on yourself so I'm afraid I don't have a lot of sympathy for you. I need you to go and break the death message to Ms Faulkner.'

As if it was somehow his fault that the man was dead when there was every chance Morea been lying in that gully since not long after he'd left the house and long before his wife had even noticed his absence. Annabel would have been told that a body had been found with her husband's ID but he could understand why Faye was making sure everything was official. 'Don't we have any uniformed officers available?'

He'd kept his tone as neutral as he could, and it wasn't an unreasonable question, but Faye scowled anyway. 'Yes. But as we need to reassure Ms Faulkner that we did everything possible to find him so that she doesn't put in a complaint about the way we've handled it, I'm sending you. If you abase yourself enough we might persuade her we're taking it seriously.'

He'd spent longer than necessary the previous evening going back over Ashleigh's initial telephone call with Annabel, and his own subsequent conversation with her, and in all honesty he couldn't see anything they could have done differently. They couldn't have saved the man's life. 'You've officially got a positive ID on him, then.' As if they hadn't known.

'We have. It's definitely him. The cards he had on him pointed us in the right direction. A tattoo confirmed it.' She made a face. 'Maybe I should say, the remains of a tattoo. And we know how he got there. They found a car he hired, parked down in Blencarn.'

'Right.' The speculation about Morea's double life looked to be correct. If he'd kept things simple and used his own car it might have been possible to find him earlier, but even then he might already have been dead.

She shrugged. 'Fascinating, isn't it? If you're brave enough you can ask Ms Faulkner if she knows anything about that. Maybe there was something wrong with his own vehicle. I'll get someone to go back to the car hire people and see if it was a regular occurrence.'

He watched the last of the coffee gurgle into the cup. 'Where did you say she lives? Windermere?'

'Troutbeck, or nearly. It won't take you long at this time of day.'

It was just after eight o'clock. He would have time to finish his coffee, gather his thoughts and get down over the

Kirkstone Pass to Troutbeck, endure the inevitable brief tussle with Annabel, and be back again before eleven and his next cup of coffee. At least it was a half-decent day and a scenic drive. The work he'd intended to do that morning would just have to wait until the evening.

The house was a small one, just up on a hillside not quite in Windermere, not quite in Troutbeck, but looking down on both with a lofty superiority. From a distance it was nothing pretentious, a former shepherd's cottage, but as Jude got closer he saw that it had been done up to a high, if not the highest, specification, from the slate sign on the gatepost to the slabs in the driveway and the smallest details on the house itself. A sporty BMW was parked on the drive alongside a larger model that he knew to be Simon Morea's. He pulled up in the large gravelled drive, got out, took a second to gather his courage while pretending to take in the stunning view across the central Lakes, and turned to the front door.

Delivering a death message had been something he dreaded as a younger officer, and had been glad to delegate as he climbed the ladder. Accident, suicide or sudden illness, the usual causes, were difficult enough in their own right, murder always worse, but in all cases the response of the loved one — a parent, a child, a partner — was distressing to behold. This case, he suspected, might be different, and that left him both interested and intrigued as to the direction Annabel's anger with her husband would take at confirmation of his final escape. He turned to the door.

'Detective Inspector.' Annabel Faulkner surprised him, rounding the door from the back of the house. She wore jeans, a fleece and gardening gloves and had secateurs in her hand. 'This is a surprise.' She stood back and made no move to approach the front door.

'Could we go inside?' he asked.

'I'm busy in the garden right now. We can deal with whatever you want to say out here.'

If that was how she wanted it, that was how it would be. Annabel was by no means a stupid woman and she must have some idea of why he was there. 'I'm afraid I have some bad news for you.'

'You've tracked Simon down, then.' She flicked the secateurs open and shut as if disinterested in what he was saying. 'Why is that bad news? Has he stripped me of all my assets in that fraud you were so sure would never happen? Or is it really bad and he's told you he doesn't want a divorce?'

'I assumed you'd think it bad news.' She wasn't just tough; at heart she was deeply unpleasant. She knew her husband was suspected dead and was choosing to toy with Jude instead. 'I'm sorry have to confirm what we already suspected. The body found in Ardale has been identified as Mr Morea.'

'Topped himself did he?' Annabel looked at him, without empathy. 'Or did someone finally have enough of him and decide to put an end to his unpleasantness once and for all?'

'As far as I'm aware,' said Jude, choosing his words with extreme care, 'at this early stage in the investigation, it looks like an accident.'

'As far as you're aware?' She tensed a little, watching him.

'I'm expecting the results of the post mortem later today, but the early indications don't show anything suspicious. I believe your husband suffered from a heart condition, is that correct?'

'Lately I've begun to have my doubts about whether or not Simon actually had a heart or whether it was just a piece of AI junk that somehow got connected to his brain.' She shrugged. 'Don't look at me like that. I did love him once, and so of course there will come a point where I sit down one evening with a glass of wine and shed a tear over what he once was. He could be very charming, when he wanted to be, and when he was in the mood he had the gift of making a woman feel like a million dollars. But when all's said and done the marriage had gone bad, the fighting was only going to get worse, and him dying has saved me a lot of hassle and a lot of money. I won't shed any crocodile tears for Simon.' That shrug again. 'I always think you have to be honest about things.'

'That certainly makes my job easier,' he said, dryly. 'Would you like me to tell you what we know?'

For a second he thought she'd refuse, showing the depths of her dislike for her husband through her indifference to his end, but even Annabel was curious. 'I suppose you'd better.'

'A walker found his body in a lime kiln in the Pennines yesterday morning.'

'In a lime kiln? Are you quite sure someone didn't have enough of him and hit him over the head with a brick? I'm sure you'd find no shortage of candidates. He had a lot of so-called friends but I'm not sure any of them actually liked him.'

'The body had been there some days but, as I say, there are no immediate signs of violence. Our initial theory is that he may have been taken ill, either in the kiln itself or else outside, in which case he may have crawled into it in order to get some shelter. It's on a relatively popular path but it seems that no-one was walking that way until yesterday, or if they did they didn't look in the kiln.' And then, because it was bound to come out in the press, he thought he'd try and surprise her. 'A colleague of his found him. Lexie Romachenka.'

She shook her head. 'I don't know the name. Still, you'll be looking at her closely I imagine. There are plenty of reasons for wanting rid of Simon and one of them would be mad jealousy that he wasn't paying you enough attention. God knows I felt like that about him myself once.'

He was watching her face for any sign of regret, but there was none. In Annabel Faulkner's eyes the death of her husband was nothing to concern herself with, a business deal gone sour but one she could walk away from without bitterness. 'Why do you think he was murdered?'

'I don't. I'm just observing that the world is full of people who would love to have done it. It doesn't mean any of them did. Now you're going to ask me where I was when he died. I expect I was in London.'

'We don't know when he died.'

'That's why I said, I *expect* I was in London. When you can be more specific about the time I can be more specific about my movements.'

Jude's thoughts turned briefly to Lexie Romachenka. 'Your late husband had a bit of a reputation as a womaniser, I believe.'

'That's an understatement.' She laughed.

'And did you know about his women?'

'Every single one of them,' she said, with certainty, 'but that wasn't difficult. He never troubled to hide his relationships and they were all casual. Not one of them was a threat to me in any way. If anything I felt sorry for them.'

'Okay. There are one or two things that are unusual about your husband's disappearance and death, Ms Faulkner, and I'd like to ask you about them.'

Still she refused to give an inch, never even looked

towards the front of the house to indicate that she might consider inviting him in and allowing him to formalise this strangest of conversations. 'I did wonder if you might have asked some pertinent questions *before* his death, Chief Inspector, rather than after it. This all smells a bit like closing the stable door after the horse has bolted.'

'There's every chance your husband was dead before you reported him missing,' he said, dryly, 'and given where he was found it's unlikely we'd have located him in time. He seems to have gone to some lengths to cover his tracks.'

'That would be entirely in character. What did he do?'

'You reported that he left his phone on the table. His body had a phone on it.'

'I think I mentioned that he had two phones. I wouldn't be surprised if he had more.'

'It seems your husband hired a car in Windermere. Did you know about that?'

'Not that particular incident no, or I would have told you what to look for. But he certainly hired cars before when he was trying to conduct what he thought was a clandestine affair. I think for Simon it was part of the drama, laying a trail and checking if he was being followed. It wasn't a serious attempt to hide his behaviour. The pictures always appeared in the media. He made sure of that.'

Jude had seen some of them, in that evening he'd spent with Ashleigh leafing through the glossy magazines Lisa had acquired from the hairdressers, more than one with a teasing caption about *married film director Simon Morea and a mystery woman*, while his wife was photographed emerging from some business meeting wearing a killer suit and a steely smile. 'You told us you were afraid of him, and yet you didn't mention this habit of subterfuge, or the fact that he might have hired a car.'

'I suspect you didn't take me seriously enough to check out the car hire outlets in any case.' She stepped back. 'I'll let you get back to work, now, Chief Inspector. No doubt you'll have all the paperwork to do. And the press, of course. I'll look forward to seeing you giving some press conference on the television and trying to justify your lack of action with a search that could have saved him, but as far as I'm concerned that's really all we need to discuss.'

'Thank you, Ms Faulkner. It's been most interesting. We may come back to you with more questions if anything else emerges.' He turned towards his car.

'You people do know how to make a fuss out of nothing,' she called after him, but he didn't respond, just got back into the car and drove up the steep hill towards the Kirkstone Pass and a meeting which, if he was lucky, would provide information to determine conclusively that Simon Morea had died of natural causes.

But it was very interesting that his angry wife had concluded that he might not.

FOURTEEN

'Okay.' Jude pulled up a chair at the table in the incident room and glanced round to see, with a degree of relief, that Faye was nowhere to be seen. That meant he could deal with this himself, collate information from those he'd deputed to do the necessary digging and, hopefully, send Simon Morea's case up to the coroner and have it recorded as a case of accidental death. No doubt it would attract a storm of media attention along with some inevitable interest in Morea's commonly-known promiscuity, but that would die down soon enough. In the meantime, matters were best dealt with quickly and clinically. He had no desire to spend more time than necessary on the case purely because the unfortunate victim of an accident happened to be well known, and he resented Faye's nervousness about it. 'Let's have a quick roundup of who's got what and then we can get through the detail. Who has the PM results? Doddsy?'

'The report came in this morning.' Doddsy seemed as resentful as Jude himself about this high-level fuss about nothing. He sat back and folded his arms, an unusually defensive gesture for him.

'Right,' said Jude, noting it and not liking the implications. 'Chris, did you get a chance to look at the CCTV?'

Chris Marshall, the other detective sergeant, nodded his head. 'There won't be anything there that'll surprise you, but we've been able to trace Morea's movements for part of the route and that should pin down the time of death, at least.'

'Good. Ash, what have you been up to?'

'Chasing down some witnesses,' she replied, promptly. 'Not with any great success, but I think we can be sure of Morea's whereabouts at one point, at least.'

He nodded, pretty sure what he was about to hear from each one of them. He worked regularly with them and they knew how he operated, each one comfortable with their role. Faye, with her micromanagement and many insecurities, unsettled them as much as she did him and without her they were more relaxed and productive.

'Okay, let's get on. You can start, Doddsy, because I'm counting on you to tell me the PM shows us the man died of natural causes and we can all stop worrying and get on with putting this to bed.' If he was correct and, as Doddsy's body language suggested, there was a problem it was better to get to it first.

'Was anyone worrying?' asked Chris Marshall. 'It never occurred to me that it was anything out of the ordinary, apart from the fact Morea was famous. It's unfortunate, perhaps, but I've seen a dozen cases like it.'

'I hope you're right. I got harangued by the man's wife this morning, and she clearly thinks lots of people would absolutely have loved to see the back of him and a fair few would have enjoyed giving him a helping hand.' And, much as he disliked it Annabel was rich, influential and therefore difficult to ignore. 'I don't see any evidence for that and I don't want to. So, Doddsy. Tell me the death was a result of cardiac arrest due to a long-standing heart condition, and we can go on from there.'

'Okay.' Doddsy glanced down at the iPad on which he'd uploaded the PM report. 'It was indeed a cardiac arrest, and it was indeed probably due to a long-standing heart condition.' But he left it somehow unfinished.

There was more coming, then. Jude knew Doddsy too well and the look on his friend's face told him this wasn't going to be as simple as he'd hoped. He cursed, inwardly. 'But?'

'Not *but*. *And*. There was considerable animal disturbance to the exposed parts of the body — head, hands and so on — and decay had set in on the rest, but significant parts of the corpse, including the torso, had been protected by the clothing and the position of the body. In addition to all the usual stuff — nothing out of the ordinary, just old scars from operations and the like, all of which are consistent with Morea's medical records — Matt Cork identified what he says is unidentified bruising on the torso, just below the heart.'

There was silence, while all four of them considered the implications of this. 'Does Matt say what he thinks it is?' asked Jude.

Doddsy shrugged. 'You know him. He's as cagey as they come. He won't commit himself to anything, but he did say it puzzled him. It was almost perfectly circular, he said, and about six inches across. Here's a photo, for those with strong stomachs.'

He turned his iPad to them and Jude give it the most cursory of glances. He didn't need to look closely. 'What about a fall? Could that have caused it?'

'That was my initial thought, but he said not. He said

he'd expect a bruise from a fall to be more irregular in shape and this is one you could have drawn with a pair of compasses. So I called Tammy and asked if the forensic people had come up with anything from his clothes, and they had. When they moved the body they found circular scorch marks on the front of Morea's rain jacket, left hand side, just below the heart.'

Now Jude understood why Doddsy had been so subdued about it when everyone else had seemed confident the matter would be quickly wrapped up. 'Right. Let's be clear. Basically you're describing a bullet wound, aren't you? Only without a bullet.'

'I think what I'm describing is a blank weapon being fired at a man with a known heart condition,' said Doddsy, and pushed the iPad away in irritation.

'Bloody hell,' said Chris, speaking for them all. 'How clever is that?'

Jude's immediate response to this bombshell was irritation. There was nothing he disliked as much as a clever criminal, and his annoyance was amplified by the fact that they all had other things to do. 'Not clever enough. Does whoever really did it think they can get away with it?'

'Do you think that could have been murder?' Ashleigh asked. 'I mean, it's not easy to prove intent if it was a blank cartridge.'

'Let's find who did it, and then we'll be able to say. At the very least it's assault. There's a lower bar for manslaughter, for sure, but I would definitely be looking at that.' If whoever had pulled the trigger and ended Simon Morea's life had known about his heart condition then murder was a definite possibility, and it seemed that this part of his medical history, at least, was public knowledge. 'The deeper we dig the more we'll find. If it's someone who knew and wanted him dead then yes, I'd definitely be looking at this as murder. Whoever did it we'll get them.'

'For the life of me I don't know how you can prove it,' said Doddsy. 'Even if you can be sure what caused it, even if you find the weapon and you find the perpetrator. Even if they admit they were there and fired the weapon. They'll just claim it was a prank.'

It was unlike Doddsy to be so negative. 'Let them. We'll go back to the forensics and see what else they can tell us. I take it there's no sign of the gun or we'd have heard, but we'll keep looking and maybe we'll find it. If we do — when we do — we'll track down the perpetrator. We'll identify a relationship with Morea, we'll look for motive and opportunity.' It might sound like Policing 101, but it sometimes helped to remind them all of the procedure. God knew what they'd find in the detritus of Simon Morea's private life when his public one was so contentious. Messages and photographs, overheard conversations and loose remarks, obvious gains in money, or in jealousy or anger satisfied, all of them possible motives for revenge, even if that revenge was only intended to teach him a lesson. 'And we start now.' They'd be lucky if Faye didn't have a heart attack of her own when she found out, and he'd make sure that he was as fully-informed as possible before he broke it to her. 'Beginning with what happened. What do we know for certain? He hired a car, he drove down to Blencarn. Then what?' He turned to Chris Marshall. 'What do we know from the CCTV?'

'I've put together a timetable, as far as we know,' the younger man said, prompt and efficient. 'Morea booked the hire car by phone a week past on Friday and picked it up in Windermere the following morning. That was the day after his wife last heard from him. Is that significant?'

'I doubt it. I get the impression they didn't speak unless there was something to be fought over.'

'Okay. He left his own car at the house so I would imagine he walked into Windermere to pick up the hire car, for which he paid with the company credit card found on his body. I can't tell you the route he took but he collected the car around nine o'clock and was spotted on traffic cameras on the A66 at Penrith at 10:23. Beyond that there are no cameras so we don't know what time he arrived at Blencarn, where he left the car.'

'It'd take him twenty minutes out to Blencarn from there, give or take,' said Doddsy, who lived in the area. 'Maybe a little longer at that time of day, maybe a little less on a Saturday.'

'Okay. So he'll have arrived in Blencarn no earlier than quarter to eleven and then, or at some point thereafter, he parked the car in the middle of the village, where we found it.'

'I can add to this,' said Ashleigh, placing her hand on a sheaf of witness statements. 'These are the results of the door-to-door calls we did in the area. Most drew a blank, but we found a local woman walking her dog who noticed a man fitting Morea's description, walking towards Kirkland. That would put him on the path towards Cross Fell, which intersects with the path that Lexie Romachenka took just to the east of the lime kiln where he was found.'

She'd brought a large-scale Ordnance Survey map, which she opened and spread out on the table. Jude had done the Cross Fell walk a number of times but not for some years. Other than that he'd approached from Blencarn, as Morea seemed to have done, rather than taking the route that Lexie had chosen from Ousby, his memories of the details were so vague as to be irrelevant, his recall of the lime kilns barely more than a thought.

Annoyed with himself for this lapse, he pored over the map.

'I wonder how many people walk this way regularly?' he asked tapping a finger on it. 'It's nothing like as popular as the walks in the Lakes, but I'd be surprised if you did that walk without meeting anyone.'

'In September?' asked Doddsy, with some scepticism. 'The weather wasn't great. And Lexie didn't meet anyone.'

'No, but on the path she took the gate was locked. She climbed it, remember. Others might have been put off by that and turned back, but the other route was unobstructed.'

'We know he went that way,' Ashleigh pointed out, 'and if we look more widely we may find someone else who saw him — or who saw someone else. So far we've only covered Blencarn and Ousby but I think we should make a wider appeal for witnesses. There's a good chance anyone walking in that area will have come from a much wider radius than we covered. I can get that done today on all the usual channels.'

'Good.' The trail was cold so time wasn't of the essence and much information, if it existed, would already be lost, but that was no reason to go slower — the opposite. The more time passed, the more people's memories faded. 'I expect the papers will already be onto it.' Something about Annabel Faulkner had made him think she was the type to get her story in first and so, no doubt, the first of the calls would be coming into the Press Office sooner rather than later. There would have to be a press conference — something both he and Faye hated, and a job over which they regularly tussled, with him inevitably emerging the loser by virtue of his junior rank. 'I doubt anything will come up, but you never know. Doddsy, can you get on to Tammy for me and explain the situation? If they haven't left the scene yet, ask them to go over it again and see what they can find. If there's a gun it might have been abandoned somewhere in the river, or just chucked into the bog.'

'If we do find anyone who was there they may have heard a shot,' said Ashleigh, but without any great enthusiasm. 'But I confess. I'm not optimistic.'

Neither was Jude. In the countryside, a shot would hardly raise an eyebrow. There was always someone out for rabbits or pigeons, even without the organised shooting for grouse on the moors, and with a fair wind you could sometimes hear the echoes from the army firing range at Warcop. The sound of a shot from a blank cartridge, at close range, would be lost. They would have to look elsewhere.

'I'll get his phone checked sooner rather than later,' he said. The technical forensic department were notoriously slow in following through on this sort of request, not just because of the paperwork involved but because of their tendency to pick and choose who they worked for. 'That could take a while, but I'll get Faye to have a word. And beyond that, if it's murder we need a motive. Let's think about who we need to talk to — and talk about — to find one.'

'It's a pretty open field, wouldn't you say?' asked Ashleigh. 'At least, if the papers are anything to go by.'

'Ash told us about your evening in reading trashy showbiz gossip,' said Chris, and laughed. 'Your dedication to duty knows no bounds.'

The celebrity reporters had described Morea as divisive, bruising and controversial. He wouldn't be short of enemies. 'I spoke to his wife this morning. Not only was she not remotely bothered that he's dead, but she also suggested, without any prompting, that someone might have bumped him off, and told me there were plenty of people who would have loved to see the back of him, though she stopped short of naming them.'

'She goes straight to the top of the list for our killer, then,' said Chris, cheerfully. He had a tendency to treat murder investigations like a game of Cluedo, and while some disapproved of this attitude Jude thought it was probably a defence mechanism. 'Assuming it was murder, of course. And don't tell me it can't be her because she drew our attention to it, because it sounds like she's a smart woman and if she did it she must have known she'd have to be very lucky for it to be written off as an accident. I expect that's why she was so insistent on reporting him missing. A double bluff. She has a reputation as an absolute ball-breaker in business.'

By the sound of it, Jude and Ashleigh weren't the only ones who'd found Simon Morea fascinating enough to waste some of their time off on. Chris must have frittered away an hour or two down celebrity internet rabbit holes as well. 'It's interesting there was no-one else who thought his absence looked suspicious, yes. So let's have a look at her. What do we know about her?'

'Not much,' said Chris, 'yet. Give me an hour and I'll come up with more. I can tell you that she's fantastically wealthy, both through inherited wealth and in her own right. I know that she's Morea's first wife and he is her second husband. I know they've been married ten years. In the past she's been a major investor in a number of his film projects, though I assume that isn't currently the case, given the state of the marriage.'

'She told me she'd refused to invest in any further projects.'

'That's interesting, because I think his last couple of

projects struggled to raise enough investment. Annabel keeps that kind of money as spare change.'

'Interesting for sure, but I'd say that would be more of a motive for him to murder her than the other way round,' said Doddsy, glumly.

'Maybe. But then you look at his philandering, which he seems to have carried out openly and with complete disregard for his wife, not just recently but throughout their marriage, and that suggests the opposite,' said Chris.

'She mentioned a prenuptial agreement,' said Jude, 'and seemed adamant that it was watertight. It was the reason she wanted him back, or so she said, so that she could divorce him before he asset-stripped the marriage, or as much of it as he could. I wonder how true that actually is? I can't imagine that a seriously restrictive prenuptial agreement would be fully enforceable if he decided to challenge it. She may have had advice to that effect from lawyers and needed rid of him before they reached the divorce courts.'

'So she chose to draw our attention to him being missing, possibly after she'd already killed him?' said Chris. 'That's high risk.'

'You don't get where she did by being risk averse.' Jude thought once more of Annabel. Did she really have that much to gain from the death of her husband?

'Or she could have had him killed,' said Ashleigh. 'If she was responsible for his death you can bet your life she won't have been so stupid as to be anywhere near the actual event. She'll have a triple alibi for every second of the time between him being last seen and his body being discovered.'

'Let's have a look at her in a bit more detail.' Jude nodded to Chris. 'I'd like you to take that on.'

DEATH ON THE SMALL SCREEN

'Bored of the celebrity gossip already?' said Chris to Ashleigh.

She laughed. 'I'm happy to let you have that pleasure.'

'Ash,' went on Jude, 'I want you to take charge of identifying and following up witness statements. There must have been people who went up in the area who we haven't yet identified. There's also the possibility that whoever it was went up from a different route, possibly some distance away, and it might be worth asking around as far away as Melmerby. Have a look at the paths. You'll see where the obvious places are to head off in that direction, and there may be some less obvious ones, too, and of course you don't need to stick to the marked routes at all. And then we need to look very closely at Morea himself.'

'That'll be nice,' said Doddsy, rather distastefully. He was a fastidious and a moral man.

'Yes. I imagine a deep dive into his private life — which he seems to have lived in public — will be interesting. We need to find out who his relationships were with, and whether they ended with any kind of rancour. We need to look at former partners who might feel bitter at being dumped—'

'Was it always him that ended the relationships?' asked Doddsy.

'According to the magazines, yes, but we don't have to fall for an image they put across, even if it was one that suited him to project. It may not always be the case. And I'd also like to know if any of them had partners who might have been jealous and chose to take their annoyance out on Morea, rather than on the wife or girlfriend he dated.'

Ashleigh made a face. 'That's a lovely job for someone.'

'But it has to be done. I'll see if I can get Faye to authorise access to his bank accounts.' He didn't expect any problems there. Faye would be scrambling as hard as he was to fight this particular fire. 'There's the phone, of course. And I'd like to meet again tomorrow and see whether we've come up with any suspects.' He paused. 'And yes. I think we need to look a bit more closely at Lexie Romachenka. Because it seems a hell of a coincidence that she found him.'

FIFTEEN

'Mind yourself, Gerry,' said the barman, slamming down the metal grille in front of the bar. 'I hadn't realised you're still here. You need to go now, son. We're closing. Didn't you hear me call last orders?'

Gerry Cole heaved himself to his feet. He hadn't noticed how time had flown. Now his last pint was empty and the admiring crowd of friends, acquaintances and strangers had thinned out like smoke on a breeze until only the barman and one of his neighbours, already fastening his coat, were left to keep him company.

'We're closing,' said the barman again.

'Come on lad,' said Ed, the neighbour. 'Let's get you home. I think you've had a few too many.'

Gerry had had more than a few too many, but it wasn't often he found himself the centre of attention and even less often that he had a tale to tell and plenty of people not just wanting to listen to it but buying the drinks for him, too. He'd have been a fool to have said no, the price of pints these days.

'It's once in a lifetime,' he said, in response to a question no-one had asked. He wasn't even a big drinker, in the normal way, but today he felt important.

'Can you manage to get him home okay?' the barman asked Ed.

'I can get him to the end of the lane, aye. Come on, Gerry lad. At least I can set you on the right path. Lord knows you've done that for me on the odd occasion.'

'It was a good night, wasn't it?' said Gerry, plaintively, allowing Ed to steer him out of the door. The bar darkened behind them as the barman snapped the lights off.

'It really was. I never had you down as a story teller.'

Even drowning in his drink Gerry sensed an undertone, knew the village was laughing at him. They would be talking about him for a week. 'Every word of it was true.'

'Right?'

'Right.' And it was. For one night only Gerry had become a teller of tales, a man who could hold the attention of a crowded room. He saw everything, doing his work around the village. He cut the grass at the verges and he cleared the drains, he mowed the churchyard, he clipped the hedges, he cleaned and painted the old-fashioned fingerpost at the centre of the village that pointed the way between Ousby and Melmerby and along to the path up Cross Fell via the village of Kirkland. Day in day out the things he saw had been irrelevant, small, fragments of other people's lives that no-one cared about, but that had changed. He had been the one to talk to the lass who'd found the body. 'The police were right interested.'

'We were all interested,' said Ed, putting an arm out to steady him as he struggled to put one foot in front of the other. The two of them matched one another, step by step, along the rough and uneven road. The lights of a car came towards them, slowed to pass safely, moved on and stopped a few hundred yards behind. A car door opened and shut.

'I see everyone when I'm working.'

'You told us.'

'I remember them all, everyone who goes past. All of them different.' There were the middle-aged women who came up to do the same walk every week, on their own or with their friends, walking dogs as big as wolves and every bit as mean. There were the young lads yomping about like they were training to be commandos, and the kids doing whatever expedition it was they did for school or the scouts these days. And there were the couples walking up there like lovers, thinking because they only had eyes for themselves, no-one else would see them. He hadn't bothered mentioning them to the police. He might do that later, when he'd found out how much that young lass from London valued her secrets. 'I must have seen the one that died. This Simon Morris or whatever his name was.'

'You must have done.' Ed's voice was shaded with laughter, as if this scene amused him, but Gerry was too full of himself and his self-importance to be bothered by the man's obvious jealousy.

'I must have seen him, only I didn't know who he was. Did you see me on the telly? They asked me about it.'

'You were absolutely brilliant.' Ed managed a jocular nudge to Gerry's ribs without knocking him over. 'You've the memory of an elephant, always have done.'

'It was me they wanted to talk to.'

'If that poor lass hadn't gone screaming off like she did they'd have asked her,' teased Ed, 'being as how she's that bit better looking than you.'

The woman, Lexie her name was, hadn't wanted to talk to the people from the telly. She'd been waiting in her car when the police arrived, to tell them what she'd seen, and somehow the local press had got there a second after, before anyone else knew there was anything seriously wrong. The girl had gone even whiter than she'd been to start and had burst into tears, and a police constable had had to take her home. 'It wasn't a nice thing to see. The body.'

'You saw it, did you? You've a stronger stomach than me.'

'I had to make sure he wasn't alive.'

'You're just a nosey old bugger, Gerry.' Ed laughed, at him rather than with him yet not altogether unkindly. 'Look, that's me at home, or nearly. Are you sure you don't want me to see you up to your front door?'

Gerry was very drunk but not, he told himself, incapable, and he still had the remnants of his pride. 'I'm fine to get home.' It was another few hundred yards to his cottage on the edge of the tiny hamlet of Townhead, and even in the dark — and tonight was gothic, horror-film dark — he couldn't go wrong. 'That Simon sounds like a bit of a lad, doesn't he?'

'Good night, Gerry. Are you sure you'll be all right for that last bit home?'

'You're a good lad, but yes. I'll be fine.'

Nevertheless as Ed, who had already passed his front door, turned at the last house in the village under the dim light of a fading and inadequate streetlight, Gerry paused. His quavering, queasy stomach rolled and the street seemed to rock gently around him, so he sat on the low stone wall by the road for a moment to let his eyes adjust to the darkness that lay in front of him. He felt mellow.

'Important.' He said the word out loud. He'd appeared on the telly, with a microphone thrust in front of him on one of the news channels. *Tell us what happened*, they'd said, and he had done, at length, though most of what he'd said hadn't made it to the screen.

The news, which had been on the telly in the pub, had gone on to show a press conference, in which a particularly serious-looking detective (in fairness, these people didn't have much of a reason to be jolly) had asked for anyone with any information to come forward. That meant Gerry. It meant telling the police he'd seen the girl who discovered the body all lovey-dovey with a man he now knew to be dead. He'd thought so before and the pictures in the news coverage had confirmed it.

The problem was, the evening had been a fun one and if he told them everything he knew it meant he had nothing left to trade on. He'd wait until he'd seen how much the woman was prepared to pay for him not to say that. And she would, because if she'd wanted to tell the police she'd been up there before with the dead man she would have done, and yet she'd denied it flat out when he told her he'd seen her. If she paid up he'd be able to buy his own pints for years to come without worrying about how much duty the Chancellor slapped on it in the Budget or how much it ate into his bills or his rent. If she didn't he'd tell the police what he'd *suddenly remembered* and then he'd be the talk of the village once more, and no doubt recipient of a pint or two in return for his tale.

Win-win.

On balance he hoped she'd pay up. It would be nice not to count the pennies, or be reliant on the generosity of others.

On the far side of the pale pool of streetlight, Ed clicked his front door closed. Sliding unsteadily from the wall, Gerry turned towards home. The rain had stopped at last but the beck, burbling along to his left, was full, in places over-full, slapping against the footbridge that spanned it. As he walked, stumbling a little, along the muddy verge, he thought again of that willowy blonde with her posh accent, her obvious posing for a non-existent camera and the sudden, panicked flight when the camera presented itself in reality. Yes, there was definitely something off, there, and if the police really were pursuing it as suspicious as the gossip had it, then she knew something.

At the end of the lane he had a choice. The stepping stones in front of him took to a path that veered away from his cottage but which offered him a short cut across a field and through his back gate. The bridge, twenty yards or so downstream, meant a longer walk in the dense darkness of a tree-shadowed lane. He weighed them up. The stones were under water, though not by more than an inch or so, but he didn't fancy the bridge, either. The lane beyond it was broken and pitted from the recent rain and his phone, on which he had showed a hundred people photographs he'd taken of the lime kilns, had run out of battery a while before, so he'd have to stumble along it in the dark. When he looked, he fancied the lane was full of shifting shadows.

The stepping stones it was, then. They were flat and stable and even though they were ghostly under the milky swirl of onrushing water his courage was high. He stepped out to the first one and the water lapped into his shoes. For a moment he hesitated, caught barely balanced between stone and bank. He should go back. But now he just wanted to be at home, and there was a sound and a shadow behind him, like a phantom under the trees, that made him think of all the things he'd ever done wrong. He hadn't seen anyone in the lane and he didn't believe in ghosts, but it was a strange night and a man had died up on the fell.

He hurried on, more concerned about getting across than how he did it. And then something — someone —

swiped his back foot from under him. He struggled, swore, but couldn't free his foot. With a yell, he pitched sideways into the beck.

It wasn't deep. It didn't have to be; it was fast. It grabbed at him as he thrashed around in his struggle to get up, pitching him face-forward again. This time he lost all contact with the ground and the angry waters of Ardale Beck carried him away.

SIXTEEN

The morning was bright, clear and fizzing like an elderflower pressé. In London Lexie, whose Clapham flat looked out on the rusting fire escape of a crumbling 1960s office building, had yearned for sunshine like this but today she couldn't welcome it. She'd slept badly, and waking only reminded her why.

Nico. Why did it have to be her who found him? Why couldn't she just have let him lie? After Hugh had left and she'd found herself alone the enormity of it had crept over her even as she tried to fight it. She'd cleared up after supper and even managed to watch the local news and see the detective who'd been to talk to her speaking for the cameras, with a degree of detachment. You could see he didn't enjoy the spotlight as real performers did. He was uncomfortable, stared at his script and in consequence looked wooden and out of control. That was what happened if you didn't love the camera; it didn't love you back. Someone should give him a few tips, a bit of media training.

Then she had gone to bed and the dark had rolled over her.

Her phone bleeped and she stretched out a hand, fumbling on the bedside table for it and dragging it under the bedclothes. Hugh, with a cheery emoji that immediately brightened her mood. She called him back.

'Up early for the cow sale, then?' she said to him.

'Up since well before dawn,' he said, 'and it's calves on sale today, not cows. Are you all right? I was worried after I left you yesterday. I don't like to think of you on your own.'

'I've been lying awake all night,' she said, solemnly, 'worrying about Buttercup. Or was she called Bluebell?'

'Buttercup,' he said, and a contented, rumbling chuckle was accompanied, in Lexie's imagination, by his generous smile. 'You'll have to come and meet her. She's dying to give you the once-over.'

'I don't think I've ever been introduced to a cow before.'

'I thought you said you worked with them.'

She giggled. This was a million miles from the conversations she'd shared with Nico, sophisticated, brittle and meaningless. 'There are cows and there are cows, I suppose. I hope she approves.'

'We'll find out when you come,' he said. 'I have to go now, get the calves ready for the sale ring. I just wanted to make sure you're okay.'

Lexie hung up with a smile, but in her heart there was confusion. She desperately wanted to see him but she wasn't usually the needy one in a relationship. With Nico it was always the women who came when he called.

The phone pinged again, this time with a picture of a cow. *Buttercup sends her love.*

All mine back to Buttercup, she messaged back, and lay there for a moment with the duvet pulled up over her head, both uplifted and yet depressingly clear-headed. In London, after a late night partying, she'd have had no hesitation about hunkering down and letting the ticking hours soothe her hangover, but yesterday she'd eaten healthily and drunk nothing (after her early morning coffee) other than herbal tea and that one glass of wine when Hugh had left. There was nothing to do but get up, and put on a brave face even if there was no-one to see it.

But she wanted them to see it. She wanted someone to see how well she was coping and admire her for it, and then ask her if she was okay and offer her help. She got up, yawned, stretched and padded over to the window to receive the sun's blessing. Retrieving the pink glass heart from the drawer where she'd placed it on the day she'd arrived, she hung it up and admired it as it spun slowly round in the sun, catching the light and breaking it into rainbows on the wall and on the sill. Nico was dead. Everything would be all right.

It was all right for the fifteen minutes it took her to have a shower and get dressed, but when she came down the stairs a white envelope, stark on the doormat, broke the mood as surely as if it were the black spot, tipped to a pirate. She picked it up. Another letter. She flipped it open. *You will regret it forever, bitch.*

Who could have done that? For a mad moment she suspected everyone. Marge, Sonia, Linda and Mikey Satterthwaite, Becca, random strangers, even Hugh, but that madness soon passed. She'd watched Hugh driving away and the envelope hadn't been there when she went to bed.

Shaking, she made her coffee and took it out to the front garden. This was less private than the back but it did catch the morning sun, and the owners of the property had put a tiny wrought-iron table and chair there for this purpose, so she might as well make use of it. Besides, if anyone came loitering through the village with a white envelope in their hand she would see them from there and challenge them. Taking her coffee, she posed herself carefully on the chair that faced out to the village street. Becca was putting her bag into the boot of her Fiat 500, looking faintly harassed while exchanging words with Linda, who in turn was standing by her car looking exasperated. After a moment, the front door of the Satterthwaite home opened and Mikey, Linda's younger son, came dashing down the path and jumped into the car. Becca drove off, Linda got into her own car and headed in the other direction. It was ridiculous to suspect any of them.

But she'd wanted one of them to come up to her, unprompted. She'd wanted Becca to come across. In her mind the scene played out. *You know you mentioned someone leaving you a note? Well, I saw someone delivering something yesterday. She didn't ring the bell but I knew you were in, so I thought it was odd.*

She? Lexie would say. *What did she look like?* And then Becca would deliver an accurate but scathing description of Annabel Faulkner.

It had to be Annabel. If it wasn't, then it was someone acting on her instructions. Nico had always been so proud about the fact that he'd put one over on his wife, handling his relationship with Lexie so differently that she'd never suspect, but everyone knew Annabel was Antarctic-cold and ruthless as a winter storm, not to mention having both the money and the brains to plan and execute her revenge.

The sun drifted behind a cloud and the September morning rustled with a chilly breeze. Left with no warmth and no audience, Lexie took the coffee back inside. She had work to do, and the previous two days had been a total write-off, one for good reasons and one for bad.

The note was still in the kitchen, and she kept looking at it as if she might learn something from it, but there was no clue. It must be the same sender — the same red type, that same giant font. *You will regret it forever, bitch*. And, oh yes, she was regretting it, had regretted it for a long time. Wasn't that why she'd ended the relationship? But wives like Annabel didn't care how their husbands' infidelities ended or why, or who initiated the split. They only cared that the betrayal had happened, and for them the pain was an ever-open wound. The Annabel Faulkners of this world never suffered as much from anything as they did from their injured pride.

She should tell someone. The first note had been a one-off, a prank perhaps, and something she could afford to ignore, but the second escalated matters. It would be common sense to tell the police, but she sensed she hadn't made a good impression on Jude Satterthwaite and it would be bound to come to his attention. Besides, if she spoke to him, or to anyone else in the police, she would provoke questions she didn't want to answer. They would ask her who she thought the letter writer was, and the next question would be: *why would Simon Morea's wife want to harass you?* After that they would explore further; Nico's triumphant subterfuge would fail and leave her to deal with the fallout. They would make the connection, others would learn of it, and she would never work in film again.

At least she could get on with the work she had in hand. She'd set up her laptop in the living room, which wasn't ideal and not somewhere where she could work for a long time at a stretch, but today she was looking for a location for a pilot programme in a comedy series, so she had clips and stills of life in a grim northern town to evaluate. That arrangement lasted barely ten minutes before she was up again, pacing the cottage. It was impossible to concentrate, too busy listening for the soft step on the doorstep, the click of the letterbox.

There was the man in the pub. He surely hadn't been responsible for the letters, but there had been something on his mind. She felt bad about badmouthing him to Hugh the previous day because he hadn't been creepy in the sense she'd implied. He had been threatening. *I seen you with that lad*, he'd whispered in her ear. *The one that's dead*.

If Hugh were here, would she tell him the truth? She didn't know. But that was the jeopardy, because gaining his help and support meant confessing all, and who knew what that would cost her?

SEVENTEEN

'I've never been one to make a connection where there isn't one,' said Doddsy, laying down the phone and looking at Jude, who had just come into the office they shared, 'but I'm going to stick my neck out on this one. That's a call in to say there's a man found dead in the beck in over at Townhead and I don't like the feel of it.'

'Townhead?' Jude was just back from speaking to Faye, a bad-tempered briefing which had moved them no further forwards. Sometimes chewing over the same old thing opened up new ideas, revealed things they'd missed but today it only emphasised their frustrations. Now this. There were a dozen cottages and hamlets with that name but Doddsy's frown meant he could guess which it was — a bare handful of dwellings on a dead-end road. Lexie Romachenka had passed through it on the day she stumbled upon Simon Morea's body. 'The one at Ousby?'

'That's the one.'

'I hope you're going to tell me it was an accident.'

'You wanted me to tell you the last one was an accident,' Doddsy reminded him, 'and you weren't happy when I did. We don't know yet. In the circumstances I'd normally say it looks like it. It was a dark night, river running high, drink taken. So yes, accident. But we said that about Simon Morea and yet, here we are.'

Jude sat down, his brain already engaging with all the things he could do to approach this new twist before he had to present the news to Faye. 'What happened?'

'All I know is that a farm worker discovered a body jammed against the footbridge as he was on his way to work this morning. Like I said, the beck's running high just now. The lad lived locally and was last seen on his way back from the pub last night a bit the worse for wear.'

'Who is he? Do we know? What was he doing there?'

'I have a name, yet unconfirmed, but I don't have any reason to question it. His name is Gerry Cole and he lives in Townhead and is well-known about Ousby. He does odd jobs around the village for the parish council. Cuts the grass, paints the signs and the like.'

'Gerry Cole?' This got worse. 'I know that name. Wasn't he—?'

'The man who met Lexie Romachenka immediately after she found Morea. Yes.'

'And the man who went up to the lime kilns to have a good look around before we got there. And then went on telly telling the whole world what he'd seen. And now he's died in what looks like an accident shortly after Morea dies in what looks like an accident but which we're sure wasn't, and less than forty-eight hours after we found the body. Christ.'

'An understatement,' agreed Doddsy, who was a regular churchgoer.

'Okay. We'll get someone down there.' Briefly, Jude toyed with the idea of going to the site himself but he thought that was high-risk. This was definitely a case to play down publicly if the press were likely to be interested, and Faye was already jumpy about how much time he spent out of the office. 'I'll get Ashleigh onto it.' She'd spent the previous day down around Ousby, doing the door-to-door inquiries. She knew the area; the locals would be used to the sight of her, so there would be no sign that the matter had escalated; and she was good with people. She could offer a blank and inoffensive *no comment* as easily as she could charm witnesses and lull suspects into a false sense of security until, overly reassured of their own cleverness, they gave themselves away. On that last note, he rather wished he'd sent her down to speak to Lexie Romachenka. Maybe he still could. 'I want to know where Lexie was last night. And I sure as hell want to know where Annabel Faulkner was.'

The two police constables who had arrived first at Ardale Beck as it rippled through the scattering of dwellings that comprised Townhead had closed the road by Ousby church, just outside the village and far enough away from the incident for the scene to be out of sight. A thin but penetrating rain had begun to fall over the already sodden Eden Valley as Ashleigh parked her car outside the church, ignoring the cluster of people who'd gathered there to see if they could find out what was going on, and made her way to Charlie Fry, the constable on duty.

'What a great day to be out in the country, Charlie,' she said, ironically. 'Just what you joined the force for, eh?'

Charlie's sense of humour was not fine-tuned. 'I've had worse days,' he said, 'and seen bodies in worse nick, too.' In case she didn't know what he meant, he nodded up the path to Ardale.

As well he might. Plenty of people besides the police would see these two deaths, so close together in time and space, and begin joining the dots. No doubt some fantastical patterns would emerge among the interested onlookers given time, imagination and a lack of facts. 'What can you tell me? Anything?'

'Nothing, except that the lad was in the pub until closing time last night and took a lot more than he usually does. He lives in a cottage over by.' Charlie jerked a head in the general direction of the farm. 'He walked up as far as the village end with a mate, name of Edward Walker, who offered to see him safe home, Gerry being well the worse for wear and not used to it, he says. Apparently Mr Cole turned down the offer and the last Walker saw of him, he was sitting on the wall staring down the lane.'

'I suppose we know where this man Walker was afterwards?' In the circumstances it was wise to explore all possibilities and one of them was that the two men had had a fallout and had come to blows, especially with one of them unusually drunk.

'We do. He walked straight in to an almighty telling-off from his wife, who he'd told he was going to be in the pub for an hour at most and he was there for three.'

Ashleigh would speak to Ed Walker later. 'Did anyone else see him?'

Charlie looked at her, his eyes slightly narrowed, as if her line of questioning offended him. 'This looks to me like an accident. The lad was making the most of his moment of fame. Isn't that all?'

Ashleigh sighed. She'd very much like it to be all. 'It's in the context, Charlie. Because of what happened earlier this week, and because he was round and about when Simon Morea was found. You know we have to treat everything as suspicious and in this case, even more so.'

'I can't see anything obvious on the body.'

He wasn't privy to the discussions she and Jude and Doddsy had shared. They hadn't seen anything obvious on Simon Morea, either, until the post-mortem and the forensic examinations had revealed a probable killer's secrets. 'Can I get up a bit closer to where he is?' There was a white van parked up the lane, indicating that the CSI team were already on site.

'Aye. They've taped it off further up. Tyrone reckoned you'd want everyone kept well away from it, but you can go a bit further on.'

'Thanks.' Leaving him standing in the middle of the road in characteristic pose, arms folded across his broad chest, she walked along the lane, observing what must have been Gerry Cole's last walk. In the dark he would have seen nothing of the trees turning, the autumn colour leached from their leaves by the grey drizzle. He would have made his way, perhaps by torchlight, perhaps not, along the uneven lane. There was a narrow grass verge between the road and the beck, but no hedge or fence to protect the unwary. There was no real need. Most of the passers-by were sober and responsible, and the water level was usually well below the road.

At the bend a line of police tape hug across the road between two spindly rowans, and Tyrone Garner, a junior constable and Doddsy's partner, stood in front of it. There was a white tent on the bank of the river and she stopped at the line of tape surrounding it. She nodded to him, but her focus was on the tent.

'Here we go again.' Tammy Garner, pulling down her mask as she stepped over the tape towards her, had a relatively cheery expression. A fresh body, albeit one that had been in the water overnight, wouldn't be anything like as ugly as one that had spent a few days out in the open, exposed to whatever curious — or hungry — creatures might be snuffling through the undergrowth. 'You know I'm the last person to do your job for you, Ash, but I'd say this one is pretty straightforward. Too many drinks and then into the drink.'

Charlie had thought the same, and it was the obvious answer. 'Do you know where he went into the water?' asked Ashleigh, looking past Tammy to where the ground lay sodden, the grass flattened and streamlined by the rushing water.

'No, but it can't be far from here. He must have gone in upstream of here. The beck narrows beyond the ford, but I'm guessing he was trying to cross there, or more likely at the stepping stones. See?'

She gestured at a series of stones. The water was about ten feet wide at that point, and they would normally have stood well clear of the surface but today the chasing flurries of Ardale Beck tripped over them, disturbing its flow.

'And he was found under the footbridge?' Ashleigh looked at that, too. It was a rickety affair and the water was so high that it was almost submerged. Below it someone had rigged up a crude barrier of chicken wire to catch anything that was washed downstream. It had surely never been intended to catch a human body.

'Yes. The man who found him pulled him out.' Tammy's mouth twisted a little, almost in disappointment. It had been the right thing to do — the only thing to do — but if the overnight rain and the high water of the now-subsiding beck had left any clue as to what might have happened or where Gerry Cole had entered the water, there was every chance that his would-be rescuer had overwritten them with the marks of his own good deed. 'I can't blame him, but I don't suppose we'll find out how he went in. Two in one week, though.' She gave

Ashleigh a sidelong look. 'Don't tell me there's not a connection.'

'Don't you start,' said Ashleigh amiably, though the suspicion was drumming in her head that there had to be. 'I'll be passing this to smarter brains than mine. Did you find anything else?'

'A stick caught up under the bridge.'

Ashleigh looked at the debris that was continuing to accumulate against the wire. 'You're going to have to be a bit more specific than that. I can see a hell of a lot of sticks caught up in there.' New ones were bobbing merrily down the beck all the time, scooped up from the banks or torn from the living trees by the power of the flow.

'Okay. It's a walking stick. A shepherd's crook, more like. I'm guessing it was his. There.' She pointed to the bank. The stick was perhaps six feet long, its handle curled and carved into a sheep's horn. 'A nice one, I'd say, but not exactly distinctive. You can buy them anywhere. And if I'm a judge it's relatively new. The one my dad had was scarred by all sorts and he could have told you a tale to go with every mark, but this one's as clean as a whistle. You'd think he'd have used it to see how deep the water was, wouldn't you?'

'Thanks, Tammy.' Ashleigh walked back down the lane, smiled at the first reporters who were gathering there, fobbed them off with a bland remark about unexplained death and blanked all further questions with a stern *no comment*, before heading down to Ousby. It was time to talk to Ed Walker.

EIGHTEEN

'Okay,' she said to Jude when she was finished in the village and had taken the precaution of driving back towards Melmerby and parking up in a lay-by where nobody in the arriving press pack could set up their microphones to listen in. 'You know what I'm going to say. I have a really, really bad feeling about this.'

'Yes,' he said, with a gusty sigh. 'I do, too. I know all the first reports say it seems like an accident, but how often have we heard that? And you know me. I have a nasty suspicious nature and the older I get the more I find myself wondering how many accidents have been neatly engineered. How many crimes we miss, because they don't look suspicious.'

When Ashleigh thought about it, which she did more often than was comfortable, she too wondered how many people got away with murder purely by engaging with the ever-present dangers around them, especially in Cumbria, where the landscape was wild, often empty, and always unforgiving. A trip, a push in the back; a long, long fall and there you had it — a perfect, unsolvable crime.

'Morea's the current example, isn't he?' she said, reaching for the flask of coffee she'd had the foresight to bring with her. It had been a hectic start to the day and it was already almost lunchtime. 'If he'd been there a bit longer the body would have decomposed. Matt wouldn't have spotted bruising and there'd have been no way to link the mark on the coat to his death.' The coroner might have thought it was odd but there would have been no evidence of foul play.'

'Exactly. And here we are, another man dead, apparently by accident, in the same place and with a connection, albeit a loose one, to the first. But you've been down there and I haven't, so tell me what makes you think it's suspicious.'

Where to start? 'Okay.' Ashleigh unscrewed the flask and took a welcome sip. 'The beck. On first sight it looks as if he drowned. Let's assume for now that that's the case. The water isn't that deep. Eighteen inches, maybe, though it may have been higher overnight.'

'It's not the depth,' he reminded her, as if she didn't know you could drown in a puddle. 'It's the force. It doesn't take a lot of water to knock you off your feet and for you to struggle to get up again. I can't recall the figures off the top of my head, though I did look them up once. But I get the point. Unless he passed out at the least opportune moment and fell in, it does sound a bit dodgy.'

'Exactly. Do you know the place?'

'I noticed it when I was there the other day. There's a footbridge just downstream from the stepping stones and the ford. I wonder why he didn't use it?'

'I'm worried about the footbridge, though apparently it doesn't take him straight home. There's a shortcut via the stepping stones and I can see that after a few drinks he might think he was invincible.' Ashleigh sighed.

'Or else just fail to compute the risk. Okay. Let's assume he either took the stepping stones or slipped in off the bank. Straightforward, no?'

'No. There's a kind of makeshift grille against the upstream side of the bridge. Within seconds of falling in he'd have been swept up against it. If he was conscious he should easily have been able to use the bridge to pull back to his feet.'

'Wasn't he drunk?'

'Yes, but by all accounts not so drunk that he was incapable.' And cold water sobered you up, especially in circumstances like that.

'You say there are no obvious injuries, but could he have hit his head in the fall?' Jude was thinking aloud, now. She knew the signs. Some people took it as questioning their judgement, but it wasn't that. He was just going over for himself the thought process she'd already been through.

'I haven't seen the body but yes, he could have hit his head on the stepping stones.'

'Fair enough. And how was the body found in relation to the grille? Was it stuck?'

'I've spoken to the witness who found it. He had no trouble at all hauling it out. It was held against the grid only by the flow of the water.'

'Right. And I know it's early in the investigation, but on the basis of what you've seen and what you've heard, what do you think happened?'

Ashleigh took a deep breath. 'On the basis that these things don't quite add up, and given the particular set of circumstances around Simon Morea's death, I'd say this is extremely suspicious. If there are any signs of injury on the body that rendered him unconscious immediately before he entered the water, I think we should be considering the possibility of manslaughter at best.'

'And murder at worst?'

'Yes.'

There was a long pause, in which she stared out at the grey horizon which, on a good day, offered a green and pleasant view. A pair of damp sheep, their fleeces weighed down by the rain and stained by the red Eden Valley mud, stared back. Some might have scoffed at the suggestion of murder based on the slenderest of evidence, but Jude knew when to listen as well as when to speak, and he had learned to trust her instincts. These days he no longer warned her to tread more carefully before she made so sweeping a statement. Time had too often proved her right.

'Okay,' he said after a while. 'I'll believe you, and not just because what you say backs up my own misgivings. How do you think this perfect murder was carried out?'

'I cheated a little,' she admitted, 'because there is something else and while I don't think it affects my view of whether it was murder or not, it perhaps offered a means for it.' She outlined what Tammy had told her about the shepherd's crook. 'She assumed it was Gerry Cole's, but I asked in the bar and I asked Ed Walker and no-one remembered him having a stick with him last night. It's not difficult, is it? You creep up on a drunk man who's concentrating on getting across the stepping stones. You don't even need to get close. It's a good length, that stick, five feet or so. Add that to an arm's length. And remember, it's dark. If you can reach out from the shadows or the bushes or whatever, you can hook a man's ankle and before he knows it he's in the water and he can't get up. If you can lift the crook a little and manage to keep hold, he won't be able to get out, no matter how much he thrashes around.'

'Are you suggesting someone managed to hold him like that for long enough for him to drown? Really?' He sounded sceptical.

'Possibly, especially if he had hit his head and was disoriented. But remember — the footbridge is just a few yards downstream. An alternative is that he got swept against it and whoever tipped him in raced down to the bridge and then used the stick to keep him down.'

More silence. This would be unwelcome news for him, as it had been an unwelcome thought for her. It would have been so much better, so much easier, if they could have ascribed it purely to an unfortunate accident. 'I'll tell Matt Cork to look out for some bruising or marks around the ankles, shall I?'

'And elsewhere on the body. The back or the chest. Yes.'

'Right. So you know what my next question is going to be. Who do you think did it?'

She looked at the sheep again and they turned away, as if the question perplexed them as much as it did her. 'I haven't a clue. Without going into much detail, my initial impression is that no-one really disliked him.' Gerry Cole's neighbours had described him as harmless, a bit odd but always friendly, and keen to belong. He'd lived alone in a cottage on the fellside and, while he had no close friends, he had no obvious enemies, either. 'Do you have any ideas?'

'Maybe. I already had a bad feeling that the two cases would be connected, and everything you've said backs that up. I've asked Chris Marshall to do a quick check on Annabel Faulkner for me, because she's certainly clever enough to think this up, but I doubt she'll have been anywhere other than provably tucked up in her own home. If she wasn't, someone would surely have seen her and if they did they might remember. She wouldn't risk that.'

'The pub was busy last night, and there were a few people there who aren't local, but that's hardly unusual. It's a good pub and there are plenty of visitors at this time of year.'

'We'll obviously check up on Lexie.'

'I'm sure Becca will know whether she was at home or not last night.' It slipped out, sounding churlish and jealous when the truth was that Ashleigh had long accepted that the future of her relationship with Jude wasn't in her hands.

'Yes, or my mum. More likely Mikey, because he's even nosier than I am and there's not a light goes on or off in that village without him knowing about it. But I don't know. It would need a degree of physical strength and for that reason it doesn't feel like a woman's crime.'

'Whatever a woman's crime is.'

'Fair point. I can't see Lexie doing it, but I can see Annabel. Which means I want to know a lot more about Morea. Nothing's come up yet from all the women he's had relationships with and in fact none of them seems obviously to have nursed a grudge, though of course we shouldn't rely on what the gossip magazines report when we're looking for motive.'

'It's certainly hard to imagine any wannabe actress tramping up to Cumbria to drown a complete stranger on the off-chance that he might identify her,' said Ashleigh with a sigh.

'Lexie went walking up there.'

'I don't think she's typical. What about any jealous partners?'

'Exactly!' There was a thud, as if he'd smacked the desk for emphasis. 'We need to cast the net a little wider. I don't think I told you that Lexie seems to have a new beau.'

'Beau!' said Ashleigh. 'Listen to you. What an old-fashioned word.'

'I chose it deliberately. He arrived at the cottage in Wasby just as I was leaving the other night. I was struck by the chemistry between them on the very brief time I saw them together and it felt like a very old-fashioned relationship. He must be twenty years older than she is and he looks at her absolutely adoringly while she seems devoted to him.'

'Have they known each other long? Because if so...'

'I wondered that. It would be very tidy if for some reason he regarded Morea as a potential rival, even though Morea and Lexie barely knew one another, but I'm told he and Lexie only met a few days ago. Adam introduced them.'

Ashleigh's view of Adam Fleetwood was, she acknowledged, a biased one. She disliked the way he oozed honey to those who could bring him some kind of benefit and vinegar to those who didn't. She fell into the latter category, not least because her association with Jude had irrevocably tarnished her in his eyes. 'So Lexie's going out with a friend of Adam. Interesting.'

'I don't know if they're particular friends. But here's the interesting thing. I looked him up, on the off-chance.'

'Of course you did,' said Ashleigh, indulgently.

'It was worth the effort. His name is Hugh Cameron and he was at school with Simon Morea.'

'Really? I didn't know Morea was a local lad.'

'He's Cumbrian born and he spent six years at boarding school in the county. Lexie's Hugh is the same age and was there at the same time. So I think we might have to have a close look at Mr Cameron, too.'

NINETEEN

'I know we only met a few days ago,' said Hugh, accepting the mug of tea that Lexie had pressed on him and looking across the room at her, 'but I think I know you well already. And that's why I can sense that something's upset you.'

'Oh.' Lexie felt herself going pink with delight at the thought that this sensible, capable man cared, and that he'd noticed, and then she saw that he was going pink too, perhaps because he'd seen that she was blushing. It was like that awkward stage as a teenager when the rules of the game were new, when neither party knew what to say or how to say it. Just when she thought she knew the rules, just when she thought she could play at love and win, walking off with the spoils of victory — freedom and an undamaged heart — someone came along and tripped her up. Here they were, two mature adults, experienced in the ups and downs of life, suddenly finding themselves playing a new variant with convoluted new rules. At one level, she loved it. At another, she was terrified.

'It's nothing really.' That was always the safe answer.

'I'm just a bit shaken up by all this stuff that's going on. Did you see that some other poor man died down at Ousby yesterday?'

'I could hardly miss it,' he said, his face sombre. 'It was all over the local news this lunchtime.'

'It threw me a bit, that was all.' Her skin was crawling with anxiety. Already she was lying to him. In a true relationship you had to be honest, all the time. Love wasn't based on secrets. Her relationship with Nico had flourished on sex and drama and subterfuge, a game played out, she now saw, for his benefit rather than hers. Even in the simplest matters, truth was above everything and those two anonymous notes, slipped under the door by someone who'd managed to remain unseen, were niggling at her like an infected insect bite. After much deliberation she'd torn them both up and put them in the bin at the end of the village street, reluctant even to have them in the house, and now she regretted it. She'd thought if they were out of sight they'd be out of mind and yet she experienced a nervous twitching every time she passed the front door, always looking for the next white envelope on the mat. And without them, she had nothing to prove that they had ever existed.

'I can tell.' He was looking at her as if he were about to ask more. She thought he cared, but how much would it take to put him off, so that he went away and never bothered to come back? A lie? The truth?

She was lying to him now, if only by omission. She couldn't bear it if he were to discover she didn't trust him enough to be honest, and the look on his face suggested his heart was already over-full of questions.

'So soon after you were there,' he said, into the silence.

If she told him the truth he might think she'd killed

Nico, and God knew she'd had enough reason to, but she was tired of lying. 'There is something.'

'It isn't me, is it? I haven't done something to upset you? I don't mean to push you too fast or anything.' Hugh looked slightly crestfallen.

Too fast? By comparison with most of the men she knew, the speed of his courtship was glacial. Too many people she knew would have tried to sweep her off her feet on a first date, before she'd had time to think it through, weigh up their merits and her own feelings, and conclude they were the bad bet they always turned out to be. By the time she realised the truth it was always too late. It was a luxury to have time to think about a man before she could get it wrong. 'No, it isn't you. Something happened to me and it's making me uneasy.'

'Something apart from this Simon Morea thing?'

In a different world she would have produced the two notes and presented them to him with a flourish, watched his face cloud over and then flare into fury as he read and understood them. Now she had to rely on her own words and she didn't think she could do justice to her fears. 'I think I must have upset someone in the village. Or something.'

'How could you possibly do that? You've barely been here a week and you're so… so nice!'

She sipped her tea and smiled. 'I haven't the faintest idea. But I've had a couple of nasty notes.' She told him about them, in detail, the times they came, the glaring scarlet type that carried with it both threat and insult. When she was done she sat back and looked at him, delighted by the outrage on his face.

'That's terrible!' He was scowling, snatching a glance out of the window as if he was preparing to go charging through the village until he found the perpetrator. By contrast, Nico would have been delighted at such a twist in the plot and told her that the whole thing was her imagination, that she was an unreliable narrator, that none of it had happened as she thought, a subtle implication that she was simple-minded and incapable of understanding. But Nico had made an art form out of gaslighting her and Hugh didn't know the meaning of the word. 'We need to find out who it is. We need to put a stop to it.'

He really was the unlikeliest of white knights. 'I don't know how to do that. I haven't a clue what I've done. I'm so new here I haven't even had time to make proper friends, never mind enemies.'

'It surely can't be to do with what happened up at Ardale?'

She shook her head. That reminded her of another secret she'd kept from him. A sudden urge came over her, to tell him everything, but she remembered in time her mother's stricture to stay silent. She had to think about it. 'The first note came before then. On the day I arrived. I'd only met a couple of people. My neighbours. Becca next door and Linda over the road. I can't believe it was either of them.' In films, perhaps, because plots so often turned on the twist that no-one was really what they pretended to be, that the kindest face hid the blackest heart. In real life, not only was there the fact that both of those women struck her as incapable of such deed, there was no reason for them to hurt her.

'I know Becca,' he said, 'though only slightly. She was going out with Adam for a while. And no, Becca would never in a million years do something like that. The opposite, in fact. She's quite the upright member of the community.'

'I know.' Adam, in passing, had disparaged her as a do-gooder but Lexie didn't think that was such a bad thing.

'She's been lovely to me. I wondered if I should talk to Linda's son. The one who's the policeman.'

'Oh, no. I really wouldn't. From what Adam says about him he's really not a very nice person at all. Very fierce and very austere. Unforgiving.'

For a moment Lexie thought of the film project she'd been toying with in her too-many idle moments. The events of the past couple of days had put it out of her mind and now her heart flashed with a second of shame. It would be a good story but she'd have to reconstruct it because it was obvious Becca still felt something for the detective, and she didn't want to hurt her new friend's feelings in any way. Like Nico, like all the rest of them, Adam might not be all he pretended to be. 'I liked him. He came to talk to me after they found Simon.'

'I remember. He was just leaving when I arrived.'

'Yes. I know all about him and Adam, but that's not the reason I can't talk to him.'

'It isn't?'

'You have to promise never to tell.'

He paused to think about what she'd just said, probably to process it. He would be wondering what terrible secret she was about to unload on him, reminding himself that they barely knew one another, that it was far too soon to trust one another with life-changing secrets. 'Yes. All right.'

'It's nothing wrong,' she said steadily. 'It's just something I did in the past and it made me think badly of myself and I didn't tell you because I don't want you to think badly of me as well. But I don't want to have any secrets from you so I have to tell you.' And if it changed things, if he walked away, it was better to do it now before she really did lose her heart to him.

'Go on,' he said, still watching her steadily.

'I think I know who sent those notes. I think it's Simon Morea's wife.'

'Why?' he asked, bewildered. 'Why would she do that? Is she unhinged? You only knew the man slightly.'

Here it came. 'I told you that. I told everybody that. But it isn't true. I knew Simon better that anyone could guess. He and I had been having an affair for over a year.'

He was such a thoughtful man, this treasure she'd stumbled on. He didn't rush to rage or judgement or offence. 'The one you came here to get away from? I thought he was called Nico.'

'His middle name was Nicholas but he never used it. He told everyone he hated it, but I used it for him. It made it easier to hide the affair, if we both pretended to be someone else.' It had taken her several months to realise that Nico had been toying with her affections for his own purposes and several more to extricate herself from the relationship, but she'd never quite understood what had felt so wrong. Now it was beginning to fall together, all the constituent parts starting to lock together into a coherent whole.

'It sounds to me as if he wasn't good for you,' he said, simply.

'I'm not a child. I knew what he was like, but I did rather lose my head.' There had been so much glamour. There had been so many possibilities. If they had come to fruition there would have been such a cost.

'He must have been serious about you. He didn't hide the other affairs, did he?'

'No. And I thought he was serious, too. I really thought he wanted to be with me and he didn't want his wife to find out because she's so fierce, and she could have caused an awful lot of damage to his career, even though he was so well regarded. She funded him a lot, you see, and although he was a creative success he never made commercial films. He saw himself as an artist, not as a moneymaker.' He had been so fake. No-one she knew had loved the material trappings of fame as much as Nico, no matter how much he pretended otherwise. 'The first letter came on the day I arrived here, and that was before I found his body. It must be someone who knew about the affair. It has to be his wife. I can't think of anyone else.'

Hugh got up and came to sit beside her on the sofa, a shambling figure of a man, self-conscious at such open emotion. She made a space for him and they bumped together in a brief but awkward hug and then broke apart, but he kept that seat with his thigh touching hers and his hand upon her arm.

'I understand,' he said, nodding like a schoolchild stumbling on the right answer. 'He was staying with her until he could afford to leave her. Where was he going to get the money from to do that?'

When Nico had been whisking her from party to party and bedding her energetically at the end of the evening, whispering sweet nothings about fame and critical acclaim in her ear — and money, she remembered, he had always offered her the prospect of the money he claimed not to care about as if he knew she could be bought — she'd never had time to think about why. The high-octane affair, fuelled by his fame and his charisma, had been enough. 'At the time I thought he loved me, but of course he didn't. He loved my money.'

'The money you're going to get?'

'Yes.' She hung her head, ashamed of her foolishness.

'You'd better tell me about this money of yours, because he doesn't sound like a man who'd wait for a year or more to get his hands on it.'

'That's the point,' she said, with a shaky laugh. 'I don't

have it yet. It's in a trust fund so he had to wait. My great-grandfather set up a trust for the family when he left Russia, and he put all his assets in it. He died not long afterwards and the money remained locked up. The trust had no executors and no-one knew what to do about it. But it expires this year and it goes to his last remaining descendant.'

'And that's you?'

'Yes. I made the mistake of telling Nico about it one day, because I thought it was a fun story and he might use it in one of his thrillers.' She'd been like the rest of them, hanging round the rich and famous, hoping to get lucky, and had been thrilled to find some detail that caught the attention of such a famous man. 'After that, he started calling me and inviting me out and of course it went to my head.' No wonder he'd wanted to keep a secret from his wife. If he'd got his hands on the money it would have gone horribly wrong and she'd have found herself dumped, or else he would have resumed his impudent affairs and flaunted a never-ending chorus line of younger, sexier women in her face, exactly as he had done with Annabel. Leopards never changed their spots. 'Now I realise all he wanted was my money and that his wife must have suspected. And now he's dead and I can't tell the police what I've just told you, because they'll think it's me.' Her bottom lip wobbled. 'When I first heard it was him I was so shocked. I thought it was an accident, a horrible coincidence, and they're not saying it's murder but I know they think it is because they're not saying anything else about it, either.'

'Oh, my word,' he said, sounding as comforting and reassuring as she imaged her father would, if she'd ever known him. 'This is a pickle, isn't it? Let's have a think. I see why the police might want to look at this.'

'I didn't kill Nico.'

'No, I know you didn't. But until they find out who did, you'd better not say anything at all.'

She'd known he'd understand. 'Now there's this other man who died. They're not saying anything about him either, not even his name, but it's just such a weird coincidence.'

'Fell in the river when drunk was what I heard.'

'People add two and two and make ten. The press are already interested in it and some of them will know I worked with Nico. What if they make the connection?'

'Are they likely to?'

She considered. 'I never told anyone except my mum where I was going when I left London and I haven't been in touch with anyone.' After the first few days the messages from friends and colleagues had stopped coming. 'But you never know. Someone knows I'm here.' Annabel, with the shoulders of a martial arts champion and the cold-eyed stare of an assassin. 'Because of the letters.'

'You should come away from here. Come back with me. I can keep you safe.'

Oh, how she was tempted. This was what she always wanted to hear, someone offering to look after her. Swimming with the sharks was exhausting, and she'd been doing it for too long, but it was too soon. 'I don't know. Shall we see how things go? It would be nice to come and meet Buttercup.'

He squeezed her hand. 'Only if you promise you'll call me if you need anything. I can be with you in half an hour, as long as I don't meet any sheep on the road.'

Despite her rising anxiety, she smiled. 'I don't know what I'd have done if I hadn't told you. Just knowing you know has made me feel safe.'

He kissed her on the cheek. 'I'm not saying you

shouldn't tell the police. But perhaps not now. Perhaps wait until they've finished their investigation.'

'I think if you'd ever met Nico you'd understand why I behaved like I did.'

'I do understand. He made people behave in ways they didn't like. He brought out the worst in them.'

'You knew him?' He had Nico exactly right. Her lover had appealed to people's baser feelings and made them feel they were justified, had led them on into trouble and left them to bear the consequences of their own actions. He was a clever man, a user and an abuser.

'Yes. It's my turn for a confession. Or honesty, as I'd rather think of it. Whatever. I was at school with him and I hated him. He had a brilliant mind, understood people. I expect that's why he became as good as a filmmaker. But I wasn't…I'm not…very clever, and he exploited that. I never understood why he behaved the way he did and it made me angry. I was just a kid, then, at school when I wanted to be at home. I didn't know how to respond to him, so of course I did the only thing I knew. I was bigger than him, so I bullied him.' His mouth twisted in disgust. 'I think, now, that I wanted him to hate me, to be afraid of me, and I ended up hating myself.'

'It's not your fault,' said Lexie, and grabbed his hand.

'But it was,' he said, simply. 'I hadn't given him a thought for years, until you mentioned school. Then I started thinking about it and I wondered if that was why I never found anyone. Because deep down I'm not very kind and people know.'

'Nonsense.' They were clasping hands tightly, now. 'This is my fault. I shouldn't have tried to make you talk about it.' Lexie was full of remorse. No wonder he'd been so resistant. 'I didn't mean to. I only asked because I was afraid you might have known him. I knew he was at school up here. If you were still in touch he might have said all sorts of awful things about me. Hugh, I'm so sorry!'

'I would never have believed a word he said,' he said with dignity. 'And besides, I needed to think about my past. It's right to tell you what kind of cruel person I am.'

'A cruel person?' she said, and almost laughed. Was this what Hugh thought of as a bad thing, a game changer? How could he believe something as trivial as this, a teenager's growing pains, would change her view of him? 'A cruel person who's so kind to me, and so good to everyone, and...and has a pet cow?' The giggle rose within her. 'Just because Nico...Simon...was such a terrible man doesn't mean we have to allow ourselves to be dragged down by him.' And anyway, he was dead and they were both free of him.

Outside, a figure moved on the path. Lexie twitched; Hugh jumped up and ran to the door. For a second she froze and she heard the click of the letterbox and him moving about in the hall, and then the figure faded away down the path and he came back in to the room holding out a piece of paper.

'It's the parish newsletter,' he said, 'that's all.' They stared at each other and, in their relief, they both began to laugh.

But nobody is going to kill me, said Lexie to the image of Annabel that appeared in her head. *Least of all you. Because I have someone who cares about me and all you have is too much money and a heart full of hate.*

Hugh had gone. It had been a glorious afternoon, laughing and talking, and she had several times been tempted to take him up to her bedroom and undress him, pull him down on top of her and make love to him in the cool peace of that September afternoon but she hadn't suggested it. She didn't want to seem forward and scare him off and besides, she knew now that there would be many more chances. The anticipation would keep her going until the moment was right. He had still been concerned about her safety, still keen for her to come and stay with him, but she'd refused. She would take care, act as normal but not go out anywhere where she wasn't in somebody's view.

She went upstairs to her bedroom and looked out, twirling the pink glass heart and admiring its sparkle for a moment, and then turned away. Her suitcase was on the top of the wardrobe and she heaved it down onto the bed and opened it up. In the pocket inside the lid was a plastic bag. She opened it, took out the gun it contained, and placed it in the drawer of the bedside cabinet.

Just in case.

TWENTY

'Okay,' said Jude, already regretting that he'd been in too much in a hurry to stop for the coffee he usually picked up from the machine in the corridor. Part of the reason he hadn't gone for that shot of caffeine was that it would take him too close to Faye's office and he didn't intend to talk to her until he had something positive to offer against her anticipated frustration with the case. He wished he'd asked someone else to fetch him one. 'Let's hear it. I want an update on Simon Morea, and anything we have about Gerry Cole. Before we get to that, I have to tell you, I've spoken to Matt Cork and it's not what I wanted to hear.' Just as with Simon Morea, he had hoped to hear it was an accident, and just as with Morea he had been confounded. 'He hasn't completed his full report but he did tell me that in his opinion Ashleigh's suspicions are correct. There are signs of bruising around Gerry Cole's left ankle, consistent with the hypothesis that someone tripped him up and tipped him in to the water.'

Chris Marshall, seated on the other side of the table, let out a low whistle. Of all of them, he was the least given to improbable suggestions and always slightly impressed when they turned out to be correct. 'There you go. They can consider themselves lucky he didn't fight back.'

'I don't believe it was luck. There are also marks on the top of his back as if something had held him down. There's every chance someone made sure he drowned.'

'So what did he do to deserve that, then?' asked Chris. 'Poor bugger. I'm going to bet he had nothing to do with cocaine-fuelled London parties and the like, but maybe he got sucked into it somehow. Supply, maybe?'

There was a photo of Gerry Cole on the table, which Chris and Ashleigh must have been discussing before Jude arrived. He picked it up. A man in his sixties, perhaps, at a local fishing lake, proudly holding an enormous trout. There was an innocence about the beaming smile with which he faced the camera. 'I'm going to say you're right. Not supply, necessarily, but I'm sure the deaths will turn out to be connected.'

'I've been digging a bit deeper into his background this morning,' said Ashleigh, 'and to be honest, it seems he's led a pretty blameless life. He was sixty-four, and had lived in the Eden Valley all his life. He moved to Ousby after his wife died. He took on that cottage at the end of the road and did it up to keep himself interested in life. He's good with his hands. Since being widowed he's been perceived as a little eccentric, but not in any way threatening or aggressive. He lives an unflashy existence, is a regular at the pub but doesn't drink a huge amount.'

'Wednesday must have been an exception, then.'

'Yes, I think it was. He'd been the centre of attention that day. He'd been on national television. And I think that's where the motive to his murder lies.' Ashleigh looked around the table, to general nodding. They'd all seen the television clip. 'It's hard not to see a connection to Morea's death, and I think this is it. He told everybody about how he worked around the village and how he saw everyone who went up that path, either from his work or his house. He told the whole world he never forgets a face. If I had to put money on it I'd say that's what sealed his fate.'

'So what do we think? Someone who'd seen the clip hot-footed it to the village and lay in wait for him, followed him up the street from the pub after he left? That has to be someone who knew where he lived,' said Chris.

'Everybody knew where he lived,' said Ashleigh. 'He told them. He's on the telly gesturing towards the end of the lane and saying *my cottage overlooking the path to Ardale.*'

'Were there any strangers in the pub?' said Chris, moodily. 'I don't suppose there had to be. They could have waited outside.'

'I believe there were plenty of visitors, but no one was paying attention to them,' Jude pointed out. It had all been about poor Gerry, that evening.

'One witness heard a car coming through Ousby from the Townhead direction at a little before half past eleven, but that's all.' Ashleigh checked her notes.

And then, if that had been the killer, whoever they were had melted into the darkness. 'Annabel?' asked Jude, just as Doddsy shouldered his way in with a coffee in each hand and placed one in front of him. 'Thanks, Doddsy. I need this.'

'I know a bear with a sore head when I see one,' said Doddsy, with a grin, 'and I reckon it's better for all of us to keep you properly fuelled. What are we thinking? Murder, I'm hearing on the grapevine.'

'Right now, we're thinking Annabel Faulkner. She was at home,' said Chris, nodding to Jude, 'exactly as you predicted. Out in the front garden for most of the day in a bright pink jacket you could see from the top of Sour

Howes, and sitting in the living room with all the lights on in the evening, telly on and glass of wine in hand. Needless to say she was as sarcastic as hell when I spoke to her, and delighted to point me in the direction of her nosy neighbours who would tell me everything and save her the bother. Also needless to say, the neighbours had been watching every move she made, given that she's just lost her estranged husband in suspicious circumstances.'

'Naturally, So we can definitely say Annabel wasn't in Ousby but we can't say someone wasn't there on her behalf. Have we checked out the pub?'

The pub, to Jude's slight irritation, didn't have CCTV and so there was nothing other than the unfocused memories of the landlord, Ed Walker, and the other people they knew to have been in there to help identify any strangers. Ironically Gerry, with that memory he had, possibly fatally, boasted about, could probably have done so.

'What about Lexie Romachenka?' he asked. 'I really think we need to look more closely at her. I don't like this coincidence. No-one we've spoken to seems to know of any connection between her and Morea other than that they knew one another slightly, and yet here they are. I find it strange to say the least that they were both drawn to the same place. Which, bluntly, may have been perfect for the films and is pleasant and quiet enough but which definitely isn't an undiscovered gem. It's just a quiet, unspectacular branch of a bigger path up to the Pennines.' He looked across to the OS map, now pinned on the wall and scrawled with arrows and question marks. 'But I really want to talk a bit more about Lexie. In film terms she's a bit of a nobody. She has a job as a film location scout. She worked on a film which Morea directed but says she hardly knows him. My understanding is that she might take instructions from him indirectly about the types of location he wants but they'd be passed on by an assistant of his rather than by Morea himself. It's unlikely they'd work closely together. If they did, any such connection would almost certainly be brief and low key.'

'She's a good-looking woman, though,' said Doddsy, 'and we know he had a bit of a weakness in that direction.'

'She's very good-looking, for sure, but she wasn't unique in that. If they'd had a relationship I would have expected to find something about it, but she hasn't appeared in any of the magazines in connection with him, when there must be at least a dozen other women who have. On top of that she's suddenly acquired a new boyfriend who went to the same boarding school as Morea thirty odd years ago. So this all sounds very fishy to me and so naturally I wonder if she's lying.'

'Maybe,' said Ashleigh thoughtfully, 'but that isn't exactly proof of guilt. People lie to us all the time.'

'Yes,' said Chris with a degree of scorn, 'to protect their own sordid, irrelevant little secrets. As if we care about those, unless there's a crime involved.'

'We don't,' Ashleigh said, 'but others might. If people are up to something then that can have impacts outwith the criminal investigation. I wonder if that's what's going on with Lexie. As far as we know she had no reason to kill Morea, but film and TV seems a pretty cruel industry to me. It thrives on contacts and gossip and who you know and what you know. I think Lexie's a wannabe.'

'In what way?' asked Jude, curious.

'I'm not sure, exactly. But you yourself said she's a very small fish in that pond. Maybe she loves her work or maybe she has bigger aspirations. I wondered if she might know something about what's happened — have some connection to the killer — that she daren't reveal. Not just because that might put her under threat, but because it might put her at odds with someone powerful enough to damage her career prospects.'

'Equally,' said Chris, with a degree of scorn, 'it might be that she knows something and is waiting for a chance to use that knowledge to advance her career.'

If Lexie was genuinely thinking of blackmailing a killer, she was playing a very dangerous game. 'Could she be working with the murderer?' asked Jude, thinking aloud. 'The connection to Morea might also have extended to a meeting with Annabel that we know nothing about. Annabel has more than enough money to buy Lexie's co-operation.'

'I hadn't thought of that. But the problem I see is twofold. First, Becca said Lexie mentioned some kind of inheritance she expects to come into very soon. So, depending on how much it is, she may not need the money.'

'Good point. But she might need influence, and Annabel will have that. She'd funded some of Morea's earlier ventures so it isn't as if she doesn't know how that sort of thing works. There will always be people who'll trade a favour for a bit of financial investment. She could easily pull strings to get Lexie a better job on a bigger project, for example.'

'Okay. I'll buy that one. But here's one last thing.' Ashleigh nodded to the other two. 'Jude and I discussed this yesterday. Do we think Lexie has the capability for the murders?'

'Physically?' Chris pulled up a photo of Lexie on his iPad. 'I don't know. She's quite a frail-looking creature, isn't she? Thin as a stick and no muscle on her that I can see.'

'I struggle with the idea of her killing Gerry, for sure,' admitted Jude. 'Morea, not so much. All she'd need is the gun, and it was a stage prop, so she could easily get one. But if that's the case I want to know how she lured him up to the lime kiln.'

'With Annabel's help?' Chris looked sceptical, as if his brush with the aggressively-bereaved Annabel had bruised his pride. 'Though having said that, I can't see Annabel colluding with someone like Lexie.'

'Maybe. I'd like to talk to them both again, but I'll try Lexie first. I want to know what she's really doing here, and what her background is. I thought when she first arrived and my mum told me her life story that there was really no need for it. There's so much unnecessary detail. Some story about running away from a relationship with a man no-one seems to know anything about. A convenient story about an inheritance which may or may not exist. I really, really think I'd like someone to go along and have a detailed chat with her.'

'I'll do it, if you like,' offered Ashleigh, clearly relishing the prospect.

Next day was Saturday. Lexie wouldn't be going anywhere 'There's no rush. I need some time to think about it before we do. I want to speak to Hugh Cameron, too, and I'd like to be fully informed on his background before I do.'

'Sounds like you know something we don't,' said Doddsy, 'since as far as I'm aware he's new on the scene and his connection with Morea is tenuous at best and decades old.'

Decades old meant nothing. 'I was reading Morea's obituary last night. There was a good one in one of the more serious film magazines, a real deep dive into the man and his character. It didn't make me warm to him in any way.' It had left him with the impression that any number of people might have had reason to be satisfied at the news of the director's death, and if any of them had been up in Cumbria over the previous few weeks they might have joined a list of suspects. For most of them, the hate and the spite would be posturing, like boxers at the weigh-in before a bout. It didn't mean there was reason for any of them to take that final step and kill him, but people did kill on slender grounds, or for motives that seemed slender to others but were everything to them.

'It's worth a read,' he went on. 'The thing that struck me is that Morea bore grudges. He said it himself, and seems to have been indecently proud of it.'

'Dear God,' said Ashleigh with a half-laugh. 'I wonder what breakfast time conversations between him and Annabel were like? Sparky, for sure.'

For sure. 'It struck me that perhaps the reason for killing him might not be pure dislike. If Morea took against someone he could make their lives very difficult. There are numerous examples of it. He would lead actors to think they were going to get a big part and then they'd learn from the media that it had gone to someone else. He humiliated his girlfriends by dumping them in the most spectacular and public ways possible. He characterised people in unflattering ways in films and challenged them to sue, but no-one ever did.'

'Lovely guy.' Doddsy shook his head.

'Indeed. And I thought there was an interesting detail tucked away in the obituary. He says he was bullied at school.' He sat back and looked at them. 'Anyone make the connection?'

'Hugh Cameron?' said Ashleigh. 'Surely…surely not after more than thirty years?'

'Morea might not be the only one with a long memory. He and Annabel had a home up here, so although I haven't checked it's reasonable to suppose he came here regularly. I can imagine a reconnection, accidental or otherwise, between him and Cameron.'

'I want to say that's unbelievable,' said Ashleigh, carefully, 'but it isn't. I just feel you've raised a lot more questions. Why would Morea get in touch? Where does Lexie fit in? Morea was dead before the two of them met.'

'That's what we need to think about,' agreed Jude. 'Let's leave it over the weekend.' He'd be working on it at home, but these days he was trying to learn his lesson and not put too much pressure on his relationships. He was due to go to the football in Carlisle with his father the next afternoon, an arrangement that fell foul of his work commitments so often that it had become a bone of contention between them. 'I'll speak to Cameron myself, I think. It'll be very, very interesting to see what he made of Morea.' Even though they would never know what Simon Morea thought of Hugh Cameron in return.

TWENTY-ONE

When Becca came back from work she found Adam loitering in the street outside her cottage. It sometimes seemed that one or other of her two ex-partners was always hanging around in Wasby even though neither of them lived there any more, and of the two of them it certainly wasn't Adam she'd rather see, especially not on a Friday night when he'd try and inveigle himself in for a drink and outstay his welcome. She knew when she saw him that there would be trouble; he had a visceral hatred for Jude that only the perceived betrayal of a deep friendship could provoke, and he'd always seen Becca as a tool with which to pursue it.

Fair enough. She hadn't been above doing that herself at one point. Her brief relationship with Adam had been entirely designed to irritate Jude, but it hadn't worked. When she looked back at it now she felt nothing but shame about how she'd behaved; it was hardly surprising Jude had moved swiftly on to Ashleigh O'Halloran, a woman whose blonde hair, ample figure and engaging manner made her far more attractive than Becca — and most other women locally — and whose dedication to her job made her much better equipped to cope with his enormous capacity for work.

This obvious problem never stopped Adam trying to draw Becca into his plans for vengeance, and while they were largely (as far as she was aware) harmless, she was always wary of his intentions. He had moved into Penrith when he came out of prison and rented a flat almost directly opposite Jude's house, so that he was an ever-present thorn in his flesh; he waged a constant campaign of low-level nuisance and complaints against him (in some of which he had tried to involve Becca); and he cultivated the goodwill and support of the local community by casting himself as the reformed criminal and drug rehabilitation campaigner while insinuating that he'd been hard done by and Jude was entirely to blame.

It had going on for years, to the point that irritation with Adam and sympathy for Jude were partly what kept Becca from moving on. Today she knew instinctively that she was Adam's primary target. She pretended she hadn't seen him as she got out of the car, looking in vain for Holmes and then transferring her attention to the car that was parked outside Wasby End Cottage. It wasn't Lexie's, which was smart, small and neat, but a battered saloon at least fifteen years old and in need of some TLC for the scrapes along the wing and the beginnings of rust along the wheel arch. In the driver's seat, a woman sat looking at her phone.

Becca, who had acquired the habit of curiosity from Jude and who had always been inclined to see if anyone might need help, concluded that the woman was lost. She was about to go over to her and offer direction, but Adam crossed the road rapidly and slid in front of her.

'Hola, Chica!' he said, as if they were still together, and smiled at her.

She wished she weren't so naturally polite. It would be wonderfully liberating to tell him, without any compunction, exactly where to go and that he should never come back. The problem was that his parents lived in the village and she liked them. They would be hurt, and the story of her rudeness would hound her wherever she went for years to come. And besides, Adam might turn on her, too, with the viciousness of which he'd shown himself capable, and she was much less well-equipped to deal with that than Jude appeared to be.

'Hello, Adam,' she said, but she wasn't polite enough to suppress the sigh. He saw it, and it delighted him. 'What can I do for you?'

His smile flickered up into a smirk as he looked towards the Satterthwaites' cottage. 'Is our mutual friend around?'

'If you mean Jude, then I don't imagine so. You seem to have forgotten he doesn't live here any more.' It was a waste of breath. Sarcasm passed him by.

'He seems to be around here a lot, these days.' He winked at her.

'I honestly don't know.' She felt in her bag for her key, dropped it, picked it up again. 'I imagine he's very busy with this case over in the Eden Valley. And in case you hadn't noticed, I'm very busy myself.'

'I was hoping to bump into him. I thought he'd be delighted to know that our friend over there,' (he tossed a nod towards Lexie's cottage) 'is going to make a film inspired by our story.'

Our story. 'I'm pretty sure Jude doesn't think you and he have a story,' she said drily, though they did. They had been friends and friendship, like love, left a faint but indelible imprint on lives long after it was dead.

'Our history, then. I was telling Lexie about what happened between me and him and she thought it would make a remarkable film.'

'Good for her,' she said, crossly. How dare he? What had happened between them had affected her, too. 'I don't really have time to chat now, Adam. I have tons of things to do.'

'She reckons she can get some of her film director friends to look at it, and if she can pitch it, it would make a hit. A sort of Cumbrian *Shawshank Redemption*. Imagine that winning an Oscar, eh?'

'Adam,' she said, finally losing her patience. 'Get over yourself. You're a small-time criminal and Jude's a policeman. That's never going to be big box office, is it?'

'I'd imagine his bosses will hate it,' he said, cheerfully. 'Lexie has all the contacts. And by the way, I'm an *ex*-criminal.'

'Enough, Adam.' She turned her back on him and strode up the path just as Holmes, who must have seen him and hidden himself away just as surely as he always appeared like magic whenever he saw Jude, materialised on the front step.

Holmes was a good judge of character. She opened the door and let herself in, then crept to the door of the living room where she could see out and not be seen, to make sure Adam had gone. What a nuisance. She knew nothing about film or the film industry, had no idea how easily films got made, what sort of money or contacts were required to get a film off the ground, or what the chances were of commercial success. In a sense that didn't matter. If, as she suspected, nothing ever came of it Adam would still have his fun spreading the rumour, which would travel like wildfire as these things always did, and Jude's notoriously sensitive boss would get touchy about it and make his life difficult. If the film got made it would be a bonus but even if it didn't, Adam would have achieved his objective. All he ever wanted from life was to be a constant irritant to someone who didn't care about him.

He had told her this, of course, so that she would pass the tale on to Jude, and although she resented the way in which he was manipulating her there was no denying she felt a twinge of pleasure at having a reason to speak to the man she'd long thought she'd marry. It did no harm to keep channels of communication open. A friendly word of warning would give Jude the chance to deal with Adam's new initiative in whatever way he deemed appropriate, rather than have it creep up and surprise him in an unwelcome message from the HR department.

She checked her watch, knowing he'd probably still be at work and wondering whether it was better to try and catch him when he'd have more time for a chat, but the decision was taken for her by the doorbell. Still standing in the living room she took a quick glance and though she couldn't see the path from where she was, she was comforted by the sight of Adam strolling jauntily down the street. Whoever it was, at least it wasn't him. She headed for the door.

'Sorry to interrupt you lass. I can see you're busy,' said the woman on the step. She might have been in her early sixties, broad of build and with a Yorkshire accent to match. 'My name's Mary Ford and I'm looking for someone. I wondered if you knew where she was. It's my daughter. Alex.'

'I don't think I know anyone in the village by that name.' Becca racked her tired brain, without success. As a secondary thought it struck her as odd that this woman didn't seem to know where her daughter lived. 'Do you have an address?'

'She never give it to me, just said it was the Cottage in Wasby, but it seems to me that every bloody house in this village is called something or other cottage.'

Becca grinned. 'Yes, it's a bit confusing when you aren't used to it. Is it Lexie Romachenka you're looking for? She's next door.'

'Lexie Romachenka?' said the woman, and laughed. 'Plain old Alex Ford in Huddersfield, so she is, but it seems that's not the name to play with in that London. At least, that's what our Alex says.'

'Come on in,' said Becca, intrigued. 'I don't know where Lexie is just now. Can't you message her?'

'Oh, I won't keep you, love,' said Mary, cheerfully. 'She doesn't know I'm coming. I took an executive decision. I think that's what they call it. You know what kids are like. They get to be grown adults and they think they know everything, don't give a toss for fifty-odd years of life experience and wouldn't know good advice if it bit them on the backside. *Oh, Mama, you don't understand!*' She mimicked Lexie's London voice to perfection. 'She wouldn't give me her address when I offered to come up and see her, and says she doesn't need any help. But I said to her, I get tired of seeing my girl make mistake after mistake and not let me help her. So I thought I'd come up anyway and sort her out. Especially after these threatening letters she's been getting.'

'Threatening letters?' said Becca, suddenly intrigued. Holmes was twining himself round her legs in a desperate plea for food and it would have been a good excuse to end the conversation if she'd been looking for one, but if she was going to phone Jude anyway it might be good to have a better excuse than just some gossip from Adam. 'Are you sure you don't want a cup of tea?'

'Oh, no thank you. I've messaged her and told her I'm

here. She'll be back all right, if only to send me packing. I'm not the kind of person she wants hanging round her these days, with all that arty-farty manner she puts on for her work, all that pretending to be someone she's not, though she's always been a bit like that. And always free with information about herself, especially when it isn't true.'

Mary Ford was pretty free with her information herself. Maybe she prided herself on her straight-talking Yorkshire nature. 'She did tell me a lot about herself, but she never mentioned any letters.'

'God help the lass. Maybe they never really existed. She does like to tell a bit of a story to make herself interesting. I doubt any of the friends she talks about are all they say they are, it's all such a bloody performance. I said to her, *Alex, just be yourself. Be honest about it. You're a good girl and a clever one, and a smart Yorkshire lass is far more interesting than the Russian princess you keep pretending to be.*' She grinned. 'She told you that tale, did she?'

'Yes, but—'

'She tells everyone. Not that there's no truth in it. My grandfather was a Russian like she says, but just one of the working poor and there were millions more like him. Russian princess!' said Mary and laughed.

'What about the letters?' said Becca, yet again. Who would have thought it would be so hard to get someone to answer a simple question? 'I remember now. She did ask me if I'd seen anyone put something through her door, but she said it was because she'd had a good luck card and someone had forgotten to sign it, so she didn't know who it was from.'

'She's plausible enough, I'll give her that, and a bit of an actress, too.' Mary's criticism of her daughter was underpinned with pride.

'The letters?' said Becca.

'Just the two. They weren't even letters, really. Just nasty notes from someone.'

'How awful!' Becca took a long look along the street and the only person she could think of who would take any pleasure out of hassling someone like that was Adam, but letters to strangers weren't his *modus operandi*. Adam liked to see how people reacted when he turned the screw; it was why he'd come all the way down to Wasby to seek out Jude and, when he wasn't there, had made sure his message would come via Becca instead. If Adam had had a reason to want Lexie out of the village he'd have whispered in her ear that other people didn't want her there, but she couldn't think of a reason why he would turn so swiftly and so savagely on a newcomer. He hardly knew her and on their brief acquaintance it seemed they got on well. 'I can't imagine anyone in the village who would behave like that.'

'To someone who's done them no harm? No, you're right. Decent folk wouldn't do that. I know who it'll be.'

'Who?' asked Becca, since forthrightness seemed to be the order of the day.

'Our Alex had a boyfriend. Did she tell you that? That's why she's here.'

'Yes, but she said she'd broken up with him.'

'Aye, because he was bad for her. An older man stringing her along? Because she never had a dad around to look out for her she's always looking for one, if you get my drift, and older men spot that and take advantage. She was right to get rid of him, but I'm willing to bet his wife isn't the forgiving sort. They never are.'

'But surely—'

'Yes, for sure, she should be going after her man, not after some poor woman he's manipulated, but life isn't like that, is it?'

'Well, quite.' From the outset it had seemed to Becca that Lexie Romachenka — or Alex Ford, as she now knew her to be called — was a woman perfectly in control of her own destiny, and now she found herself wondering whether Lexie was really on the run from her own domineering mother, rather than from the married lover she'd had the sense to break things off with.

'Her trouble,' said Mary with a sigh, 'is that she's a damn bad judge of a man, and I'm not sure that I shouldn't take some of the blame for that. I can never read the bastards right myself.'

Nor can I, said Becca to herself, thinking wryly of Jude and of Adam and of many a lost opportunity, just as Lexie's car turned off the main road and bumped along the village street.

TWENTY-TWO

'Mama! What are you doing here?' Breathless with anxiety, Lexie flung herself out of her car regardless of the fact that her mother was on Becca's doorstep in full view of the whole village, most of whom were about to start arriving from work or bringing their kids home from this Friday-afternoon activity or that. She wasn't a woman to have a public row, but she'd spent the afternoon wondering whether it would be forward to invite Hugh for supper, and had finally decided to do it. The boot of the car was packed with the wherewithal for a three-course meal for two and it was purely by chance that she hadn't got round to calling him to see if he was free. If he'd accepted, she'd have had some explaining to do to both of them.

Becca, thank God, was either discreet or terrified of getting involved in a row. She disappeared back inside her cottage, almost falling over her cat as she did so, and closed the door behind her leaving Mary to make her determined way down the path to Lexie.

'Alex,' she said, smothering her daughter's fury in the

most all-consuming maternal hug imaginable. 'Aren't you pleased to see me?'

'No.' Lexie was almost in tears of frustration as she disengaged herself too quickly from the one person who always put her welfare first. 'What are you doing here? I told you I didn't want you to visit.'

'I know it's important to you to live your own life,' said Mary, looking her up and down, 'but I won't be cut out of it while you need help. I'm here because you didn't sound as if you were yourself. I know what you're like. There's been all this nonsense over Nico and I think you need someone to take you in hand and sort you out or you'll stay mithering in your bed all day, and that isn't healthy.'

'I haven't been mithering. In fact I've just been out to buy myself a treat tea, since it's Friday.' Lexie gathered the bags of shopping from the boot and handed them to her mother while she felt in her bag the front door key. If there was to be a row, which there almost certainly was because her mother was in full bull-in-the-china-shop mode and Lexie herself was in no mood to back down from her determination to run her life her own way, then at least they should have it behind closed doors. Assuming, that was, that her mother hadn't already washed all Lexie's dirty linen in public. 'That's great. Of course I'm grateful you care about me. Don't take this the wrong way but when I said I didn't want you to come it was because I didn't want you to come.'

'Yes, lass, but here I am. And here I'll stay until I'm sure you're all right and the police have found out what happened to Nico. I take it they haven't worked out you were his bit on the side?'

Lexie winced. Her mother always called a spade a spade. 'It was a romance, Mama,' she reminded her sternly, because that was what she'd always pretended.

'Spare me the *Mama* nonsense, please,' said Mary, carrying the bags through to the kitchen and beginning to unload them. 'My, you've enough here to feed an army. It's as well I'm here to help eat it.' She opened the fridge and began stacking the perishables in it. 'If you ask me it's forgetting who you are and where you came from that landed you in this mess and now you need to get out of it. Getting a grip on reality will be a start.'

She had no idea. To try and make your name in film as a dull Yorkshire lass from a working-class, single-parent household was an impossibility. Social class wasn't a barrier in this day and age but being boring unquestionably was, and to people like Nico the unfashionable north was duller than beige and more to be poked fun at than an avocado bathroom suite. In circles where to be the wrong sort of different invited mockery it was better to be an identikit south of England blonde with a romantic history than a provincial. 'I suppose you can stay for tonight, but there's only one bed so you'll have to sleep on the sofa.'

Mary slammed the fridge closed, peered through this door and that and settled herself in the living room. 'That'll do me fine for one night. Tomorrow you'll come home with me, where I can look after you. And if you don't come then I'll stay here as long as it takes, sofa or no sofa.'

'I'm thirty years old!'

'Thirty years old and still needing your mum to dig you out of the holes you get yourself into with men.' Mary folded her arms across her formidable chest. 'You can't deny that.'

Truth. 'And I suppose you think you'd make a better job of choosing for me?'

'I've got age and experience on my side even if I didn't make good choices for myself.'

'But that's exactly it. Nico was my choice. My. Choice.' He'd been a bad choice and one she regretted, even more so now he was dead and she was stalked by the constant fear that the police would find out about the affair, but it had been her mistake, just as her flighty father — and, by extension, Lexie herself — had been her mother's. She'd chosen to get into bed with Nico and she'd chosen to leave him. *And Hugh is my choice, too*, she was about to say, but stopped herself. Now was not the moment to mention the possibility of a new boyfriend to her mother. She took a deep breath. 'I think you should go home tomorrow. The house really isn't big enough for you to stay any longer. I never asked you to interfere. I just wanted to come here and have a bit of peace. I wanted to be here. I wanted to find myself.'

She'd begun to do that. Today she'd taken an early morning walk through wet grass, looking at spider's webs spun out on the hedges and spangled with dew, watching the swallows as they dipped and whirled, lining up on the telephone wires like passengers at a departure gate, waiting to head for the sun. She was learning the joys of early nights and books, days without panic and mornings without headaches. Now her mother had arrived to ratchet up the drama and make a crisis of everything.

'Then you agree,' said Mary, as if it were a killer comment, 'that you'd lost yourself. That London wasn't good for you.'

'I love London.' But she loved the country, too, and London had starved her of that. When she was a child there had always been glimpses of the hills from that grey flat on the housing estate where she'd been brought up, and the day trips out to the moors to breathe lungfuls of fresh air that went straight to her head remained among the better memories of her adolescence. 'I like it up here, too. I'm going to recharge my batteries and then go back. Perhaps in a few weeks.'

'Don't forget I'm your mum,' said Mary, quietly.

Thirty years old, fumed Lexie, but she knew how this would go. Her mother would stay and she, Lexie, would go along with her meekly, probably eventually ceding her the comfort of the bed and sleeping on the sofa herself, all the while scheming to do things her own way and keeping her secrets. If her mother didn't know about Hugh she wouldn't be able to be rude to him, or to do anything to prevent Lexie from plunging into this new relationship. Work was a suitable excuse; she would invent locations to visit and sneak off to see him, then spend the evenings sitting watching the television to keep her mother pacified. After a few days Mary would get bored and go home and Lexie could resume the life she had begun enjoying living.

Assuming no-one ratted on her, of course. She couldn't see Becca opening her mouth on the subject of Hugh without a very clear cue that it was okay to do so, but she knew Adam was someone who enjoyed making mischief. She was a bad judge of men, but not that one. Maybe, after all, when she made her film he would feature in it as the villain and not the hero.

Realistically, though, (it was funny how Mary always brought a dose of cold common sense with her) the film was unlikely to get made. Without Nico she had no real contacts, and if she attracted the wrong sort of attention from the police it would be hard to make much progress in her career unless she traded on her notoriety. She was smart enough to see that was both short-term and high-risk.

'Okay, Mama,' she said, with a deep breath. 'Of course you can stay, for as long as you want, but I have a lot of work to do. I'll be out and about a lot and I'm afraid you'll be very bored.'

Lexie turned the ingredients for the romantic dinner into a one-pot kitchen supper for two and they spent the rest of the evening in companionable silence, watching a Netflix film that Lexie had seen before and disliked. She excused herself early and, pouring herself a sly gin and tonic, sneaked it up to her room like the rebel she'd been when she was sixteen years old. When the gin was gone (it took longer for her to drink than it usually did, and she enjoyed it more) she texted Hugh with a brief explanation because she didn't dare to phone, then settled back to bed contemplating what would be a fraught few days to come.

TWENTY-THREE

'The thing is, it's been preying on my mind,' Becca said, 'and I know it shouldn't and I know it's something you probably don't want to hear, but if I know Adam you will hear about it, sooner rather than later, so it's probably better that you hear it from me.'

She sounded wretchedly apologetic. Another time Jude would have taken a few moments to reassure her but her phone call had caught him at a tricky moment. He and Ashleigh had called into M&S where they'd picked up a pizza and a salad and were walking back to his house to continue chewing over the thorny problem of Simon Morea, Lexie Romachenka and the unfortunate, in-the-wrong-place-at-the-wrong-time Gerry Cole. He was wary of speaking to Becca while that too-comfortable relationship with Ashleigh remained ongoing, all the more so when Ashleigh was walking beside him overhearing every word. He'd seen too many people tie themselves in knots keeping unnecessary secrets so he always told her when he'd spoken to his ex but everything became much more complex with a third person listening in. A word out of place, a wrong emphasis, could make life difficult as he trod the tightrope between the woman he was sleeping with and the one he loved.

'Thanks,' he said, giving Ashleigh a half-shrug, one that said *you heard what happened, she called me*. 'It's always good to know what he's up to.'

'I'm sure it won't come to anything. And I know he only told me so I'd tell you.'

Adam was manipulative like that. 'I'm forewarned,' he said, with a half laugh. 'Thanks, Becca.'

She rang off, and he and Ashleigh turned up through the church close and cut across the curtilage outside St Andrews. It was already dusk.

'That's a new one,' said Ashleigh, who'd listened in as Becca stumbled her way through the explanation. 'Fair play to Adam. He's finally learned that false complaints against you don't work, so he's got creative. A film!'

Faye's face, when Jude tried to warn her about the very outside possibility of Adam's creative fantasies ever making it as far as the big, or even the small, screen would be a picture. He'd have to tell her, because when Adam talked troublemakers listened, and the wrong kind of gossip could be damaging.

'I should take the credit for inspiring him,' he joked. 'Do you think I'll get a name check in the award speeches when he wins his BAFTA?'

'I highly doubt whether Lexie is quite as serious about the project as he is, or indeed as he thinks she is,' said Ashleigh, cheerfully.

'I hope you're right.' Adam's persistence, the low-level drip-drip of negativity, wore down Jude's enthusiasm as water wears away at a stone. Everyone in the office, including Faye, knew what was going on and the Professional Standards Department laughed louder with the arrival of each vexatious complaint, but Jude was more cautious. There was always a chance that one of the accusations would stick. 'He's the least of my problems right now.'

'Hunger's the biggest of mine.'

They were still laughing at that when his phone rang again. He dug it out of his pocket. 'Becca, again. Pocket call, I expect,' he said to Ashleigh, but he answered it nonetheless. 'Hi, Becca. Is everything okay?'

'Yes, sorry. Silly of me.' She sounded flustered. 'I got so worked up about Adam — God, I can't see what I ever saw in him — that I quite forgot. He wasn't the real reason I called.'

Adam had once been one of Jude's closest friends, something that would now be unthinkable. People changed. They matured as they grew, not always in a good way. They grew apart and sometimes, just occasionally, they grew back together again. 'Okay.'

'Yes. It's Lexie.'

'Has something happened?' He stopped by the churchyard wall, took a look round to make sure no-one else was in earshot, and flicked the volume on. 'I've got you on speaker. Ashleigh's listening in, if that's okay.'

'Yes, of course. She'll probably want to hear it. No, it's not something bad, or at least I suppose it might be, but not dangerously bad or anything. She's had some anonymous notes. Unpleasant ones. They started just after she arrived so I can't think it would be anyone in the village, which means it must be someone she knows from somewhere else.'

Somewhere immediately above them a pair of starlings chattered in the trees. 'Did she tell you that?'

'No. Her mother turned up unexpectedly, because she was worried about her, and she told me about it. On the day she arrived Lexie asked me if I'd seen anyone at her door but she said it was because someone had left her a welcome card.'

'Did her mother have anything else to say?' he enquired, his attention caught.

'Yes. Oh God, Jude, you'd have loved Lexie's mother.' She laughed out loud. 'There's no messing about with her. I just stood with my mouth open while she talked.'

'The best sort of witness,' said Ashleigh, as if to remind them both that she was there.

'I rather got the impression Lexie's been making up stories about her background and it's much less mysterious and exotic than she claims, but that's hardly a crime. No Russian prince or anything. Still, I'll let you get on.' She hung up again, rather more briskly this time.

'It's not a crime to make up stories about yourself,' said Ashleigh, as he pocketed the phone again and the two of them made their way out into Sandgate, 'but it does rather raise the question of what else she might have been making up.'

'Or withholding,' he agreed.

'Indeed.'

They'd run a background check on Lexie as a matter of routine and he hadn't given it as much attention as he might have done, because his focus had been much more on the dead man than on the witness who had discovered him. When he had a moment he would check. He knew Romachenka wasn't her real name, but it seemed that hardly anyone in the film industry stuck with what their parents had given them, so that hadn't raised too much of an eyebrow. Lexie was definitely worth that second look they'd talked about at the team meeting.

Sandgate was busy so, out of natural caution, they let the matter drop as they made their way along Drover's

Lane and up into Wordsworth Street. Jude's house was near the bottom of the hill; on the other side of the street, as so often, Adam stood at the window of his rented flat watching out for him.

It must be so tedious, so exhausting, wasting energy on so trivial a feud. Over the past couple of years Jude had learned to ignore him, to a degree, but he remained surprised by Adam's staying power, his capacity to bear a grudge.

'I'll do the pizza,' he said, heading to the kitchen as Ashleigh checked her phone with the screen tilted away from him so he couldn't see it — something he knew meant she was checking for messages from Scott.

'Thank you.' She pocketed the phone and went for cutlery. 'That was interesting what Becca was saying about Lexie, wasn't it?'

'Very. And now I have to confess to an ulterior motive when I invited you here. I'm proposing that after we've eaten we get out the beers and the popcorn and settle down to watch a film.'

'That sounds topical. What sort of a film, or do I have to guess? It's going to be one of Simon Morea's, isn't it?'

'Correct. It's not my normal sort of film, I have to say. I'm more of a biopic man. It's a Cold War thriller set in the 1960s, and it has a local connection.'

'Is it by any chance the one Lexie scouted locations for?'

'Yes. Dark doings up on the Pennines and spies up at the listening station at Cross Fell. Apparently it's an excoriating take on our modern surveillance society, and more critics hated it than loved it.'

'I have to say that doesn't sound my sort of film, either.'

'Fortunately it's not very long.'

The microwave pinged and they settled to eat, picking over the threads of the Morea murder again and again as they did so, finding nothing new. When they'd eaten and cleared away, they went through to the living room and Jude switched on the telly. 'Here we go. It's called *The Sounds They Make, The Sounds We Hear* and it was released in the summer. It showed in a few art house cinemas but it never made it to general release. Right. Here we go. Lights, camera, action. Let's sit back and be entertained.'

He'd never been a big film buff even before he'd become far too busy to spare the time for the cinema when there were other things he'd rather do. Occasionally he used to go to the pictures with Becca if there was something she was keen to watch, but that was about it and he hadn't set foot in a cinema for years. The film which had turned out to be Simon Morea's swan song had received some critical acclaim and some harsh comments; it was slow-moving, intense and atmospheric and failed to keep his attention. Nor, judging by her yawns, did it for Ashleigh. Most of the film had been shot in the central Lakes or at the coast towards Sellafield but…

'Wait,' said Ashleigh. 'That's Ardale Beck.'

'Yep.' They watched the section twice before Jude paused it on a shot in which the camera seemed to hover above the surface of the bog, a strange kaleidoscope of weeds and water, with the lime kilns featuring more as a reflection in the water than in the film itself.

'Do you have any idea what's going on?' asked Ashleigh.

'No, but did you catch that Scottish guy's name? The baddie?'

'No, but the sound quality isn't great.'

'It's shocking.' That was probably deliberate, some comment on something to do with the perils of modern communication. 'But I'm pretty certain I heard someone call him Hugh.'

'Wow!' said Ashleigh. 'Morea really was vindictive, wasn't he?'

He and Adam had something in common. Jude pressed *play* and the film moved on. The hero was following up a lead from a contract that took him to Orkney on the trail of a communist agent who had established a sleeper cell on his defection from Russia and had gone to Scotland after the War.

Jude sat up at that. Ashleigh's eyelids, which had been dropping, lifted. 'Wait, what?' she said. 'I'd never heard anything about this until a week or so ago and here we are, listening to it again.'

'The Russia connection? There's nothing new under the sun.'

'Shall we go straight to the credits?'

'I think we need to suffer for our art.'

The film rolled on but he wasn't paying a huge amount of attention to it, and he was sure Ashleigh wasn't either. Instead he was thinking about Lexie Romachenka, aka Alex Ford. Descendant of Russian emigrés, spinner of tales, film location scout. As the film lurched towards its deliberately ambiguous and frustrating ending (a body turning slowly as it fell from the Via Ferrata at Honister but with no indication as to whose body it was) he leaned forward to watch the rolling credits. And yes, there it was. 'Hugh Cameron. That's his villain. Nice twist.' The credits kept rolling.

'Locations, Lexie Romachenka,' read Ashleigh. 'But we already knew that. It's just the story that's surprising. Isn't it?'

'No.' Lexie hadn't lied about knowing Morea, but she'd claimed they'd only met once or twice, and yet here was the story she claimed as hers, stitched into the film made by a man she'd barely spoken to and professed to dislike. 'It's interesting, though. As you say, that's not a particularly well-known bit of history. As it happens, I had heard about it. My mum knew about it and she mentioned it because Lexie had told her all about her grandfather. My dad was into niche history and she'd heard it from him, way back.' He managed a grim smile. His parents hadn't spoken for years and he'd been surprised to hear Linda mention his father's name. 'If that's true, and if that's where Lexie drew her back story from, perhaps that's where Morea heard it.'

'Even though they weren't close?'

'She says they weren't close. We've already established that Lexie's relationship with the truth is flexible, and I suspect she's one of those people who thinks it's all right to withhold information she doesn't think is relevant, rather than letting us decide what matters and what doesn't.'

'I expect she'd be concerned about what information we would release,' said Ashleigh, with a yawn, 'and I do understand that. I don't imagine anyone in her line of work is especially discreet.'

'I think we need to have a serious talk with Ms Romachenka,' he said, scowling. 'And I think we need to ask her about the letters, too. Let's not forget them.'

'I would imagine that's Annabel Faulkner,' said Ashleigh, with another yawn. 'Don't you? Because if Lexie thinks she can hide things from us I don't imagine Annabel would be any different. I wouldn't be at all surprised to find she knew everything all the time. And, bluntly, I wouldn't be remotely surprised either to find that she was the one who killed her husband. And now we've got Hugh Cameron to think about.'

'He'll be easy. Chris tracked down a former schoolteacher of his and Morea's. I'm speaking to him tomorrow.'

'Such dedication,' said Ashleigh. 'I do hope you're not cancelling the football for it.'

'My dad would never forgive me. No. I'm catching hold of this guy, Sam Benton, afterwards. He lives in Sheffield but it happens that he's in Carlisle for the weekend and he's happy to squeeze me in. I'll be very interested in what he has to say.'

TWENTY-FOUR

'I have to say,' said Jude, taking the seat to which he was directed, 'I didn't have crashing an eighty-year old's birthday party on my bingo card for this week.'

'It's my brother's party,' said Sam Benton, with what could only be described as a cheeky grin, 'and he's my kid brother, too, so he does what I say. You're more than welcome to stay for the whole night if you've nothing better to do.'

'Much as I'd like that, I've another engagement.' Liking the cut of the old man's jib, Jude grinned back at him. They were in a corner of a function room in a hotel in Carlisle, where helium balloons jostled against the ceiling and a huge foil banner with an eightieth birthday greeting hung across the centre of the room. The party hadn't started; Sam had offered to make himself available for half an hour before it began and Jude, finding that he would be passing the door of the hotel on his way back from the football, had been quick to take up the opportunity.

'I'm more than appreciative of you finding find the

time to speak to me,' he said, shrugging off his jacket and untangling the Carlisle United scarf from round his neck.

'I'm happy to. I'm only sorry to be so specific about my times, but I live down in Yorkshire these days and I'm only up here for tonight. I'm away to Cornwall tomorrow for another eightieth party would you credit it, so it was now or never.' Sam's expression switched rapidly from cheeriness to melancholy. 'The past has been on my mind more than a bit since I saw what happened to Simon, even though it's a long time since I saw the lad, or heard anything from him for that matter. He was never one to look back. I remember him leaving without a goodbye, not so much as a backward glance. It brings it all back. It's Simon you want to talk to me about, isn't it?'

'As a matter of fact it isn't,' said Jude, settling back in the chair and accepting the glass of sparkling wine that came his way via a waitress who clearly had instructions to make sure any guest, or anyone who looked as if they might be, was kept well-supplied. 'At least, not specifically.' He reckoned he knew pretty much everything he needed to about Morea, though you never knew what kind of fascinating snippets might lurk in someone else's memory. 'It's a contemporary of his. Hugh Cameron.'

He had the impression that Sam, who was in his early eighties, was still mentally sharp, but he frowned a bit at that, as though casting around. 'You don't remember all the boys' names, that's the thing. Simon...now, he was different. He stood out from the beginning. But I'm not sure about a Hugh Cameron. There were several Camerons.'

Jude had been prepared for this, and had set Chris, before he left the office on the previous evening, to hunt him out a photograph of a young Hugh. This he duly produced, and handed a printed copy to Sam, along with a class photograph that Chris had somehow been able to dig up. The old man pushed his glasses on to the top of his bald head and frowned at it for a minute, before his expression cleared. 'Ah! Ah yes, of course. That was his name. It's all coming back to me.'

'Did you teach Hugh? I'm guessing you taught Simon, by the way you talk of him.'

'I taught them both. I was their housemaster — guidance teacher, I suppose you'd call it, for the whole time they were there. Ah yes. It was a long time ago, but now when I think about it…young Hugh isn't in any trouble, is he?' He looked up, anxiously.

'Why do you ask?' Jude watched, fascinated, as Sam stared at the photos, looking from one to the other, and seemed in his mind to be isolating these two boys from the hundreds he would have cared for over his long teaching career. 'Was he in trouble at school?'

'Oh, always.' The look Sam bestowed on the photograph of Hugh was part of affection and part of regret. 'What age will he be now? Fifty? He'd be the same age as Simon.'

'That's right. He's forty-nine.'

'Ah. And to answer your question, yes. Hugh was often in trouble at school and when I look back at it now I wonder if that was necessarily the way it had to be, or whether we failed him. I've been out of the profession for twenty years but even latterly we were making progress in understanding the young people we cared for. Hugh wasn't suited to boarding school. He liked his own space and to be left alone.'

'I can see there wouldn't be much chance of that.'

'None,' said Sam, with regret. 'I wish we'd understood that better. We'd have handled him differently.'

Traditional methods notwithstanding Sam would, Jude

thought, have made an excellent and sympathetic housemaster. 'What do you mean?'

'We might have looked a little more deeply into the causes of his bad behaviour, but of course in those days rules were rules and if you broke them, you were in trouble. I tried to cut him some slack because I liked him, but perhaps I was a bit too timid.' He broke off to reach out for a sausage roll from the tray the attentive waitress was offering him.

'What do you mean? What sort of trouble did Hugh get into?'

'You can see from the pictures he was a big lad, big for his age and big as a grown man. I think he would have had a nice nature if it had been nourished, but it wasn't. He should never have been at boarding school. His parents had a big farm somewhere and they worked hard, and without knowing the ins and outs of their business it always struck me that they didn't prioritise their son. They were quite a bit older and I imagine they found him hard to deal with. I expect they'll be gone now.'

'His father still lives in Shap, I think, but his mother is dead. Hugh went and worked on the farm after he left school and he's been there ever since.'

'He'd have loved it. We had a lot of very clever boys, but Hugh wasn't one of them. He wasn't academically bright and he wasn't interested enough to ask questions. He always took things literally and I would say he was easily led. Of course, when the others laughed at him, he resorted to using his fists, and he was regularly in trouble for fighting.'

Sam looked at the photos again, and Jude waited. He knew better than to try and hurry an old man's memory. You might as well try and hurry the Solway tide. He sipped his drink, taking care not to drink it too quickly so that the waitress would fill it up. He wasn't technically on duty and he wasn't driving, but there were standards.

'Did he have problems with anyone in particular?' he asked.

'Is that what you people call a leading question?'

'It wasn't,' Jude said, 'but I'm interested you think it might be.'

'The student — we called them pupils in those days — that Hugh had trouble with was Simon. But I think you won't be surprised to hear that.' He gave Jude a sly smile. 'If you were you wouldn't be here. Are you telling me you think Hugh killed Simon?'

'The investigation into how Mr Morea died is still open.'

'Now, Chief Inspector.' Sam looked at him, the way he might have looked at a schoolboy wriggling his way out of a difficult situation. 'Maybe that's true, and maybe it's accidental and maybe you really have nothing better to do on a Saturday evening than this. His name must have come up in your investigation.'

'It's one of many,' Jude allowed. He and Faye had been very careful that no mention of the word *murder* had come into the public domain, but this speculation was inevitable. 'At the moment I'm trying to find out what brought him up to Cumbria. He and Hugh may have had connections in common.'

'Well. The thing was this. Hugh wasn't clever but he wasn't malicious either. When he lashed out it was from confusion and bewilderment. He and Simon didn't get on, not at all. They were two very different types of boy. There were others that Hugh didn't get on with, and others that Simon didn't get on with, but it was only ever Hugh who was in trouble over it.'

'Knowing what I know about Simon,' said Jude, giving

in and accepting a sausage on a stick, 'I think I understand that.'

'Boys are like everyone else. The clever ones are very clever and when those clever ones are troublemakers and in close proximity with those they don't like, it can get nasty.'

So it could. At school Jude and Adam had been close but Adam had always been able to create problems for those he didn't like. When the two of them had fallen out, he'd turned these troublemaking arts on his former friend. Jude wasn't stupid and he knew Adam well enough to understand exactly how his mind worked and that the worst thing he could do was respond. If he ever lost his temper and raised a fist, or even gave in to the temptation to shove his tormentor out of the way, the result would have been an immediate complaint and possibly a disciplinary procedure coming his way. 'Yes, I can see that.'

'I could see at the time that Simon was at the root of it, but you can't blame the victims now and we couldn't then. Simon focussed on Hugh because Hugh would always give him the response he wanted, and the other boys watched closely and learned to deflect any trouble in Hugh's direction as a means of self-protection.'

'He was unhappy at school, then?'

'Unquestionably. And yet, Chief Inspector, I liked him. I thought he was at heart a gentle boy and he responded well to gentleness, but schools can be brutal places at the best of times and ours was no different. At boarding school you have nowhere to hide. I look back now and for all the records show that Hugh was the bully, I don't see it that way. Simon had that gift of putting others in the wrong.'

'Would you say Simon knew human nature pretty well?' Jude had one eye on the clock. He had the impression that

Sam would reminisce about schooldays for ever if he were given the chance, but not only was there a party about to start around them, but Jude had left his father, with whom he had been to the football, drinking in the pub next door.

'Definitely. I think that came out in his films. I was never a fan of his when he was a lad, though people do change.'

'I don't think Simon changed much, in that respect.'

'That's a pity, but it doesn't surprise me. I liked his films, very much.' Sam was nodding, with approval. 'He had an eye for character. Often I used to see something that reminded me of someone. You could see he knew how people's minds worked. I'd wouldn't quite go so far as to say he had his moments of genius, though he surely thought he did and I was never very comfortable with any of them. His best understanding was of the dark side of human nature, and I didn't like that. He knew how to show people their own weaknesses and many people — the better people, I have to say — aren't equipped to withstand that. Certainly Hugh wasn't, although he became a very fine young man.'

The room was starting to fill up, now, with partygoers in their best outfits, carrying gift-wrapped parcels and heading to an elderly man sitting in state in a chair at the end of the room. 'You've seen him since he left school, then?'

'Oh yes. I liked to keep in touch with my boys, to see how they got on. I never heard a peep from Simon once he'd gone, of course. We were no use to him once he'd set his eyes on stardom, except as material for some of his darker films. One of them was set in a boarding school, I remember. If I'm honest I never expected to hear from Hugh again, but I sent him a letter once to see how he was getting on and he did reply to me, so we kept in touch. I saw him every year until I retired.'

'And what do you think of him?'

'A very fine man, I would say, though his sense of self-worth is very low. But there he is, with that big farm which he runs, or rents out most of it I think and runs a bit of it by himself. He bears no grudges, or at least if he does he keeps it very quiet. But I worry that we damaged him, punishing him when we should have helped him deal with matters better than he did.'

'Simon bore grudges, though?'

'For sure. I imagine he took them to his grave with him.'

'In his latest film, the villain was called Hugh Cameron,' said Jude. 'Did you notice that?'

'His latest film? My dear young man, every film, every drama-documentary, every piece of fiction Simon ever produced that I've seen has had an unpleasant character in it called after someone he didn't like. There's a hired killer in one of them called after me, and I thought Simon and I got on better than most, but I think if you look back you'll find there are evil Hugh Camerons all over the place, or violent farmers from Shap, or whatever. Simon may not have been a genius in film but I never met anyone who could outdo him in terms of remembering an old slight, and I'm afraid Hugh bore the brunt of that much more than any of the rest of us.'

TWENTY-FIVE

Jude slept little the night after he'd crashed the party. There were too many things that didn't make sense, too many lies told. He spent too much of his Sunday worrying about it, though knowing that nothing would emerge from the tech team or the lab over the weekend he made himself stay out of the office. On the Monday he was in before seven, checking in with Chris Marshall, who was also in early, but there was nothing new to learn. The messages on Morea's phone had still not been unlocked; he left Faye (who, thank goodness, wasn't in the office) a note asking her to do whatever she could to get them processed as a matter of urgency and then, after three cups of coffee, he headed back down to Wasby to confront Lexie Romachenka.

Lexie's car wasn't outside Wasby End Cottage but an older, battered model that was probably her mother's stood tucked in at the side of the road. Jude had taken the decision to call in unannounced because the best chance of getting something out of her was to catch her by surprise and he'd been reasonably certain that at this time of the morning he'd find her in. This now seemed like a misjudgement — not a disastrous one, because Wasby was only twenty minutes or so from the office and he could easily claw the time back, but one which irritated him nonetheless. He stopped the car outside his mother's cottage and debated whether to speak to Mary Ford. If Lexie was only away to the shop in Askham it would be worth waiting and if not Mary would almost certainly know where she was and when she'd be back.

The windows of the cottage were wide open as if someone was giving the place a thorough spring clean, so Mary wouldn't be rushing off anywhere. Speaking with her would cost him five minutes. He strode up the path and rang the bell.

'Are you Mary Ford?' He flashed his warrant card at the square, grey-haired woman who answered the door. There was an obvious family resemblance in the shape of the face and the set of the eyes, the stamp that nature set and which was all but impossible to erase, but in every other way the woman in front of him was as unlike Lexie as possible. She wore practical, well-worn and not obviously expensive clothes that had seen better days and no make-up, presenting a shapeless and unmemorable figure whereas Lexie had the impossible willow-thinness of someone too familiar with the camera. Her sleeves were rolled up, her hands red and wet, and she had a tea towel thrown over her shoulder. He had clearly interrupted her in cleaning. 'DCI Satterthwaite. I'm hoping for a quick word with Lexie Romachenka.'

'Police?' For a moment a look of panic came over her face. She took the warrant card and frowned at it, holding it at arms' length, the handed it back. 'I thought that was all done and dusted.'

'I'm afraid it never is until the investigation is concluded,' he said, offering her the platitude with a weary smile.

'Someone's not got her into any trouble have they?'

'No. I wanted to talk to her a little about the work she did with Simon Morea. We're looking into his background in considerable depth just now, and speaking to his colleagues. I know Lexie did some film work for him. I was in the area on another matter, so I thought I'd call in.'

She gave him a hard stare, not fooled. He formed the impression that she was thinking very rapidly. 'I can't help you, I'm afraid. Our Alex went away out at the crack of dawn saying she was meeting someone to look at some locations.'

'Did she say who? Or where?'

'Nope. Only that it was over Shap way, and something to do with some adventure show they're making for children's TV.'

'It's good to see she's got someone up here with her after what happened last week,' he said. 'You're her mother, that's right?'

She put her head to one side. 'I suppose it's your job to know everything. Yes. I'm taking her under my wing for a bit. I'm a proper mother hen, me. You'll know she had a tough time with some man down in London that broke her heart?'

'She told us that.'

'She had the courage to tip him out, but you don't recover from that kind of thing in five minutes, and on top of that there's all this nonsense up at Ardale. Folk need to be gentle with her,' she said, including him in that instruction.

'I don't suppose you happen to know who the man was, do you?'

Mary smiled at him, much as his mother used to do

when, as a child, he might ask her a precocious question. 'Do you think young lasses like that tell their mothers anything more than they have to? No, I don't know anything about him, except it seems he was after money from her. Not that she has any, but he maybe thought she did. She thought he loved her, of course.' She sniffed.

'But you don't know who he was?'

'Only that she always called him Nico. That was it. He could be anyone for all I know.'

'Did she know him through work?'

She shrugged. 'She knew a lot of people. She's a bit of a social butterfly, our Alex, but she's never been one for sharing her life with me. I don't ask questions and I doubt I'd approve. It's my job to look after the lass when she needs me, that's all. Shall I tell her you called?'

'Yes, if you don't mind. It's not important, though. I was just passing.'

'Is that right?' she said, and closed the door.

He stood for a second, then turned (almost tripping over a pair of walking boots crusted with red Eden Valley mud that stood on the step) and headed back down the path. Inside the cottage, Mary Ford stood squarely in the living room window, watching him; in response, he crossed the road, went up the path to his mother's cottage and round the side of the house. She was in the garden, as he'd known she'd be.

'What a pleasure!' she said. 'We don't normally see you in working hours.'

'I told your neighbour's mother I was just passing and she didn't believe me,' he said, 'so I thought I'd come in for five minutes to make a lie into the truth and scrounge a coffee while you tell me all you know about Russian airmen in Orkney.'

'Goodness me, Jude,' she said, leading the way into the

kitchen which, handily enough, looked out onto the street and Lexie's cottage, 'your mind does go down some strange rabbit holes. I'm afraid I can't tell you very much. It was something your father had a bee in his bonnet about, once, a long time ago. You know what he's like — a repository of strange facts. He'd read a book about it and insisted on telling me all about it.' Years ago, she'd listened to her husband, though Jude thought he'd never really listened to her. 'That must be twenty years ago now. I think you'd still have been living at home.'

'It's niche, though. I mean, it's not well known historical fact, wouldn't you say?'

'I'd certainly never heard of it before.' Linda flicked the kettle on.

'That's what I thought. And yet I've heard about it twice in the past week, from different sources.'

'You have an extraordinary way of thinking,' she said, spooning coffee into the cafetière. 'You're more like your father than I thought.'

He was looking out of the window pondering whether that was intended as an insult or a compliment when a sporty blue BMW with blacked-out windows crept silently along the street and pulled to a halt outside Lexie's cottage. He moved swiftly across the kitchen to the window, taking care to conceal himself behind the curtain.

'Jude,' said his mother, part amused and part exasperated. 'What on earth are you doing now?'

He raised a finger to his lips even though no-one could hear her and she, understanding, kept away from the window. The car started up again, pulled up and disappeared down the street.

He recognised it as Annabel Faulkner's. It remained out of sight for as long as it took for him to make a bet with himself about what would happen next and then, exactly as he had expected, a woman in a grey raincoat with the hood pulled up walked up the path and bent towards the letterbox.

He hadn't foreseen that the door of the cottage would spring open as she reached out. Interesting. He craned his neck to try and see what was happening. Mary Ford snatched at something the other woman had in her hand. There was a slight tussle and Mary stepped back inside with what looked like a white envelope in her hand. A few more words were spoken over the threshold before the second woman — he was sure now that it was Annabel — followed Mary into the house and closed the door behind her.

'What was that about?' asked Linda, intrigued.

'I don't know.' But he thought he did. Annabel, caught in the act of delivering something — perhaps another of those threatening messages — to Lexie. 'I think an irresistible force just met an immovable object. I might have to go and find out who wins.'

'Are you sure you know what you're doing?'

'I'm just going to have a listen. Lexie's mum's cleaning and the windows are open through the whole house.' It was surprising that Annabel hadn't spotted that as she made her approach, or maybe she was just so brazen she didn't think she'd get into any trouble if anyone interrupted her. All she'd have to do was pretend she was lost and ask the way and if Lexie had answered, perhaps she might even have welcomed the confrontation.

He slipped out at the back of the house, keeping out of the sightline of the front door and crossed the road. From Becca's garden, concealed behind a thick cotoneaster that climbed the wall and where Holmes hunted for mice and spiders in the dusk of a summer evening, he had a clear view of the back of Wasby End Cottage. The through lounge had windows front and rear and on this mild September day they were open. A smell of glass polish drifted towards him on the breeze.

'Yes,' Mary was saying, her voice high with tension. 'Of course I know you. Do you think I'm stupid just because I've no money and not much of an education? Do people like you think you can buy brains, like you think you can buy everything else?'

'Your daughter has no-one to blame but herself for the negative attention she attracts,' said Annabel, in the same cool boardroom voice she'd used in the police station on the day she'd looked Jude in the eye and lied to him. He'd known it then and here was further evidence of her dishonesty. She'd told him she knew every one of her husband's mistresses and that had been true, but she'd also told him she'd never heard of Lexie Romachenka and that, he now knew, was a highly significant lie. 'She should have kept well away from my husband.'

'Handmaidens like you always blame the woman not the man,' snapped Mary, contemptuously. 'My daughter's a good lass. She only wanted love and she believed him when he told her that was what it was.'

'She should have known that if she wanted love Simon was the last person to get that from. He didn't know the meaning of the word.'

'He loved her well enough to know he'd better keep her as his secret,' said Mary. 'Don't get me wrong. I think she was a fool and she ought to have known better than to fall for someone because of his charm and his glamour and his money. Your man's a worthless bastard, but maybe you knew that and you deserve one another.'

'Worthless bastard understates it,' said Annabel, and laughed.

'Aye. But he thought she was different, or he wouldn't

have cared about whether you knew or not instead of going through all those hoops to keep her secret. Worthless maybe, but he knew she had to be protected from the likes of you.'

'Your loyalty is charming,' said Annabel, with a tinkling social laugh, 'but he probably kept her secret because I'd given him an ultimatum and said if there were any more serious affairs he'd regret it. He'd be lucky if I killed him. Lexie Romachenka meant nothing to him. If she did he'd have taken chances for her but he never even came after her when she left.'

'Maybe he did come after her,' said Mary, her voice so low now that Jude had to strain to hear it. 'Don't you think that's why he was here? She's told me all about him and he's the kind of man who won't take no for an answer.'

Annabel snorted. 'That's certainly true.'

'That's what happened, isn't it?' Mary went on. 'I can see it. He came here. You found out. You knew he was like a stray dog let out for the night, and you followed him and killed him.'

'Your imagination does you credit, Ms Ford. You should be in the movies. That's an outrageous claim. I hated the man and I was determined to make him pay, but I'd rather have made him suffer while he was alive. I would have seen him ruined, slowly and publicly. He would have hated that more than he feared death.'

'And what about Alex?'

'Alex?'

'My daughter. Lexie. What about the letters?' A blur inside the house must be Mary, waving the white envelope she'd snatched from her unwelcome visitor. 'That's why you're here, isn't it? Sneaking around and getting revenge on her, too, when the only mistake she made was following her heart.'

'Give that back to me!'

'Shall I open it? Shall I see what it says? It's not going to be an invitation to a beetle drive, is it?'

'It's private and I accidentally approached the wrong house.'

Jude had heard enough. Leaving a few broken branches behind him he disengaged himself from the clutches of Becca's tiny shrubbery, brushed a few dead leaves and a large and agitated spider from his jacket, and strode back through the garden to Wasby End Cottage. As he'd expected, the front door, was unlocked and so he pushed on, into the living room where both Annabel and Mary, facing off like a pair of boxers at the weigh-in, turned to him in surprise.

'Good morning, Ms Faulkner, and good morning again, Ms Ford. I'm afraid I couldn't help overhearing that conversation, and in the light of it I have some questions to ask both of you.'

Mary Ford, who either had the courage of a lion or else was so foolish she didn't know fear, looked Annabel Faulkner in the face and laughed. 'You ask away. I'd love to hear the answers.'

'May I ask what you're doing here, Ms Faulkner?'

Annabel Faulkner glared at him. 'You have a caterpillar in your hair, Chief Inspector.'

'I overheard the conversation,' he went on, brushing it away. 'Since you won't answer, let me try again. From what Ms Ford has said, and from what I've heard elsewhere, I understand Lexie Romachenka has received at least one threatening message. Are you in any way responsible for that message?'

Annabel looked down. Both she and Mary seemed to have forgotten where the conversation had started. Mary still held a white envelope twisted between her fingers.

Jude held his hand out for it.

'If you're going to make baseless accusations about murder on the basis of what this person, who is clearly acting in bad faith, has to say,' said Annabel, watching as Mary handed it over, 'then you can expect to hear from my solicitor. I hope your legal team are prepared.'

'I didn't mention murder,' he observed, 'and nor has anyone from the police.'

'Of course you're talking about murder. Everyone knows you don't make this effort for every accidental death. Someone of your rank, paying attention to insignificant little Lexie Romachenka? Pull the other one. It's got bells on it.'

'When you speak to us you'll certainly be entitled to have a solicitor present,' he said, disliking her ever more.

She watched, her face a mask but for the narrowed eyes, as he slit the envelope open and pulled out a single sheet of paper with a message on it in huge type and red ink. *Just because he's dead doesn't mean you stop paying the price.*

Just as he'd thought. 'Does your daughter have the other notes?' he asked Mary.

She shook her head. 'She says she threw them away.'

Annabel laughed. 'So much for your evidence, then.'

'I think this is quite enough,' he said, turning towards the door. 'Ms Faulkner, I'm going to ask you to come with me. We have some very interesting matters to discuss.'

TWENTY-SIX

'You are being interviewed under caution,' said Ashleigh, once she'd read out all the requisite details and the recording device in the centre of the table was flashing away, 'in relation to the murders of your husband, Simon Nicholas Morea, and of Gerald Cole. Furthermore, you are being questioned in relation to malicious communications delivered by hand to Ms Lexie Romachenka, also known as Alex Ford.'

'I've advised my client to say nothing.' The duty solicitor, who was presumably doing the job until Annabel's extremely expensive lawyer could make it up from London, was a young woman who Ashleigh had occasionally come across before. Normally she was cool and competent but today she looked positively terrified of her client and eager for the whole thing to be over.

Understandable. Annabel might not be the most threatening or dangerous suspect Ashleigh had ever interviewed but there were few who had presented themselves in so forbidding a manner. The interview promised to be hard going.

'I'll decide what I answer and what I don't, if you don't mind.' Annabel scowled at her, then whipped round to turn on Ashleigh. 'Fire away, then, sergeant. You know what they say. Nothing to hide, nothing to fear. Or is it the other way round?'

With a few more seconds' thought, Ashleigh concluded that Annabel's fierceness was, after all, largely bluster. In consequence she was less inclined than the solicitor to take notice of it. 'First of all, I'd like to talk to you about your husband.'

'Yes, of course you would, because you want me to confess to killing him and do your job for you.'

'Ms Faulkner!' said the solicitor, in a panic.

'I've always been honest with you,' said Annabel, ignoring her. 'I came to hate Simon but I never wanted him dead. It was much more fun watching him squirm when he was alive and when the divorce went through it would have been a whole lot more fun to watch him realise that he was only ever a success because of my money and without it he would have been a nobody. So yes, I hated him. But I didn't kill him.'

'You knew he had a heart condition?'

'Of course. It was why I wasn't at all surprised to hear a heart attack had taken him off. But we've been through all this before. I've given you information on my whereabouts at every time you've asked me about it.'

She had done that, and her movements had been verified. Without a doubt Annabel had been in London for the whole of the period in which Simon Morea must have died, and had not arrived in Cumbria until just before she'd reported him missing. It didn't rule out someone else doing her bidding, but that was something that had to be proved independently. If Jude thought it worthwhile they could seize and search her phone and laptops, find out to whom she had spoken, begin to unpick what might prove to be a dense web of deceit. If Annabel had paid someone to remove her husband she'd have done her very best to conceal it, but they could try.

'Let me bring you back to the reason why we've asked you to come here today, Ms Faulkner. When DCI Satterthwaite went to break the news of your husband's death, you told him you knew everything about your husband's infidelities and every detail about his sexual partners. In that same conversation, he mentioned Lexie Romachenka in the context of the discovery of the body, and asked you if you knew her. You said you did not.' She'd brought a copy of the notes that Jude had jotted down after that informal meeting and at this point she placed it on the table in front of her, but Annabel never gave it a glance. 'This morning, in Wasby End Cottage, Wasby, DCI Satterthwaite overheard you telling Mary Ford, who is Lexie Romachenka's mother, that Lexie was having an affair with your husband, and that you knew all about it, and had known all along. Which directly contradicts of what you said earlier.'

'Maybe I was lying to the Ford woman.'

'While delivering a threatening and anonymous message to Lexie Romachenka's cottage?'

At this point, Annabel managed a wry smile. 'It's interesting the Romachenka girl didn't tell you about the affair, then.'

'Neither did you,' Ashleigh reminded her.

'You never asked.'

Ashleigh moved on. 'In the light of this morning's events, can you confirm that you did in fact know that your husband was having an affair with Lexie?'

'Yes,' said Annabel and her eyes narrowed into that characteristic, calculating glare.

'And as far as you're aware this was the one affair he tried to hide from you?'

'Yes.'

'Why?'

Annabel shrugged. 'It was always difficult to know what Simon thought.'

'Was it because he was serious about the relationship and might seek to pursue it? And were you, perhaps, concerned that if that happened he'd leave you before you had the chance to leave him?'

'Ms Faulkner,' said the solicitor, warningly. 'May I remind you again. You don't have to answer any of these questions.'

'As I say,' said Annabel, ignoring her, 'I don't know what went on in Simon's head but I do know what drove him. There were two things. The first was his libido. He couldn't resist a pretty girl and when they threw themselves at him, which they did, because he had a rare animal charm and the cachet of celebrity to go with it, he took it as his right. I knew that when I married him, and when I did marry him it was because of that charm. Yes, even I fell for it. But I learned my lesson very quickly. And before you ask, the reason he married me rather than any of the others, and the reason he didn't dare to leave me, is that I am very, very rich. Richer than any of them.' She sat back, hands flat on the table, and a look of triumph on her face, as if money could buy everything. 'That's the other thing. That's the only thing stronger than sex for Simon. Greed.'

'You invested heavily in his film career, didn't you?'

'I did. Early on, when I loved him, I was happy to do so unconditionally, but once the gloss came off our marriage Simon and I found ourselves locked in a power struggle. We're both very proud and neither of us could bear not to be in control. But film is a difficult business and most films fail to make money. Simon's career was critically successful but without my money he'd have sunk without trace because his work never had any popular appeal and never made any profit. He had one film that made it into cinemas and that one didn't last long. Without my investment it would never have been made. He was dependent on me for my money and that was the reason we stayed married. He needed the money and I needed the power.'

'When you reported him missing you told us you were seeking a divorce.'

'When my lawyer arrives from London,' said Annabel with a withering glance at the duty solicitor, 'she'll be able to confirm that I'd spoken to her about the possibility of divorce and how likely the prenuptial agreement was to stand up in the divorce courts. She's of the opinion that it was robust.'

'You were tired of fighting your husband over money, then,' said Ashleigh.

'I never got tired of that, but in my opinion he was thinking of making a permanent relationship — as far as any of his relationships were permanent — with Romachenka and there was a reason for that. Money, again.'

Ashleigh spared Lexie Romachenka a thought. She showed all the signs of being one of those people who chase after the high life rather than riding on its crest. The cottage in Wasby wasn't over-luxurious and Lexie's clothes, though neat and trendy, were not expensive. Her flat in London was small and in an unfashionable part of Clapham. Her job was unlikely to have much security and would not, as far as Ashleigh was aware, bring in a huge amount of money. Her background was anything but wealthy. 'Go on.'

Annabel smiled at her. 'Is this something else you didn't

know? Dear me, Sergeant. You do seem to have slipped up. Of course, when I found out Simon was having an affair and it seemed serious I made it my business to find out why. I learned from an associate, who did some discreet digging for me, that the woman's great-grandfather set up a family trust for his descendants. The trust is due to be wound up at some time in the near future and the money would come to Lexie. Anecdotally, from those who have spoken to the Romachenka girl, I believe there's a substantial amount, though I haven't been able to identify precisely how much. Simon, of course, would see that as an excellent opportunity not only to spite me but also to maintain his financial stream. The price would have been tying himself to a dull little woman like Lexie Romachenka, but that need only be until she'd served her purpose and financed the film that was going to make his fortune.' She paused. 'That was always the next film, of course.' A nasty little smile. 'Simon's talents fell well short of his assessment of them.'

'Let me take you back to this morning,' said Ashleigh as Annabel paused. 'Why did you come to Lexie Romachenka's address with a threatening note?'

Now, at last, Annabel lost some of her confidence. And why not? She'd been caught red-handed. 'My solicitor has advised me not to comment.'

Beside them, the duty solicitor failed to hide her sigh.

'Had you been at the property before?' asked Ashleigh.

'No comment.' Annabel's eyes narrowed.

'I suggest to you went to the property today to deliver a threatening letter and also intending to threaten Lexie Romachenka,' said Ashleigh. 'Is that correct?'

'No comment.'

To all intents and purposes, Ashleigh recognised, anything further was time wasted. The solicitor was looking relieved because Annabel had finally taken her advice and Annabel herself, having said her piece about her husband and his lover, was now sitting back with arms folded and showed every sign of maintaining her sudden reticence. There was nothing to do but go through the formality of asking questions that would not be answered, to bring the interview to a close and release Annabel pending further inquiries.

TWENTY-SEVEN

'You made it,' said Jude as Ashleigh came into the canteen and joined him as he was finishing his lunch. 'Get yourself something to eat and tell me what you made of Annabel.'

Ashleigh glanced at her watch. 'Do I have time?'

They had a team meeting scheduled for two o'clock. Jude hadn't forgotten it, but the morning had run away from him and it was later than he'd expected. 'Grab something and take it up with you. I don't see why you should have to go hungry just because you drew the short straw and had to spend the morning with Annabel.' He swept the dry curls of ham that were all that was left of his sandwich into the cardboard packet and stood up. 'Get your lunch. I'll clear this away and we can head up together.'

'Okay,' she said, when she'd acquired sandwich, flapjack and coffee and caught up with him at the door. 'You want to hear about Annabel. I don't like her. I know we're supposed to be neutral and objective, but I don't think I've ever met someone quite as hard as that and I've met a few. She's playing with us.'

He'd thought that from the beginning, but he also thought that was her weakness. By holding the police in contempt she underestimated them. She wouldn't be the first to make that mistake.

'She didn't roll over and tell us everything, then,' he said with a wry smile. 'I didn't think she would. *No comment* all the way through?'

'No, not at all. I mean, not until we got to the questions about what she was doing at Lexie's cottage with a threatening note, consistent with other threatening notes that Lexie told her mother about. Then she clammed up completely.'

'Rather than just admit it when she was caught red-handed? She really does think we're stupid.'

'I wish Lexie had kept the other two notes,' said Ashleigh, fretfully.

'Yes. From what her mother said, they would have made the basis for a charge of harassment if nothing else. Annabel may not have intended to harm Lexie physically but she certainly wanted to put the fear of God into her.'

'And didn't mind risking being seen with her,' pointed out Ashleigh, as he held the door of the incident room open for her. 'Driving about in a car that's even flashier and more recognisable than yours, and coming up to the door in broad daylight. She'd probably have been delighted if Lexie had seen her. She'd reckon on her being too scared to say anything and she'll have been punishing her for her temerity in having an affair with the husband she didn't even care about any more.'

'Fascinating psychology.' They sat down at the table beneath the whiteboard and Chris Marshall, on the other side of the room, looked up, saw them and disengaged himself from whatever he'd been doing to make his way across to join them. While they waited Jude scanned the whiteboard where Chris had pinned up a selection of photos, maps, notes and other paraphernalia that might aid them in their thinking. The photograph of Annabel Faulkner was a studio portrait, taken from her company website, and she had obviously taken care to present herself in that, as she did in life, as a woman not to be messed with.

'What did she say that made you dislike her so much?' he asked. He'd also disliked Annabel intensely, but that had been because of the way she'd challenged him. Ashleigh's reasons might be both different and more perceptive.

'She makes such a big play of being honest,' she said with a sigh. 'Don't get me wrong. I like honesty but Annabel weaponises it and that's not good.'

'That's an excellent way of putting it.' He shook his head over Annabel, how she'd claimed to be afraid of her husband when she must have been planning a campaign of harassment against Lexie, and had probably already started it. He didn't imagine the notes that had come to her in Wasby were the first she'd sent. Maybe Lexie had received others in London, or Morea's other women had had similar notes before them.

'Doddsy's running a bit late,' said Chris, pulling up a chair. 'He did say he thought it would be worth the wait.'

Jude nodded. Faye had promised to chase up the tech people and the results would have come to Doddsy. It would be interesting to see if they'd been able to unlock Morea's phone. 'Ashleigh's just giving me an account of her interview with Annabel.'

'Rather you than me,' said Chris to Ashleigh with a grin, 'from what I hear.'

'She was quite happy to talk to me about Simon,' said Ashleigh, through a mouthful of sandwich. 'And happy to give us plenty of motivation for her having killed him.'

'Because she knows we know she can't have done it,' said Chris.

He was right. You had to be cleverer than people like that. Annabel was one of those who laughed in your face, who might all but admit to a crime and be confident that her involvement would never be proved.

'Yes. And by God, that interview will give me sleepless nights. I almost feel sorry for Morea, having been married to her. She's a complete control freak and there's a strong streak of sadism through it as well. She literally said she didn't want him dead because she had much more power over him when he was alive.'

Jude considered. Annabel, with her immense wealth and her boardroom brass neck, was an attractive and easy option as a murderer. You could pretend to be as honest as the day and that honesty itself might be a lie. 'And yet, like Macavity, when you reach the scene of crime she's not there. Provably. But I still can't get away from her as a possibility. She hated him.'

'But she didn't actually fire the shot,' insisted Chris.

'I know. We can get CCTV reviewed,' said Jude, thinking as always about the next steps. 'She wasn't afraid of showing up at Wasby in that fancy BMW so we may be able to trace her back to Lexie's cottage at other times, too. When it comes to Morea's murder it's obviously a little trickier, but I think we have enough of a case to look a little more closely at her. I'd really like to have a look at the messages between her and her husband and see what kind of threats and abuse they engaged in with one another. Those will be on the phone he left at the house. I'd also like to get a look at her phone and see if there's any kind of exchange with someone who either might have done the job for her or might arrange for it to be done on her behalf.' That meant getting Faye to authorise the seizure of

Annabel's phone, and by that time Simon Morea's triumphant widow would surely have deleted anything incriminating, if she'd committed it to a message at all.

'Exactly. The most powerful argument for her having him killed is that she was about to lose her power over him. She thought he was going to leave her for Lexie. Who, according to her, is in line to inherit a large amount of money from a family trust, which would considerably reduce Annabel's financial leverage and, in consequence, the power she could exert over him.'

'I never came across anything about a trust when I ran background checks,' Chris observed, 'but if she doesn't actually have the money that's not surprising. I'll have a look and see if I can find out more, and how much it is.'

'It'll be very interesting.' It seemed that he and Ashleigh had been on the right track in what they'd discussed on Friday night. 'Ash and I watched a film of his, and it included this bit about Russians in Orkney, and there was a reference to a trust in that. I was thinking about it on the way in to work this morning. I'm no film critic but it seemed really clumsy, like it was a plot twist shoehorned in for no reason. Now I think I know. I bet it was a sign to his wife that he didn't need her any more. She'd have understood it. Lexie might or might not; she might have interpreted it as an indication of how much he cared for her, a shared secret. But it was there.'

'I know we're talking about Annabel,' said Ashleigh to Chris. 'But it's worth remembering Lexie also lied to us. This Nico she's supposed to have had an affair with is Simon Morea.'

'She's mighty foolish if she thought we wouldn't find out at some point.' Chris had looked at Lexie's movements earlier and she, like Annabel, had been well away from Cumbria at the time when it was most likely that Simon had died, but she'd been in Yorkshire, not in London. It wouldn't have been impossible for her to have slipped away to the Eden Valley.

'She ended it,' said Jude. 'That's interesting. Maybe she realised he was only interested in her money. It isn't beyond the realms of possibility that he came after her and she killed him purely to get rid of him, because he does strike me as a thoroughly unpleasant specimen who won't take no for an answer.'

'And Gerry?' asked Chris. 'I can't bring myself to care about Morea, but Gerry seems like a decent man and he didn't deserve what happened to him.'

'I think that's pretty simple. Whichever woman killed him knew, or suspected, that he'd seen them. Knew he was a regular in the pub. Knew where he lived. Followed him home and took a chance.' Proving it would be the problem, but Jude wasn't about to let the death of a decent but relatively obscure countryman be overshadowed by that of a celebrity. 'If it hadn't happened on Wednesday it would have been Thursday or Friday or whenever the opportunity arose.' Or, if the chance of disposing of Gerry so cleanly hadn't occurred they might have resorted to a riskier way of removing him.

Ashleigh finished the last of her sandwich and crushed the empty packet into something approximating a square. 'Finding who killed Simon is a start. We can work back from there.'

The door opened and Doddsy shouldered his way in. 'I'm sorry I'm late, but I've got some gold for you.' He pulled up a chair.

'Is it the transcripts from Morea's phone? Are they useful?'

'It is, and they certainly are.' Doddsy shuffled about in the folder he'd brought with him and brought out a thick sheaf of paper. 'There's a lot in here and I only had time to run through it in the most cursory manner. They'll tell us a lot more when we've had some time to go back and see all the details, but I focussed on the bit that's most important to us, the hours immediately before he died.'

'Don't tell me. Annabel arranged to meet him up there?' Jude leaned forward. 'That's my gut feeling at the moment. She's pretending too hard to be honest. She has to be bluffing.'

'Your gut feeling has it completely wrong for once,' said Doddsy. He sat back and rubbed his chin. 'I'm bound to say I'm leaning towards Annabel too, and it may yet be her who did it. But it wasn't her who contacted him and proposed they meet up at the lime kilns at Ardale Beck. It was Lexie.'

Was this, after all, a surprise? Lexie was the one who had most to fear from him, the one who'd tried to get away. 'Those messages must be on her phone, too, unless she's deleted them. She must have known we'd look for them.' Or maybe she really was so naive that she didn't realise they could be traced.

'No, she's not that simple. She did think that through. They'd been messaging each other on this phone throughout their relationship, which makes interesting if slightly cringeworthy reading, if you've time, and I suppose someone will have to go through them in detail. He was very keen to keep the affair a secret. That's very clear. There's a lot of to-ing and fro-ing and him cancelling at the last minute because there's *too much risk*, and plenty of apologies for him being out with other women but claiming that's what he had to do to keep up the front.'

'Every trick in the book,' said Ashleigh, with contempt, and Jude guessed from the accompanying scowl that she was thinking of Scott and his endless excuses for finding himself in the company of other women.

'It didn't work. Lexie seems to have been made of sterner stuff than he expected. She dumped him. She seems to have been brave enough to do it face to face, too, and the messages that come immediately after it show he didn't take it well.'

'If Annabel is right and Lexie's due to come into a lot of money,' said Ashleigh, 'I wonder if she's smart enough to realise that might be why he was so keen not to let her go.'

'That would make sense. He never mentions money but she makes a couple of oblique references to him wanting to pursue the relationship for all the wrong reasons. I didn't know about the trust so I assumed he's just one of those men who can't stand being dumped by a woman and who just wanted to rekindle the relationship so he could end it on his own terms.'

'I wouldn't be surprised if there was a bit of that in there, too, by all accounts,' said Jude. 'And remember, Lexie's mother told Annabel that Morea was only interested in the money, though that might be an assumption rather than something she knew for certain. Either way, Lexie dumped him and he wasn't having it. Were the messages aggressive?'

'His to her were, and threatening. She told him she was leaving town for a bit, going back to Yorkshire. As far as we know she was there for a couple of weeks before coming up here. This is where it gets interesting. He kept insisting she come back to London. She refused and told him never to contact her again. Then she messaged him a week later, out of the blue, and told him she was at home with her mother and she'd caught her mother checking her phone, so she'd bought another and had a new number.'

There were burner phones all over the place. How many had Simon thought he needed? One for each affair? Now it seemed that Lexie, confronted by her mother's curiosity, had been just as underhand. 'She couldn't just change the passcode? That makes me feel like she's setting him up and keeping herself in the clear.' It was a safe bet that Lexie's new phone would have met with an accident somewhere and would never been seen again. 'Smart.'

'She probably learned that trick from him. She finally agreed to see him, but she refused to come to London. She suggested meeting in Cumbria and he agreed and proposed Ardale Beck. They were messaging one another as he travelled up, they messaged when he arrived. He messaged her to let her know he'd arrived at Blencarn and would be with her in about forty-five minutes. That's the last message on his phone and on the basis of that I think we can fix the time of his death to within an hour or so, consistent with the PM, to around noon a week past on Saturday.'

'It's not looking good for Lexie, then,' said Ashleigh, thoughtfully. 'On paper, anyway.'

'You have doubts?' Jude asked. 'If these messages are genuine it looks pretty cut and dried to me.'

'I know, but I thought, and I still think, that of the two women Annabel is by far the more likely murderer. She has a really hard, calculating feel to her. And this,' she indicated the transcripts which Doddsy had printed off, 'feels a bit off to me. How do these latest ones fit in with the earlier style of her messages, Doddsy?'

He rubbed his chin. 'You'd need to do a proper contextual analysis of it, I think, but yes, now you mention it there was a change of tone. She went from being a woman who claimed she just wanted to be left alone to someone who approached him and was only prepared to negotiate with him on her terms. Which sounds much more like Annabel than Lexie.'

Lexie had struck Jude very much as a woman trying to wrest control of her life back from others. Ashleigh was right and she didn't have the bearing of someone who sought revenge. 'Those messages are pretty damning. She wasn't in Cumbria at the time but she could easily have come across from Yorkshire.'

'And Gerry? We know for certain she spoke to him. We don't know everything he may have said and we don't know what he may have seen, but it won't have been that difficult for her to creep up from Wasby at night and take a shove at him as he walked home drunk.'

'Okay,' said Jude, his mind going. 'I think it's time to get a warrant for Wasby End Cottage, and after that I shall be very interested to have another word with Lexie.'

TWENTY-EIGHT

Jude was about to deal with a warrant for both Lexie's and Annabel's devices when the incident room phone shrilled in the background. He looked across as Chris swooped to answer it. Too often, when that phone rang in the middle of an inquiry, it was a precursor to bad news so it was no surprise to him when Chris's expression sharpened.

He turned back, just as Chris stood up and waved him across, snapping the phone on mute. 'Jude, that's Mary Ford. Lexie's mother. She says Lexie's gone missing. You'd better speak to her.'

He was across the room in three steps, seizing the phone. 'Ms Ford? It's Jude Satterthwaite here. Can I help you?'

'Yes. It's Alex. She's missing.'

Damn, damn, damn. 'Okay, Ms Ford. Let's take this step by step.' He sat down, and reached for a pen and a pad. 'First of all, when did you last see your daughter?'

'She went out this morning,' said Mary, in a businesslike fashion. She was, he sensed, a woman who didn't mess about. 'She said she was going into Penrith for some groceries and wouldn't be long. Then she messaged me to say she'd bumped into someone she knew and she was going for coffee.'

'Okay. When I asked you about Lexie's whereabouts this morning, you told me she'd gone out working and would be gone all day.'

'It wasn't true.'

It wasn't the time to ask why. Mary Ford's maternal instinct would certainly extend to protecting her daughter from the attentions of the police, especially if she nurtured the slightest suspicion that Lexie might be guilty of murder, or indeed of anything else. Later he would remind her, very firmly, of her responsibilities and of the ramifications of lying to the police. 'What time did she leave this morning?'

'About ten minutes before you arrived.'

He glanced at the clock. Quarter to three. In the great scheme of things Lexie hadn't been away for long and she, like Simon Morea when Annabel had reported him missing, wasn't a vulnerable person, but this time he took it much more seriously. If she knew, or suspected that she was about to be called in for questioning over her lover's death she might easily have done a runner or, if she had spotted Annabel in the village, she might have panicked. A murderer on the run or another victim; neither outcome was good. 'I need you to be totally truthful with me right now. Did you tell Lexie what happened in Wasby this morning?'

'I messaged her after you'd left, told her that woman, Faulkner, was the one who'd been sending the threatening notes and that she had nothing to worry about. I told her you'd taken her in for questioning and that everything would be all right.'

'She replied?'

'She said *yay! That's great! What a relief. Will bring something nice for lunch so we can celebrate.* All text speak of course. Young people are like that. That was about ten o'clock and I haven't heard from her since.'

'Okay, Ms Ford. We'll get a couple of cars out to look for her. Do you have any idea where she might have gone? Could she have planned to leave, perhaps go into hiding for some reason?'

'Why would she hide?' Mary sounded perplexed. 'She's not taken her clothes or anything. I looked in her room.' Then, in a different tone, she said: 'And there is one thing.'

It was too much to hope that Mary had remembered something that would render the whole thing irrelevant. Jude doodled a big black question mark on the pad. 'Yes?'

'That woman next door.'

'Becca Reid?' said Jude, and saw Ashleigh, who had drifted over to listen, raise an eyebrow.

'Yes, that's her. I heard her and Lexie talking yesterday and she said something about a man.'

'What do you mean?'

'A man friend,' said Mary with a degree of impatience. 'I thought at first it was herself she was talking about, but now I wonder if it wasn't.'

If Becca had found herself a man, Jude would have known about it, if only because Adam would have taken great pleasure in telling him. 'Did you have any reason to think your daughter might have been seeing someone?'

'Not especially, but it wouldn't be a surprise. Men come to our Alex like flies to a jam pot. It's not her fault, but it goes to her head and she can't resist the compliments, when in fact a man is the last thing she needs. But she didn't say owt to me about it and I didn't ask.'

Jude's concerns abated. 'Does she usually tell you about her relationships?'

'Oh yes, all of them, but never until the bomb drops, you know? If she told me about them before there wouldn't be any problem because I'd damn well be telling her how to handle things so she doesn't get damaged by it. But she has a soft heart. She keeps mum and I pick up the pieces when it all falls apart.'

It was immediately obvious to Jude why Lexie might not want to tell her mother about her potential partners. It was one thing to make mistakes, but at least they were your own. 'Okay. Then it seems to me this might be the person she bumped into. Perhaps they've gone for a long lunch or a walk and she's changed her plans.'

'And not told me?'

'Would she normally tell you?'

'Not where she's going or who she's with.'

'Okay. Thanks, Ms Ford. It sounds to me as though Lexie — Alex — may just have gone off with a friend and I expect she'll turn up when she's ready. There are plenty of places around here, and especially around Wasby, where the phone signal is poor or inconsistent. I'd be grateful if one or the other of you could let me know as soon as that happens.' He reeled off his work number so that he didn't miss the call. 'And in the meantime we'll make sure we keep an eye out for her.'

He hung up, drumming his fingers on the table. 'For a moment there I thought history might be repeating itself, but it does sound as though Lexie might not be missing at all, but has gone into Penrith and found something better to do. Coffee stretching into lunch or the like. Mary strikes me as a helicopter mother and it might be quite suffocating to spend too much time with her.'

'In fairness, I can't really blame Lexie for keeping

secrets,' said Ashleigh. 'So do we think this is her new man friend, then? The one you met. Hugh Cameron?'

'I didn't exactly meet him. He introduced himself but he never took his eyes off Lexie the whole time. So yes, I'm pretty certain that's who it must be.'

But the context was difficult. Sam Benton had been certain about Hugh Cameron's good nature but there was still too close a connection to the murdered Simon Morea for Jude to be comfortable about it. 'I'd rather not take the chance that Lexie has faded quietly away in the background and won't reappear until she pops up somewhere we can't reach her.' Especially not after that incendiary discovery of the messages on Simon Morea's phone.

'Or been murdered,' said Ashleigh, bleakly.

That was the worst option. 'I'd like to talk to her sooner rather than later. It might be worth trying to track down Hugh Cameron and see if he knows anything. I didn't get as far as details with him, so I know almost nothing about him except that he has a farm somewhere round here, but more than that I don't know.' That irked him. He prided himself on his local knowledge. Even Sam had been vague on the details.

'Would Becca know how to get hold of him?'

'She might.'

'You'd better call her,' said Ashleigh, watching him carefully. 'If you're that concerned.'

Was he? He thought he might be. Knowing that there was a boyfriend on the scene made Lexie's disappearance less mysterious; it seemed entirely natural that she might want to pursue the early stages of a relationship without introducing a potential partner to a probably-hostile mother. Hugh's potential grudge against Morea, however, made it complicated. There was now somebody in her life who might be prepared to help her out in whatever she was planning to do next. If, as seemed likely, Lexie was somehow involved in Morea's death it was possible she'd pulled the trigger herself, but an unknown accomplice made the murder of Gerry Cole highly plausible. A man as ordinary as Hugh Cameron had seemed, a man who faded into the background, might easily have been overlooked in the pub in Ousby, sneaking out unnoticed once he'd identified his quarry. 'It won't do any harm. The sooner we speak to Lexie the better.'

Acutely and irrationally conscious that Ashleigh was listening in, he reached for his phone and dialled Becca's number, half-hoping she wouldn't answer, but she picked up immediately. 'Jude. You just caught me. I'm having a cuppa between appointments. Is everything okay?'

'Yes, all fine. I won't keep you. I just wondered. Apparently you were talking to Lexie about a boyfriend. Lexie's friend. Hugh Cameron.'

'I certainly wasn't talking about a boyfriend of mine,' she said crisply. 'Don't tell me you're hunting Hugh for a murder, because I won't believe that. There's not enough to him. What you see is what you get with Hugh. But I only met him a couple of times, back in the day. You know?'

He did know, and allowed himself a wry smile. 'You can't deny Adam has the knack of picking dodgy friends.'

'Not always. We were both friends of his, once, and neither of us is dodgy. Hugh's all right. Not awfully bright, but very nice. I hate to say it but I found him tweedy and dull. Sorry if that sounds judgemental. But actually I think he might be quite good for her. I don't want to sound like her mother but she's had more than enough of the glamorous, exciting type.'

Becca was a pretty good judge of character. He smiled.

'I don't suppose you happen to know where we can get hold of him?'

'I don't have a contact. Adam would know,' she said, and checked herself. 'You won't want to call him, obviously. Okay. I do know Hugh has a farm down this side of Shap, not too far from here, actually. High Rigg Farm, I think it's called. Does that help?'

'Thanks, that's really helpful.' He hung up and turned to Ashleigh. 'Fancy a quick run down to Shap? If Lexie's there I'll be asking her to come back with us to help with enquiries and if she isn't, we might have to go looking for her.'

'You'd better not let Faye see you going on a jolly.' Doddsy, too, had drifted across to listen in. 'Though it'll be interesting to see what you come up with, given they both have a connection to our man Morea.'

'I'm certainly very keen to talk to her,' he said, checked his watch and, with a rising sense of anxiety, headed towards the door with Ashleigh following him. In the corridor his phone rang.

'Mikey,' he said, trying to hide his irritation as he answered. 'Is it important? I'm busy.'

'I should hope so. I pay your wages through my taxes, so don't you forget who your boss is,' retorted Mikey. 'As always, I'm calling with something relevant. Something just happened that made me raise my eyebrows. I'm working from home this afternoon, and given what Mum told me about the stooshie over the road this morning and you charging in and arresting some complete stranger, I thought you might want to know what's happening. Lexie's mum just called in here.'

'Right?'

'Yes, and gave me the third degree on some man she's convinced has got his claws into Lexie.'

'And naturally you knew all about it.' Mikey absorbed knowledge the way the moss in the bog above Ardale Beck absorbed water.

'Yes. I wouldn't normally have told her anything. It's none of her business, and I like Lexie, but she was so wound up I thought I'd better reassure her. It's only Hugh Cameron from High Rigg and he wouldn't hurt a fly.'

'What did she say?'

'Went off with a face like thunder,' said Mikey with a degree of relish. 'Five minutes later she jumped into her car and took off like Lewis Hamilton on a mercy mission. And from the look on her face I wouldn't want to be wherever she's going when she gets there.'

TWENTY-NINE

Lexie was losing her heart — and her head — yet again, but this time it was different. This time what she felt wasn't the heady excitement of lust at first sight, fuelled by excitement and adrenalin and attention; it was a flame much slower to take hold but one that was already consuming her. That she had ever considered trying to seduce Hugh made her cheeks flame with embarrassment; he wasn't like anyone else she'd ever met. He was slow and smiling and thoughtful and dull — or at least, that was how he'd seemed when she'd first set eyes on him — but she'd very soon realised that this wasn't all. Was this what love was, when you saw someone in a way that no-one else did, saw a truth that was visible to your eyes only? And did he, in return, see something of value in her when other people dismissed her as dross?

Alex Ford, reinvented as Lexie Romachenka, mover at the fringes of other people's exoticism, was suddenly consumed by the need for something authentic and wholesome in a way she'd never been before. There had been no words spoken when she'd turned round in the groceries aisle at the supermarket to find Hugh coming round the corner. They had stopped and stood and stared and smiled. Then she'd said *You?* as if it was a film and he'd said *You said you were going to the supermarket and I thought I'd take a chance*.

In fact, for all it felt big and exciting, this moment of drama was a little more scripted than it might have looked. She'd texted him to say she was going shopping and suggested they should meet for coffee, and he had replied that he would come in to town and message her when he got there, so their meeting was rather more prosaic than her heart would have liked. Nevertheless, she couldn't help thinking that when other men claimed to take chances for her the stakes were much less wholesome. As happened when people were in love coffee had overflowed into lunch, during which he had told her all about his farm; she had said *I'd love to see it sometime* and then he had said *why not just come down now?* And so, here she was, jumping in and out of his battered Land Rover to tramp around fields of sheep and cows in a pair of borrowed wellies several sizes too big.

'This is just fabulous,' she said, when they'd completed their tour of the further reaches of the farm and returned to the yard. 'I don't know what I expected, but it wasn't this. It's so wild. So beautiful. And the views!'

'It's not that big. Just 300 acres, all of it moorland. Mainly sheep.'

'And you work it all by yourself?' she asked, tucking her small hand into his big one.

'I get in casual help when I need it, for lambing mainly. My dad still lives in the village and comes up if I'm really desperate, though he's well over eighty now and a bit frail, so he's not much more than another pair of eyes and good advice. It makes him feel useful, though, so I keep on asking him.'

What a kind man. 'I'm so glad you get on with him,' she said, thinking of her own fraught relationship with her mother and how wonderful it would have been to have a father who cared enough to be involved.

'I'm not sure he'd say that,' he said, shrugging it off.

She sensed he and his father had a strained relationship, in a very different way from the difficult one she had with her mother, but she didn't want to press him on it. 'I'd like to meet him.'

'I'd love you to, and I think he'd like you. But right now there's something much more important. We're coming to the highlight of your tour. Over here.'

She followed him across the yard where, in a field next to the steading, a cow raised its long head, looked at them and immediately came lumbering towards them. 'Is this Buttercup?'

'It is. Buttercup,' he said to the animal as it came to a stop by the gate, 'there's someone very special I want you to meet. This is Lexie. Be kind to her, she's special. Lexie, this is Buttercup.'

'Good afternoon, Buttercup,' said Lexie, seriously. 'How very nice to meet you.' She began to reach out a hand. 'Can I pat her?'

'Yes. I wouldn't try it with some of the others but Buttercup's as tame as they come.' He opened the gate to the field and led the way in.

Feeling like a proper farmer, Lexie patted Buttercup on the nose while the animal looked at her inquisitively with its huge brown eyes. London seemed a long way away. In London she might have squealed in fake fear at any sudden movement from so big a beast until someone offered her a protective arm, but here she didn't do that. She didn't need to. Hugh was right beside her. 'I think I like your other woman, Hugh. It's so nice to find a cow who isn't jealous.'

'I think there's only one woman for me,' he said, and leaned down to kiss her.

It had been a long time coming, but it was worth it, there in that muddy gateway under Buttercup's brown gaze. 'Better stop, Hugh. We'll embarrass her.'

He laughed and took her hand. 'Let's get back in to the house and I'll show you round in there while the kettle's boiling.'

'Thank you so much for inviting me down here.' She took a sidelong glance. His hair needed cut and if he'd shaved that morning he'd made an untidy job of it. There was mud on his cheek and on the elbow of his wax jacket and the sweet and sour smell of the farm hung around him. She sniffed. It wasn't unpleasant. She probably stank of muck herself, and her mother would have something to say about it when she got home.

Her mother. Oh God. Her mouth dropped open.

'Everything okay?' he asked. He must have been watching her as closely as she had been watching him.

'Oh, nothing. I just remembered I've still got my shopping in the car and it probably ought to go in the fridge.'

'You can put it in my fridge until you're ready to go, if you want. I thought you might want to stay for supper.'

How she'd love to. But her mother. Oh God. 'Look, Hugh, we need to talk.'

The disappointment that clouded his face hurt her in a way she hadn't expected. He'd be expecting the worst. He'd be expecting her to tell him he was too old for her, that the farm was lovely but that she was too young and too metropolitan to live out in the sticks, that she was bored with the quiet of the countryside and was intending to take the next train south. In fact it was so much more prosaic than that. She had to speak to him and level things up between them before her mother found out about him.

Mary would be going spare and would get the story out of her within minutes of Lexie's return to Wasby. 'I think I need to tell you what I'm like.' She corrected herself. 'What I used to be like. You told me all about you and I should have said then.'

'Shall we go into the kitchen?'

'Actually I like it out here.' That way, when she'd shattered his illusions she'd be spared the awkwardness of an exit; she could just get into her car and drive away with tears streaming down her face, leaving a solitary figure, ever-diminishing in her rear view mirror. 'I forgot to call my mum and tell her I was coming. I really care for you. I know it's only been a week.' *But I already love you more than I've loved any other man.* 'I've been thinking about this a lot since I came to Cumbria.' That affair with Nico had been one that had forced her into a lot of self-reflection and it had been a harsh and a sobering experience. 'I realise now that I've been pretending to be someone I'm not.'

'A lot of people do that,' he said. 'You're still young. I spent part of my youth trying to make other people like me by being something I wasn't, and it only turned me into a bully.'

'You aren't that. That was decades ago, not the real you. And it wasn't your fault.' Like everything toxic in her life it had been Nico's doing. 'I like you.' *I love you.*

'It's thanks to you that I realised how much I like being me. I don't mind if other people think I'm boring. I'm just me.' The look he gave her was a plea. *I am what I am. Don't go.*

'Right?' She was grateful he'd taken it so easily. 'But it's hard when everyone around you is glamorous and exciting and rich, and when they talk about yachts in Monte Carlo and the goodie bags they got at the Oscars and how the only reason you didn't see any pictures of them on the red carpet is that they were wearing the same dress as Halle Berry. And you know they're lying, or at least exaggerating, but you get sucked into it. And if everyone around you is pretending, it's natural for you to pretend, too. So I invented a new me and that's what I've shown you.'

'A completely new you?'

'No. But I took the only things about me that were exciting and made something of them. I changed my name. I told everyone my Russian great-grandfather was a prince when he was only a peasant. I told them I was brought up on a small estate in rural Yorkshire, not a council estate in Huddersfield. Everybody loved the stories. They made me so interesting.' *Ooh, Lexie Romachenka with those gorgeous Slavic looks.* 'But I made myself very unhappy.'

'I could tell that.'

Her mother had said that, too. *Anyone looking at you will see how pale you are, Alex. Anyone can see you're unhappy.* It would be nice if she could get Mary out of her head for a while. 'I got myself into a real pickle. That's how I ended up in that awful thing with Simon.'

'The Simon I bullied,' he said, with a flatness to his voice.

'No!' she said, so cross at this injustice that she would have stamped her foot if the cumbersome wellies hadn't made it impossible. 'The one who bullied you. He did, don't deny it. It's what he was like to everyone, making their lives miserable and playing the victim.'

'You never said…' he began.

'I told you some of it, but not all, because it was complicated. He always insisted it was a secret, even wanted me to call him something else.' That had been a red flag too, and she hadn't realised its importance. 'He kept it secret because he didn't want his wife to find out, and I thought it was because he cared for me, and I got scared because I didn't care for him. He got aggressive, so possessive. And I realised that he wanted my trust fund. He wanted it so much he was prepared to divorce his wife and marry me for it.'

'Bastard!' he said, and she almost laughed. She'd been expecting something a bit more old-fashioned, like *cad* or *swine*.

'And do you know the worst thing? I lied to him about the money. I mean, sort of. The trust fund does exist, but it doesn't have much more than a few thousand in it, and they're roubles not pounds, Russian roubles. Even if I could get them they'd be worthless. I lied to you, too. I don't have any money.'

He was silent for a while, thinking about it. Nico would have rushed straight into recriminations and abuse, and there would have been a passionate, performative reconciliation afterwards. 'Do you think that matters to me?'

'It seems to matter to everyone else,' she said, bitterly.

'But not to me. I like you for what you are, not what you pretend to be. Which isn't to say that what you were pretending to be wasn't interesting or exciting, but I like what's underneath. I didn't see you just as a gorgeous woman, though that's what you are. I saw much more than that. I saw a girl in tweeds who smiled a lot and loved the country. And when I did, I understood that the reason I never had a long-term relationship was because I always thought I had to be glamorous and exciting and date glamorous and exciting people, and I'm not like that.'

Why did people laugh at Hugh? They should listen to him instead. Lexie took his hand. 'It wouldn't have mattered if Nico hadn't died. He kept wanting to come and see me or for me to come back, and in the end I had to block him. I never heard anything from him after that.'

She moved away from the gate, pulling it behind her, and Hugh moved beside her. 'What was he doing up here?'

'I don't know. When I heard it was him I was terrified. I thought he might have been coming to try and find me. Then there were the letters. I told you about them. My mum says that was his wife. I was so scared and I did come here, and then when I found him…'

'For a moment I thought you were going to tell me you'd killed him.'

'No. I'm not that sort of person.' Thank God; it would have changed how he saw her and he would have rejected her, appalled. 'But I sold myself to him for less than my worth. I think that's as bad, in its own way.' Nico was better dead, but she, at least hadn't killed him. 'It'll take me a long time to get over that. To learn to like myself again. And you need to know that.'

He was silent again and she knew he was thinking of school. 'It isn't easy, but I'll be with you every step of the way, if that helps. And for what it's worth, I like you.'

'You keep saying it.'

'Because it's true.'

She felt herself going pink in the face and it wasn't because of the keen autumn wind. They had reached the farmyard, now, where chickens scratched among the mud and jostled each other in the search for food. 'I'm going to sort myself out. Explain myself to my mum. She'll be furious. She says I'm a terrible judge of men and I always have been in the past, but you're different.'

'Text her. Tell her you're going to be late back. I haven't checked the barn for eggs yet, and I was thinking if there are enough I could rustle you up an omelette.'

'I can't help it,' she said. 'I'll always be a bit of a drama queen. It's in my nature.'

'Maybe my life needs a bit more drama.'

They turned towards the house and as they did so her mother's car came bouncing up the lane to the farmyard and a few seconds later another car appeared behind it in the lane, a fancy dark blue Mercedes, and she recognised Jude Satterthwaite driving.

Drama was here on the farm, in spades.

THIRTY

'There's something not right about this.' Jude spun the Mercedes down the narrow lane that led towards High Rigg Farm.

'I know.' Ashleigh had her phone on her lap and kept checking it as if she were hoping for someone to contact her with something new, something that would change everything. 'It isn't right, is it? I can't see Lexie Romachenka as a killer. I know she had the motive, but it all feels like fluff with her. There's never any intent. But what about—'

What about a blank cartridge in a gun, a dramatic scene staged for no-one but its participants to see? Lexie might easily have done that. 'Maybe she didn't mean to kill him. She could easily have got hold of a stage prop. I did a bit of digging on that while you were talking to Annabel. Modern stage guns can't be fired at all, which is interesting, but older ones can. That film of Morea's was set in the 1960s and he might have been tempted to use older, authentic ones if they were available. Those old ones do fire blanks and while they wouldn't do any serious harm, they can do for your heart, for sure. Your hearing, too. So we can add the means. Lexie could easily have got hold of one. As for the opportunity, her mother will no doubt give her an alibi but if she did it, we'll crack it. There must be CCTV and ANPR cameras and so on. I don't care how long it takes.'

'You think it's an open and shut case, then.'

He swithered again. Sometimes he thought one thing, sometimes another. 'As a matter of fact I don't think I do. On the face of it, yes, but it feels a little too convenient if Lexie turns out to be staring us in the face all the time.'

'Are you saying she was set up?'

He drummed his hands on the steering wheel, impatient at the constraints of the narrow, high-hedged road. Ahead of them they caught glimpses of another car in the same direction. 'Exactly that. I keep thinking of those messages and how Doddsy read them out, and he's right. There's a definite change of tone. After she switched to the new phone she became almost dictatorial.'

'You might expect that, if she'd ditched him.'

'You might, but she told him never to contact her again and then she messages him to tell him to contact her on a different number and the tone of the conversation is much less like her. The earlier ones show that Lexie's a very modern texter. She uses emojis and abbreviations and hashtags. She's all *lol* and *lmao* and all the rest of it. She doesn't use completed sentences and she doesn't use punctuation, whereas these were much more correct. So yes, I think someone else sent those later messages.'

'Annabel?' asked Ashleigh, craning her neck as the car slowed for yet another bend. 'What's that car?'

'I'm pretty sure that's Lexie's mum.' That meant trouble.

'I wonder about Annabel,' went on Ashleigh, still

paying considerable attention to the car ahead. 'She pointed the finger at Lexie.'

'But I don't think she would have overlooked that particular detail of tone in the messages. And if it turns out that Lexie was definitely somewhere else — because, of course, we now know pretty much exactly when Simon died — then it'll be too easy to prove it wasn't her.'

'Could it be Hugh Cameron after all?' Ashleigh asked. 'Is it possible he was in it with Annabel? If that's the case then I'd start to worry about Lexie's safety.'

'As her mother claims to. No, I don't think it's him. Look if I get close enough to that car, can you run the number through the app and double-check who it's registered to?'

The car squeezed into a gateway to allow a tractor and trailer coming the other way and Ashleigh, taking the chance, snapped the number into the app on her phone. 'Yes, you're right. That's Mary Ford.'

'Right.' Jude waited in the lay-by for a moment to let Mary out of sight. He knew where she was heading. 'Mary Ford, who Mikey saw tearing out of Wasby like a bat out of hell when she realised her precious daughter might have rushed into a relationship with a man, when the last one nearly ruined her life. Mary Ford, who complained about the kind of life her daughter was living in London. Mary Ford, who had every reason to hate Simon Morea, a man who had used and abused her daughter for his own purposes. Who was suffocating Lexie with motherly love at the time that Lexie's messages to switched to a new phone. Yes. Of course it's Mary. Now I understand.'

'I wasn't expecting that,' Ashleigh said, 'but the more I think about it, it fits. Mary would guarantee that Lexie was in Huddersfield at the time of Simon's death and I'll say she probably was.'

'But was Mary?' asked Jude. 'We don't know. She could have taken a day off work or called in sick and not told Lexie. It's a bit of a trek, for sure. Two and a half hours, maybe, plus the walk? But it's easily doable within the working day. And do you know what else?'

'What?'

'Boots. When I saw Lexie after she found Morea's body, her walking boots were on the front step. They're new. And when I was down there this morning there was a different pair on the steps that I thought must be Mary's. They were older, they were cheaper, they were worn, and they were crusted with that bright red mud you get in the Eden Valley.' It wasn't evidence in itself, and the boots would need to be analysed by a forensic geologist, but when that was done, and when other experts had looked at the patterns of use of language in the text, and a whole load of other things, he was confident that Mary Ford would be left standing as the only person who could have killed Simon Morea.

Mary's car lurched its way through a potholed gate signed High Rigg Farm, and bounced up the uneven track. At the end of it, the grey slate farmhouse crouched against the backdrop of bare hills. A mile or so away, traffic sped along the M6 and a train slipped in and out of view beside it. On the other side of the yard Lexie was bending down and laughing, pointing at a chicken, and the tall figure of Hugh Cameron stood close behind her. Jude pulled up the car in a gateway at the edge of the farmyard and he and Ashleigh got out.

'Should we intervene?' asked Ashleigh.

'Not yet. Let's keep a watching brief just now. I'd love to know what's being said.'

'Mama!' said Lexie, her voice quavering a little so that

Hugh moved beside her and placed an arm around her shoulder.

'Alex.' Mary had marched up to the two of them and stopped in front of her daughter. 'This has to stop. Now.'

'I don't know what you mean.' Lexie looked baffled.

'You do. Get in the car, come back home with me. We're going back home and you're staying there until you're well again. You can fetch your car later.'

'But I *am* well. I was never ill. I just made some really terrible choices and now I've had time to think about them. That was what you were worried about, wasn't it? But it's fine. I'm just going to live a much more mature and sensible life from now on.'

'Mrs Ford,' began Hugh, moving forward.

'It's *Miss* Ford,' she snapped at him.

'Miss Ford. Look, let me introduce myself. I'm Hugh. Lexie and I met a week or so ago and we get on really well. But honestly, you don't need to worry about Lexie. I know you're concerned about her, of course you are, that's natural, but I promise you my intentions are good. We like each other a lot but we aren't going to rush anything. So please, why don't you come in and have a cup of tea and we can talk.'

'There's nothing to talk about.' Mary thrust her hands in the pockets of her coat. 'My lass is all I care about. Why are you still single at your age? Because you couldn't find a woman who'd take you?'

'I—'

'Mama!'

'Honestly, Miss Ford,' said Hugh, showing no signs of being rattled. 'I'm still single because I never found the right woman. And with respect, I don't think you know anything about me, and Lexie's a grown woman who'll make her own decisions.' He gave a shrug and looked immovable. 'I hope you'll be able to leave us to feel our own way through this relationship, and perhaps in the end you and I can be friends.'

'Friends!' said Mary and laughed in disbelief. 'A man single in his fifties? That's a red flag if I ever saw one. If it's her money you're after, you're in for a disappointment. She doesn't have any.'

'Lexie's been honest with me about the money. It's fine. I never wanted it, I don't need it and I don't care about it.'

A brown cow, interested, shuffled towards the gate where the Mercedes had parked and Jude, who had recent reason to be nervous of the animals, took it as a cue to move forward. No-one paid him any attention.

'So you say. And if it's just a bit of the other you're after, don't even think about taking my girl and having your fun with her and then abandoning her.'

The gate nudged open. The cow, delighted, ambled towards the farmyard.

'Buttercup!' said Hugh, distracted. 'How did you get out?'

'Oh no!' said Lexie. 'Oh, I'm sorry! That's my fault! I didn't shut the gate properly!'

'Listen to me! Because if you do, if you dare try anything with my girl,' shouted Mary, her voice pitching higher with every word until it was all but a scream, as Hugh surged past to try and manoeuvre the cow back into the field, 'you'll pay for it like—'

'Like Simon Morea paid for it,' said Jude, softly, behind her.

'Yes, just like I made Morea pay!' said Mary, regardless, then turned and saw the two police officers. Her mouth dropped open.

'Thank you, Ms Ford,' said Jude, formally. 'I'd like you to accompany me and Sergeant O'Halloran to the police station. We have some questions to ask you about the murders of Simon Morea and Gerry Cole.'

'Mama,' said Lexie, stepping in front of her mother, her eyes wide with anxiety. 'Is this true? Oh God, I knew you hated him but I never thought you'd—'

'Don't be daft. If I go to prison,' said Mary to her daughter, 'who's going to look after you?'

'I expect Lexie will be able to look after herself just fine,' said Jude, pleasantly, as Mary's hand moved from her pocket. He took a guess at what was in there. 'Don't be silly, Ms Ford. We know the gun's a stage prop. It's not going to kill anyone. Why not just hand it over, eh?'

'Stage prop?' said Mary. 'Don't be ridiculous. This is real. He died, didn't he?'

Lexie was in the way. Jude surged forward and wrestled her to one side but Mary moved with her, pointed the gun over her shoulder and fired towards Hugh. The noise echoed round the farmyard; the cow, terrified, surged past them towards the barn. Beyond it Hugh stood alarmed but unhurt.

'What the hell—?' he asked bewildered and Lexie flung herself towards him and Jude and Ashleigh between them overpowered Mary and relieved her of the gun.

'It's a prop!' Lexie shouted. 'It isn't real! Mama, where did you get it? What are you thinking of?'

'Then how did I kill him?' said Mary, bewildered. 'If it isn't real, how did that bastard Morea die?'

THIRTY-ONE

Hugh, who was the only one unruffled by events, had put the kettle on and made a pot of tea and then gone out to calm Buttercup down and return her to her field while the two detectives had bundled Mary into the Mercedes and waited for a police van to come and take her away. Lexie stood watching them and thought, detachedly about her feelings as the van arrived and her mother, handcuffed, was handed over and driven away. It was her turn now, to explain, but how could she? She hadn't killed Nico, but if it wasn't for her, if she hadn't confided everything in her mother because there was no one else she could confide in, it wouldn't have happened.

Killing Nico had been bad enough. That attempt on Hugh was worse. She would never forgive her mother for that.

She settled in the big farmhouse kitchen with a cup of tea and watched Hugh moving about, watched the two detectives having a conversation out in the yard, saw them exchange glances and head towards the house. Her turn, now. Head held high she settled herself at the table where they would see her as they came in, and then she remembered that it wasn't a game, or a play but real life and real death.

'Are you all right, Ms Romachenka? Or is it Ms Ford?' asked the sergeant, coming in ahead of her boss and fixing her eyes straight on Lexie as if she was concerned about her, and maybe she was.

'Maybe just call me Lexie.' Lexie's old world was crumbling. Her mother had killed Nico. She must have killed the other poor man. She had to have taken leave of her senses. 'I'm fine. I'm really fine.' Hugh would look after her. 'I'm more worried about Buttercup.'

'The cow?' asked DCI Satterthwaite, and he and the sergeant exchanged wry smiles. She'd thought, in the moment, that he'd been more comfortable about the prospect of taking on the gun than he had been about poor, gentle Buttercup.

'It was my gun,' she said, before they could ask her. 'Though actually it wasn't. It was Nico's. I stole it from him.'

'It's not real, obviously,' said the sergeant, smiling and sitting down opposite her at the table.

'Mama must have thought it was,' she said miserably. 'That's what she used, isn't it? I didn't know. On the telly it never said.'

'There's a reason we don't tell people everything we know,' said the sergeant. She might have been neat and tidy when she'd arrived but in the melee outside she'd acquired a fair coating of muck and both she and her boss were covered in mud and straw, like a pair of scarecrows. She hoped they didn't have to pay their own dry cleaning bills. She smiled. They'd never said Nico had been murdered, not publicly, though everyone had guessed. But her mother…

'I don't understand why she didn't realise what had happened,' she said, miserably.

'Well, you know how it is,' said the sergeant, as if she were sharing a confidence. 'I probably shouldn't speculate, especially not with you. But I'm going to guess she didn't wait to see. She would have put the gun against his coat, pulled the trigger and then run for it.'

Lexie shot a look at the chief inspector, who was staring out of the window but was almost certainly listening while his sergeant played fast and loose with process. She liked their approach. They made her feel somehow safe. 'You don't think I—?'

'We will have some questions to ask you in a more formal setting,' said Satterthwaite from the window, 'but I think that can wait. You must have had a real shock.'

'I can tell you about the gun, though,' said Lexie, pleadingly. 'Let me do that. I never dreamed she'd shot him. I never even noticed it had gone missing.'

'We'll be asking you about the gun later,' said the sergeant, 'but right now it's not the most appropriate—'

'But I want to tell you. I want to tell you now.' The story was boiling in her head and in her heart, the truth she had to tell, as quickly as possible. In time they would press her uncomfortably for the details because (she wasn't stupid) she could see how they might think she was an accessory, how she might have helped her mother, but she knew Mary would swear to her innocence. She knew, too, that the gun would land her in trouble but she would face up to that. For now, the story spilled in all its messiness — the affair and the secrecy, and the money — and only stumbled when she came to leaving Nico. 'It was awful. There was such a scene.'

'Surely not,' said DCI Satterthwaite, deadpan.

She liked that. He was right, too. Everything had to be

staged and dramatic with Nico, and in life she thought he made more of a success of it than he did on screen. 'Yes, but it wasn't good. Horrible, in fact. It took a lot of drink to give me courage to tell him.' There had been drugs involved, though she thought she wouldn't mention that, but when she saw the looks on their face she knew they wouldn't be at all surprised. She supposed you didn't get to be a detective without knowing about the traps people fell into, and drugs in a seedy pub in some back street came from the same place, and did the same damage, as those taken in penthouse flats and London clubs.

'I told him it was over,' she said, remembering the fury in his eyes. 'He went crazy.' He had, after all, been out of his mind on cocaine. 'He told me he wouldn't let me leave. He said he loved me.' He hadn't. Nico had never loved anyone but himself. 'Over and over again, shouting and screaming, and I stood there and kept telling him I was going to end the relationship. And then he produced this gun.'

'That gun?' asked Satterthwaite, nodding in the general direction of the farmyard. The gun had gone with Mary in the van, safely in the custody of uniformed officers.

'Yes. And it's realistic. So realistic. I thought it was real, because I don't know anything about guns. I was so scared.' He had marched up to her and placed the gun against her chest and laughed and said *are you still going to leave me?* 'And so, of course, I agreed to stay.'

The sergeant had been taking notes but she looked up at this and caught Lexie's eye. 'That must have been awful.'

'It was. When I said I'd stay with him he laughed and put it down and told me it was a fake, and when I looked closely I could see he was right. I'd already seen him for what he was, and that only confirmed I was right to leave. so I waited until he was asleep, and then I got up and I walked away in the middle of the night.'

'And the gun?'

'I took it with me.'

'Why?'

Lexie drew a deep breath, remembering the night she'd taken a last, long look at night-time London from Nico's penthouse. The dawn had just been breaking after a long night, and she'd seen it lying on the table. 'I don't know.' Because it made her feel exotic and important? Because it made her feel safe? 'I think it was because I knew it wouldn't be long before he found another woman and I didn't want him to do the same to her.' The gun, fake though it was, had made her feel powerful. She had walked through Battersea and Vauxhall with it in her handbag, until she'd finally flagged down a cab. 'I called my mum that night and I told her what had happened and that he'd threatened me, and that I'd taken it, and she came right down on the first train to fetch me home.'

'Did you tell her it was a stage prop?' asked the sergeant, interested.

'I don't think so. I don't remember. I was in such a state. She took me straight home and I just slept and slept, for days it felt like. I hadn't realised how exhausted I was. It was unreal. And then I told her I was going up to Cumbria to get away.'

'She knew everything about your affair?'

'Everything. Not at the time, but I did tell her some of it because I had to tell someone, and she's my mum and I trusted her. I'm such a poor picker of men. I always pick the losers. I pick the rich ones, who flatter me.' Her lip quivered. 'It wasn't the first time, and I always went home, and she always told me it would end in tears and I remember her saying that if any of these men ever threatened me…' She picked up her tea, with an unsteady hand. 'She did say she'd kill them.'

The door opened and Hugh poked his head around it. 'Am I interrupting?'

'No, we're doing fine. I think we're just about done,' said Satterthwaite, cheerfully. 'For now, at any rate. That was fascinating and I'm glad you got it off your chest. But now we'll head back to Penrith and formalise it, shall we?'

THIRTY-TWO

Mary Ford had the same duty solicitor as Annabel Faulkner had had, and the solicitor had taken great pleasure in reminding Ashleigh that her previous client (who was now represented by her own London lawyer) had had nothing to do with the murders about which she had been questioned. Annabel was still facing a charge of malicious communications, though swearing she would fight them all the way. Mary Ford was very different. Her job was done, or so she seemed to think. She had protected her daughter from a monster and she was proud of it.

'Our Alex and I never got on,' she said to Ashleigh, sitting in the interview room with both hands flat in front of her on the table, 'but that didn't change owt. She's still my daughter and I'm still her mother and that's a relationship that ties you together until death, like it or not.'

'You didn't like it?'

Mary shrugged. 'She was difficult. She was always looking for a father figure, that's what it was. I did everything I could for her but I couldn't be father and mother and she was wayward. A dreamer. Like her father.'

'Were you ever married?' asked Ashleigh. You didn't need a degree to see that Mary's crimes were rooted in her psyche.

Mary shook her head.

'Who was Alex's father? Did he have any part in her upbringing?'

'If you call a couple of hundred pounds every month a part, then aye. He was a mistake I made and I realised it early on. He was gone before Alex was born and the best I can say for him is that he paid his way until she turned eighteen. There was no one after that. But she fantasised about him, saw him as a hero. Told people he'd died rather than admit he'd left her.'

There was a silence in which Mary met Ashleigh's gaze and Ashleigh tried to read the complications behind it. Mary, she sensed, didn't like men. It was that simple. Maybe she didn't like women either. In fact, there was even possibility that Mary Ford simply didn't like people and bore all relationships like a burden, trading in obligation and responsibility rather than love. Poor Lexie.

'What about your daughter?' she asked. 'She's an attractive young woman. I'm sure she's had her fair share of admirers. How did you feel about that?'

'Our Alex,' said Mary, after a moment, 'has an empty head and no judgement. I told her, over and over, if she had to have a man she should choose a sensible one, if she could find one. They're thin on the ground.'

'She was very open about her relationships?'

'Aye, in the end. When she was a lass she told me everything but that soon stopped. She's a flighty one. She wouldn't be told.'

'Would you say your relationship with her was positive?' asked Ashleigh, with interest. Yes, she could see the psychologist having a field day with Mary Ford.

'To start, aye, but she was a difficult teenager. Older men, always. She's never shown any interest in anyone her own age. Very strong-willed. And then she got it in her head that she was going to be in films and went down to London, and then it all went wrong.'

'Tell me what you knew about your daughter's relationship with Simon Morea.' Mary was in a mood to confess and so it was worth letting her talk.

'I went down to London,' Mary said. 'After she started going out with him. She never told me his name but I knew there was a man and she'd lost her head over him. She wouldn't introduce me, but I found out enough, because the lass couldn't tell me enough about how important this mysterious boyfriend was and how famous. You didn't have to be that clever to work it out, and if she'd told anyone else, they'd have worked it out, too. The lass was right under his spell. I knew all about him. He was a bad lot, the worst. The very worst. He'd have ruined her.'

He probably would. There was nothing Ashleigh had read, or heard, about Simon Morea that made her think otherwise. To men like him the Lexie Romachenkas of the world were disposable, vehicles allowing them to flex their power and their muscles, and then dispose of them. 'She told him she had money.'

'She told everybody lots of things. The lass is a liar. She wants to be loved and admired and she'll say anything to make someone care. But I told her. *They don't want you. They want your youth and your prettiness, they want the money you haven't got*. She said he'd marry her. I told her how that would go. The best she could hope for was that he'd drop her before he got old and the worst was that she'd a long marriage with him and gave the best years of her life to looking after him. Then she'd end up spending years wiping his backside and when he shuffled off she'd be left with nothing but her own company and her old age.'

The duty solicitor, Ashleigh noticed, was completely rapt by this. 'Okay. Let me be clear. You knew who Lexie's partner was before she told you.'

'I knew,' said Mary steadily, 'and I knew how it would end. I'd seen her put her neck in that noose many times before but this man was out to trap her. I don't know what made her see sense and leave him but when she did, I was ready for her.'

'What happened, Ms Ford,' asked Ashleigh, 'on the day Lexie called you and told you she'd split up with her lover?'

'I got the train straight down and fetched her back. She told me what had happened and how he'd pulled a gun on her and she'd talked him out of shooting her.'

'You believed her?'

Mary thought about it. 'You get to know someone when you live with them. She can tell a story, but that bit was true. When I got her home and tucked her up in bed, I found the gun. She'd brought it with her. I never said to her I'd seen it, but I asked her about him and she said she was sure he'd come back, because of the money. I said to tell him there was no money but she was too scared to do that. She said he'd kill her because being made a fool of was the worst thing that could happen to him.'

'Did it occur to you to go to the police?'

Mary shook her head.

'So what did you do then?'

'The lass was in a state. I put her to her bed and I got her phone and unlocked it. I knew her passcode. I knew he had a separate number he called her on so I thought he'd believe it if she did the same. I had an old phone and so after a few days I used it to contact him and pretend I was

Alex. I said I wanted to meet, but it had to be somewhere no-one would see us. He agreed. It was him that suggested up by the lime kilns.'

'You asked to meet him,' Ashleigh said, carefully, 'with the intention of killing him. Is that correct?'

'He'd have been back at her if I hadn't. They never go away. They see her and they think they can do what they want. They can't. Not with me at her back.' Mary seemed calm. 'After that it was easy. I knew she had the gun with her. I took it when she was sleeping and I went up to meet him.' She laughed. '*Who are you?* he said. *Where's Lexie?* And I told him then, that he'd never trouble my girl again, and I walked right up to him and put the gun at what passed for his heart and pulled the trigger. He went down like a stone and I walked away and went back home like nothing had happened.'

'Did your daughter suspect?'

'Not a thing. I made sure she didn't miss me when I was out. Kept her quiet with sleeping tablets.'

'You drugged your daughter?' said Ashleigh, and noticed the solicitor's expression mirroring the shock she felt.

'She needed the rest,' said Mary, stubbornly.

'Okay. But you say you believed the gun was real. Did it occur to you that when his body was found, Lexie might be the one to attract attention? She would have had the reason to do it? She would have owned the weapon. There would have been messages luring him up to Ardale, messages purporting to be from her. Did that occur to you?'

Mary smiled. 'Aye,' she said, 'it did. But she would have been safe, then, wouldn't she? Locked up, maybe, but safe from all those men.'

THIRTY-THREE

'Did I miss anything?' Ashleigh asked. She and Jude were in the pub at Askham. 'You know how I hate to miss out of the dull graft of an investigation.' She grinned at him. In the days since Mary's arrest she'd been out of the office and he'd been too busy even to catch up with her in the evening.

'Not much,' he said, reaching for his pint. Tonight they'd come out for an evening meal and she had offered to drive. Askham had been his choice, partly because they rarely went to the pub there and partly because there was a chance he'd run into Mikey without having to go all the way to Wasby and risk running into Becca instead. 'It's a nasty mess, I will say that.'

'I wonder if Mary is insane,' she said, contemplating her glass of lime juice and soda.

'From what I hear that's the line the defence are going to take and Faye thinks they have a fair chance of success.' He frowned. 'I'm no psychiatrist but I'm not quite so sure. I think she thought she'd get away with it and if she didn't then Lexie would be the obvious suspect.' Mary had struck him, as he'd read over the transcript of the interview, as someone who wasn't all that smart, someone who had good ideas but failed to think through the potential flaws in them. In that she was more typical of the ordinary criminal than the criminally insane. 'We have her car on the motorway cameras. She travelled up from Huddersfield to Blencarn and back on the day of his death.' Just as they had done for Simon Morea, they had managed to pinpoint Mary's location on the Kemplay roundabout, just five minutes after he had passed through.

'Bad not mad then? And what about poor Gerry?'

'As you suspected. She realised he might have seen her after the television interview he did, and she couldn't take the risk. My mum always complains about middle aged women being invisible but it certainly came in handy for Mary that night.'

'I feel a bit sorry for her,' said Ashleigh.

'Do you? I don't. It may well be she gets off with manslaughter rather than murder for Morea, or it may well be that the jury decide he was a menace and deserved to die and don't convict, but what she did to Gerry was cold-blooded and no way an accident.' But it would be hard to prove. 'My big fear is that she might get away with that one, too.'

'Damn and blast.'

'Exactly. But if she does go down for killing Simon Morea it'll be for a very long time.'

'I'd love to know more about the relationship she had with Lexie.' Ashleigh frowned. 'It's very controlling, isn't it? We shouldn't be surprised to come across a possessive relationship within a parent-child dynamic, I know, but this one feels a bit odd.'

Jude thought of Lexie — beautiful, smart, successful and popular, albeit with the wrong kind of person — and of her mother, who was dull and misanthropic, growing older and risking losing her daughter to a man. It didn't matter how suitable the man was. Her attitude to Hugh had shown that. It had been chance that the man she had chosen to murder was the one who might arguably have deserved it, but it could have been any man who stood between her and a lonely old age. 'I think Mary was jealous of her daughter.'

'It seems a pretty feeble reason to me.' Ashleigh speared a chip with her fork and dipped it in a pool of tomato ketchup.

'Possibly, but the comparison between them is stark. I'm not really surprised Lexie made the most of the tiny bit of an exotic background she had. I'm not surprised she wanted to reinvent herself. From what I've heard since Mary was arrested, she had a fairly grim childhood. Mary was pretty much a recluse and friendships weren't encouraged. Her mother made a big thing of looking after Lexie, of being everything to her, and I think there was an unspoken contract, in her mind at least. She would look after Lexie and when she got older Lexie would look after her.' Hence the comment about growing old alone. Mary had been expressing her own deepest fears. 'And then these men kept coming along, and Lexie was so unused to that kind of attention and flattery that she fell for it every time.'

'I was so sure it was Annabel,' said Ashleigh, and laughed. 'Some detective I am, eh?'

'She would have made a fine criminal. She tried so hard to pin it on Lexie, didn't she, and then we have Mary doing pretty much the same thing. Annabel didn't know who did it, and maybe she believed that Lexie was guilty, but she was determined to point us in her direction.'

'A thoroughly nasty woman. But let's not get too cocky,'

said Ashleigh, jovially, 'since you were thinking it was Hugh Cameron.'

'Yes, for a while, but there was an obvious flaw. They didn't meet until after Morea was dead, and Hugh had no motive.'

Ashleigh emptied her glass. 'Hugh's a lucky man, isn't he? When she went after him with that gun she thought it was real. She'd have killed him, instead of just frightening that poor pet cow of his half to death.'

'Never mind the cow. There was a moment when I thought it was real, too, and we'd got it wrong.'

'Imagine if it had been and we'd been a bit later. Imagine if we'd been concentrating on Lexie rather than Mary. God. I can't stop thinking of that. She would have killed him, wouldn't she?'

'Another man coming between her and her daughter? Yes, you're right. She would, if she could.' He focussed on his own meal. It was Friday. He was ready for another pint. 'I hope it works out between the two of them. Hugh seems nice enough, and he might be good for her. She probably needs someone who'll adore her for what she is, not because of what she can do for them, and he does strike me that way.'

'Talk of the devil. That's Lexie over there, isn't it? Just coming in,' said Ashleigh, with the slight concern of a detective about to be caught in a social situation with the witness in a live murder investigation. 'Damn, I suppose we'll have to move on somewhere else.'

'Not until I've finished my pie. She won't want to talk to us if she's with Hugh.'

'She's not,' said Ashleigh, drily.

He looked up. Lexie was with Becca, and the two of them were laughing like old friends as they walked into the bar. Jude looked down at his plate and toyed with the idea of leaving his meal half uneaten and getting out before they could get sucked into a conversation, but his stubborn streak asserted itself. He and Ashleigh had as much right to be there as anyone else. He hadn't wanted to talk to Becca, if only because he needed to wean himself off that habit of drifting down to Wasby on a whim in the hope that he'd run into her, but here she was, and he wasn't going to let her chase him away.

She'd seen them. For a moment their eyes met and she shifted towards the bar, as though the meeting was as awkward for her as it was for him but Lexie, completely unaware of the dynamic, came surging over to the table.

'Sergeant,' she said, 'Chief Inspector. I know you're off duty. I know you're not supposed to talk about the case and I'm not going to. I wanted to say thank you. And don't say you were just doing your job.'

'I'm sorry about what you had to go through,' he said, neutrally. He'd already learned that Lexie liked to talk. Best just let her ramble on until Becca had settled elsewhere with the drinks.

'I've had a difficult relationship with my mother all my life. She never did trust men, you know, after my dad disappeared almost without trace as soon as he knew there was a baby on the way. I don't know if she loved him, but I think she must have done, because she never forgave him.'

Becca had ordered a Coke and a glass of wine and was looking round the bar, but the other tables were occupied and in any case Lexie was sliding into an empty seat at their side. She came across to them, sat down beside Jude, slid the Coke towards Lexie, and took a large sip of wine. 'Lexie's decided to stay in Wasby for a while longer. Did she tell you? We were just coming out for a drink to celebrate.'

'Yes.' Lexie lifted her glass in salute.

'I take it Hugh's all right?' asked Ashleigh.

'Yes, poor man. I don't think he quite understood what he was getting himself into and he got an awful shock. He thought the gun was real and he's already beating himself up for not having stepped in to save me, even though I was never at risk. But actually I think he was more worried about poor Buttercup. I swear he loves that cow more than he loves me.'

When she talked about Hugh, her eyes lit up. He might be a good twenty years older than she, but perhaps that was what she needed.

'So, no damage done then,' said Jude, noncommittally.

'Except you crashing through my garden and breaking bits off my cotoneaster,' said Becca, taking another, too large, sip of her wine. 'Anyway, here's to your new life in Wasby, Lexie. And here's to true love.'

They raised their glasses and Jude looked first at Becca and then at Ashleigh. But both must have been thinking of true love in a melancholy way, and neither would meet his eye.

THE END

ACKNOWLEDGMENTS

Most of the support I have received from this book has been intangible and came in the way of support from readers who liked the previous books and asked when the next was coming. Without them, I might well not have written it.

But I did, and in the writing there are those to whom I owe a debt of gratitude. They are, if I may call them that, the usual suspects - Graham Bartlett, who provided invaluable advice on keeping the policing realistic; Keith Sutherland, who is always a willing and eagle-eyed proofreader; the talented Mary Jayne Baker for the cover; and my husband, Alan, for his editorial input.

To those I would like to add Liz Taylorson, who read an early draft and offered insightful comments fingering exactly what the issues were, and professional pirate (yes, really!) George Collings, who advised me about the use of stage weapons. (It's okay, George is an actor, not a villain.)

Thank you to you all.

ALSO BY JO ALLEN

Death by Dark Waters

DCI Jude Satterthwaite #1

It's high summer, and the Lakes are in the midst of an unrelenting heatwave. Uncontrollable fell fires are breaking out across the moors faster than they can be extinguished. When firefighters uncover the body of a dead child at the heart of the latest blaze, Detective Chief Inspector Jude Satterthwaite's arson investigation turns to one of murder. Jude was born and bred in the Lake District. He knows everyone — and everyone knows him. Except his intriguing new Detective Sergeant, Ashleigh O'Halloran, who is running from a dangerous past and has secrets of her own to hide. Temperatures — and tensions — are increasing, and with the body count rising Jude and his team race against the clock to catch the killer before it's too late…

The first in the gripping, Lake District-set, DCI Jude Satterthwaite series.

Death at Eden's End

DCI Jude Satterthwaite #2

When one-hundred-year-old Violet Ross is found dead at Eden's End, a luxury care home hidden in a secluded nook of Cumbria's Eden Valley, it's not unexpected. Except for the instantly recognisable look in her lifeless eyes — that of pure terror. DCI Jude Satterthwaite heads up the investigation, but as the deaths start to mount up it's clear that he and DS Ashleigh O'Halloran need to uncover a long-buried secret before the killer strikes again…

The second in the unmissable, Lake District-set, DCI Jude Satterthwaite series.

Death on Coffin Lane

DCI Jude Satterthwaite #3

DCI Jude Satterthwaite doesn't get off to a great start with resentful Cody Wilder, who's visiting Grasmere to present her latest research on Wordsworth. With some of the villagers unhappy about her visit, it's up to DCI Satterthwaite to protect her — especially when her assistant is found hanging in the kitchen of their shared cottage.

With a constant flock of tourists and the local hippies welcoming in all who cross their paths, Jude's home in the Lake District isn't short of strangers. But with the ability to make enemies wherever she goes, the violence that follows in Cody's wake leads DCI Satterthwaite's investigation down the hidden paths of those he knows, and those he never knew even existed.

A third mystery for DCI Jude Satterthwaite to solve, in this gripping novel by best-seller Jo Allen.

Death at Rainbow Cottage

DCI Jude Satterthwaite #4

At the end of the rainbow, a man lies dead.

The apparently motiveless murder of a man outside the home of controversial equalities activist Claud Blackwell and his neurotic wife, Natalie, is shocking enough for a peaceful local community. When it's followed by another apparently random killing immediately outside Claud's office, DCI Jude Satterthwaite has his work cut out. Is Claud the killer, or the intended victim?

To add to Jude's problems, the arrival of a hostile new boss causes complications at work, and when a threatening note arrives at the police headquarters, he has real cause to fear for the safety of his friends and colleagues...

A traditional British detective novel set in Cumbria.

Death on the Lake

DCI Jude Satterthwaite #5

Three youngsters, out for a good time. Vodka and the wrong sort of coke. What could possibly go wrong?

When a young woman, Summer Raine, is found drowned, apparently accidentally, after an afternoon spent drinking on a boat on Ullswater, DCI Jude Satterthwaite is deeply concerned — more so when his boss refuses to let him investigate the matter any further to avoid compromising a fraud case.

But a sinister shadow lingers over the dale and one accidental death is followed by another and then by a violent murder. Jude's life is complicated enough but the latest series of murders are personal to him as they involve his former partner, Becca Reid, who has family connections in the area. His determination to uncover the killer brings him into direct conflict with his boss — and ultimately places both him and his colleague and girlfriend, Ashleigh O'Halloran, in danger…

Death in the Woods

DCI Jude Satterthwaite #6

A series of copycat suicides, prompted by a mysterious online blogger, causes DCI Jude Satterthwaite more problems than usual, intensifying his concerns about his troublesome younger brother, Mikey. Along with his partner, Ashleigh O'Halloran, and a local psychiatrist, Vanessa Wood, Jude struggles to find the identity of the malicious troll gaslighting young people to their deaths.

The investigation stirs grievances both old and new. What is the connection with the hippies camped near the Long Meg stone circle? Could these suicides have any connection with a decades-old cold case? And, for Jude, the most crucial question of all: is it personal, and could Mikey be the final target?

Death in the Mist

DCI Jude Satterthwaite #7

A drowned man. A missing teenager. A deadly secret.

When Emmy Leach discovers the body of a drug addict,

wrapped in a tent and submerged in the icy waters of a Cumbrian tarn, she causes more than one problem for investigating officer DCI Jude Satterthwaite. Not only does the discovery revive his first, unsolved, case, but it reveals Emmy's complicated past and opens old wounds on the personal front, regarding Jude's relationship with his colleague and former partner, Ashleigh O'Halloran.

As Jude and his team unpick an old story, it becomes increasingly clear that Emmy is in danger. What secrets are she and her controlling husband hiding, from the police and from each other? What connection does the dead man have with a recently-busted network of drug dealers? And, as the net closes in on the killer, can Jude and Ashleigh solve a murder — and prevent another?

Death on a Monday Night

DCI Jude Satterthwaite #8

An ex-convict. A dead body. A Women's Institute meeting like no other...

It's an unusually challenging meeting at the Wasby Women's Institute, with local resident and former drug-dealer Adam Fleetwood talking about his crimes and subsequent rehabilitation...but events take a gruesome turn when prospective member Grace Thoresby is discovered murdered in the kitchen.

The case is particularly unwelcome for investigating officer DCI Jude Satterthwaite. Adam was once his close friend and now holds a bitter grudge, blaming Jude for landing him in jail in the first place. To complicate things further, the only thing keeping Adam from arrest is the testimony of Jude's former girlfriend, Becca Reid, for whom he still cares deeply.

As Jude and his colleague and current partner, Ashleigh O'Halloran, try to pick apart the complicated tapestry of Grace's life, they uncover a web of fantasy, bitterness and deceit. Adam is deeply implicated, but is he guilty or is someone determined to frame him for Grace's murder? And as they close in on the truth, Jude falls foul of Adam's desire for revenge, with near-fatal consequences…

A traditional detective mystery set in Cumbria.

Death on the Crags

DCI Jude Satterthwaite #9

Everybody loves Thomas Davies. Don't they?

When policeman Thomas falls from a crag on a visit to the Lake District in full view of his partner, Mia, it looks for all the world like a terrible but unfortunate accident — until a second witness comes forward with a different story.

Alerted to the incident, DCI Jude Satterthwaite is inclined to take it seriously — not least because of Mia's reluctance to speak to the police about the incident. As Jude and his colleagues, including his on-off partner DS Ashleigh O'Halloran, tackle the case, they're astonished by how many people seem to have a reason to want all-round good guy Thomas out of the way.

With the arrival of one of Thomas's colleagues to assist the local force, the investigation intensifies. As the team unpick the complicated lives of those who claim to care for Thomas but have good reasons to want him dead, they find themselves digging deeper and deeper into a web of blackmail and cruelty … and investigating a second death.

A traditional British police procedural mystery set in Cumbria.

Death at the Three Sisters

DCI Satterthwaite #10

Three feuding sisters. A faded spa. And a woman, dead in the water…

As they head towards retirement, Suzanne, Hazel and Tessa Walsh are locked in bitter disagreement about the future of the lakeside beauty spa they jointly own. Should they keep The Three Sisters going as their parents wished, or should they sell to a neighbouring hotelier who seems determined to acquire the failing business, even at a preposterously high cost?

When their employee, Sophie Hayes, is found drowned close to the spa one cold January morning it rapidly becomes clear that it's no accident: Sophie has been murdered. But who could possibly want to kill her — or was she mistaken for someone else? As DCI Jude Satterthwaite seeks the answers he and his team dig ever deeper into the complicated and embittered relationships between the sisters and their neighbours.

As the investigation proceeds Jude becomes convinced that Sophie's murder may only be the beginning and it's not long before a shocking and tragic turn of events proves him correct and he and his team find themselves in a race to prevent a further, final tragedy overtaking the Three Sisters. Can he uncover what deadly secrets the sisters are prepared to die — or kill — for, or will he be too late?

Death in Good Time

DCI Satterthwaite #11

A murdered undertaker. A missing clockmaker. A family secret.

In life, eccentric aristocrat Lady Frances Capel was known for her habit of setting challenging puzzles, but the problem she leaves behind after her death looks unsolvable. When the undertaker is found dead at her funeral, DCI Jude Satterthwaite is left with a headache for a whole host of reasons, and a case he'd very much rather not be working on.

Jude's suspicions that the key to the mystery lies in Lady Frances's will and with a decades-old family secret are confirmed when he receives a cryptic message from reclusive local clockmaker Gil Foley, but when he follows up Gil has vanished. Convinced that this has something to do with the undertaker's death, Jude finds the stakes raised sky-high when he realises that his ex-partner, Becca Reid, is involved in Gil's disappearance.

With both Becca and Gil in grave danger, Jude and his colleague DS Ashleigh O'Halloran find themselves in a race against the clock. Can they solve the mystery before time runs out and a second life is lost?

Written as Jennifer Young

Jo writes romance and romantic suspense under the name of Jennifer Young.

Blank Space

Dangerous Friends Book 1

He's made a lot of enemies. She has some dangerous friends.

Bronte O'Hara is trying to move on from her ex-boyfriend, Eden Mayhew, but when she finds an injured man in her kitchen in the run-up to an international political summit in Edinburgh, a world she thought she'd left behind catches up with her with a vengeance.

Eden's an anarchist, up to his neck in any trouble around — and he's missing. The police are keen to find him, certain that he'll come back, and that when he does, he'll have Bronte in his sights. What does he want from her — and does she dare trust a handsome stranger with her life?

With danger and romance in equal measure, Blank Space is a contemporary take on the romantic suspense tradition pioneered by Mary Stewart.

After Eden

Dangerous Friends Book 2

In the aftermath of a violent G8 summit when she almost lost her life, Bronte O'Hara finds herself fighting against her feelings for Marcus Fleming, the policeman who saved her. When Marcus is cleared of any wrongdoing over the deaths of three people during the undercover police operation, Bronte isn't the only one who struggles to come to terms with the outcome. The friends and relatives of those who died are determined not to let the matter rest, whatever the cost. Some are looking for closure;

some want justice. And someone is determined to use Bronte in a bid to gain revenge…

Storm Child

Dangerous Friends Book 3

Scotland can be a dangerous place.

When their car comes off the road in a blizzard, Bronte O'Hara and her boyfriend, detective Marcus Fleming, stumble across an unconscious teenager in the snow. After he's rescued by two passing strangers, the boy simply disappears, and even Marcus's police colleagues don't believe their story — until the youth's body is found.

It looks like the accidental death of a young criminal, but Bronte and Marcus are convinced that things aren't as straightforward as they seem. Who was he? What was he doing out in the storm? Who else might be in danger?

And who will stop at nothing to make sure that Bronte and Marcus never find out?

Looking For Charlotte

Divorced and lonely, Flora Wilson is distraught when she hears news of the death of little Charlotte Anderson. Charlotte's father killed her and then himself, and although he left a letter with clues to the whereabouts of her grave, his three-year-old daughter still hasn't been found.

Flora embarks on a quest to find Charlotte's body to give the child's mother closure, believing that by doing so she can somehow atone for her own failings as a mother. As she hunts in winter through the remote moors of the Scottish Highlands, her obsession comes to threaten everything that's important to her — her job, her friendship with her colleague Philip Metcalfe and her relationships with her three grown up children.